BLACK

GIRLS

MUST

BE

MAGIC

ALSO BY JAYNE ALLEN

Black Girls Must Die Exhausted

BLACK GIRLS MUST BE MAGIC

A Novel

JAYNE ALLEN

HARPER

An Imprint of HarperCollins*Publishers*

Originally published as *Black Girls Must Die Exhausted: And Baby Makes Two* in 2019 by Quality Black Books.

BLACK GIRLS MUST BE MAGIC. Copyright © 2019 by Jaunique Sealey. All rights reserved. Printed in the United States of America. No part of this book may be used or reproduced in any manner whatsoever without written permission except in the case of brief quotations embodied in critical articles and reviews. For information, address HarperCollins Publishers, 195 Broadway, New York, NY 10007.

HarperCollins books may be purchased for educational, business, or sales promotional use. For information, please email the Special Markets Department at SPsales@harpercollins.com.

Designed by Jamie Lynn Kerner

Library of Congress Cataloging-in-Publication Data has been applied for.

ISBN 978-0-06-313792-9 (pbk.)
ISBN 978-0-06-321130-8 (library edition)
ISBN 978-0-06-323742-1 (international edition)

22 23 24 25 26   LSC   10 9 8 7 6 5 4 3 2 1

BLACK
GIRLS
MUST
BE
MAGIC

1

"Is it mine?"

Across the table, Marc's face crinkled with intensity as he spoke. Handsome Marc. Elusive Marc. My ex-boyfriend and sometimes-friends-with-benefits Marc. The glow of the Los Angeles brunchtime sun served as a perfect accentuation to his richly hued brown skin and made his eyes look like bottomless flowing pools of melted chocolate. Light danced across his pupils, and I couldn't tell if it was simple curiosity I was reading there or something more. Being very new to pregnancy, I hadn't had a chance to really miss alcohol, at least until now. Turning water into wine would be the first of many miracles I needed in this moment. It hadn't even been two months, but damn, I really missed wine. And before today, I'd also been missing Marc. He had an uncontrollable effect on me; every time we shared space, there was an undeniable thrill that even the deep disappointment of his unavailability couldn't diminish.

"Is that what you want?" I shot back at him, inhaling

sharply and swallowing hard, bracing myself for a harsh response. I hoped he wouldn't notice how much I cared about his answer. It didn't matter anyway. *Too late now, Tabby*. I picked up my water glass, trying to imagine it contained a crisp Chardonnay. Maybe I could get drunk on my own imagination.

The cloud across Marc's face darkened. "Does that matter to you?" he challenged. "It's a little late, don't you think? To be asking that kind of question?" His eyes traveled downward to my still-flat belly and lingered on my just slightly swollen breasts. They had become so sensitive that I could almost feel his gaze physically. When his eyes met mine again, his intense stare caused a traffic jam of words in my throat.

"I mean . . . I guess," I fumbled. "I . . . I remember you said you didn't?" My mind continued to spin through deeper thoughts I lacked the courage to say. His glare cut into my contemplation. I started to get the feeling that however I answered the question was going to upset him in some way. But regardless, I owed him the truth. He had a right to know, no matter how it changed our current friendship.

"It doesn't matter what I *said*, Tabby. And I didn't say I didn't. I said I didn't *know*." His eyes drifted below my breasts again and stared intently, as if he could see inside me to find out for himself.

"Marc, you're confusing me." I wiped my forehead with the first two fingers of my right hand out of pure nervousness. Why *was* I so nervous? "Look, the reality is that yes, I am pregnant—not even two months. And when this conversation started, I was unsure how you'd take the news, but now I *really* have no idea. So, to answer your question . . ."

Marc used the pause to cut me off and make his next interjection. "The baby's mine, isn't it? That's why we're here? Just tell me—I can't take this anymore, Tabby."

Oh no.

"Marc, the baby . . . it's . . . it's not yours." I got the words out as quickly as I could. "It's mine. *He's* mine." Marc's face registered the slow spread of shock.

"Tabby, what in the hell does that mean? How is that even possible? What do you mean it's not mine—or *he's* not? How do you even know *he's* a he?" Marc's words came in a flurry of hard consonants. At this point, he had leaned so far forward that I could almost feel his breath on my face.

"Marc, I know because I went to the doctor." I said the words slowly, trying to regain control of the spiraling situation. "Timing forced me to make a decision, so I did. I found a donor, and I moved forward with having a baby." Confusion clouded Marc's face. I continued, "Only one embryo cleared all the testing—a boy." Trying to explain something so complicated, thinking about those weeks of waiting and uncertainty and constant fear of loss, the pang of tears began to threaten my eyes. Still, I forced myself to finish. "And, after Granny Tab died, I knew I didn't want to waste another day before meeting my child. Son, daughter, it didn't matter. All I wanted . . . Marc, all I *want* is a healthy baby. And if I didn't try, maybe I'd lose the chance to ever know . . ." Those words pleading for health were my truth as much they were my daily prayer. It was out of my control now. All of it. The tears that welled blurred the view of Marc in front of me, mercifully hiding his reaction.

"You had a baby with a stranger?" Even though Marc's

voice sounded more like a hiss, I was glad that he'd managed to whisper. "Tabby, I thought you were just freezing your eggs! A donor?" Marc spat the words out and looked away, his hands closed in tight balls on the table. After a few seconds in suspended animation, he finally looked back across at me, his voice now almost an octave higher than his usual, slightly raspy baritone.

"Why are you even telling me this?" This was the exact question I'd been starting to ask myself. It had all made sense before the conversation started. As Marc finished speaking, he made a gesture to the server to come over. He probably wanted the check immediately so he could run for cover like he always did. It'd be fitting, since the last time he ran away from me when we were dating was basically what forced this decision in the first place. But what I wasn't going to do was to allow him to make me feel bad about it. I sat forward, grounding both of my feet on the floor beneath me.

"Yes, Marc. I had a baby with a donor. And thank God I did. You knew that I didn't have much time or many options. Maybe you thought I was joking, but my egg reserves were low. Way low. The doctor said if I could, it'd be better to make embryos to even have a shot. I got pregnant, but many women in my situation don't wind up as lucky.

"Even now, I still have to clear another round of screenings and tests, just to make sure that everything is progressing well. Timing forced a decision and I didn't have a second to waste or wait—not on you and not on anybody else."

"Wow, Tabby, this is some heavy shit." Marc finally leaned back in his seat with a sigh, slouched and deflated. He signaled "one more" to the approaching server, who acknowledged with a nod. "Sorry, did you want something else?" He gestured toward my half-full water glass.

"No, I'm fine," I said. Regret was fading my patience. "Look, Marc, this is not heavy, and it's not your problem. There's no *problem* here at all, only a blessing. I'm only telling you because . . . because, you know . . . we had . . ."

"Oh damn, Tabby, we were freakin' while you were getting pregnant? Are you serious?" At this, his body shot upward, and all of a sudden Marc was sitting stick straight again. "Why didn't you tell me? Were we even supposed to be doing that?" Marc was practically yelling at this point. I had no idea why he cared so much. I tried to stay as calm as possible, and turn my voice into a lullaby.

"Technically no, Marc, we weren't. But with everything going on, I just needed something familiar, and . . . we have . . . history. I had a lot of decisions to make, and it was nice to be able to count on you for that . . . comfort." My cheeks reddened. After the years of mine that Marc wasted, I finally had an admission of my own. The expression on Marc's face was hard to read. His eyes were wide, in contrast to the narrow slits that they had become earlier, and his mouth was still slightly ajar, even though he didn't seem to be making an effort to say anything. I was willing to answer other questions for him, but at that point, it seemed like anything I offered might be too much.

"I mean, a son . . . a son? Tabby, what are you going to do? You're going to raise him all alone? As a single mom? Who will be his father figure? His role model?" His words felt like a sharp stab.

"Marc, Black women have mastered raising men as single

mothers." I said, trying not to sound defensive. "My Granny Tab did it with my dad. I have plenty of examples to lean on. And, I will have the village."

"The what?" Marc's brow crinkled.

"The village. You've never heard that it takes a village to raise a child? I don't need anything from you, and I'm not asking you for anything, but I'm hoping that we're *actually* friends. Maybe one day you'll be a positive part of my child's life. But, for right now, I have to get past this next round of tests. I just want him to be healthy. I want me to be healthy. The rest, I'll worry about after."

"Tabby, you're crazy. You know that?" The sides of Marc's mouth tipped slightly upward for the first time in our tense conversation. His hand reached for his refreshed drink on the table. Ice clinked against the glass as he pulled it up to take a generous sip. He shook his head after he'd finished and just looked at me.

"I'm not crazy, Marc. I'm just doing what I can to live the best life possible, whatever that looks like for me." And with that said, just like the old days with Marc, I knew I'd be leaving our time together with more questions than answers, more doubt than certainty about the future of our relationship. Somehow, he'd also succeeded in making me doubt myself again. In some ways, Marc had a point. What if I had made the wrong decision? All the things I had felt so certain of started to feel flimsy after our conversation. As my thoughts whirled, Marc seemed to be relaxing into the understanding that the news I'd just delivered was actually *not* his problem. I watched his face soften further while his eyes continued to study me as if I were some sort of newly discovered being sitting across from him. And then he started to laugh subtly to himself as his demeanor shifted.

"Okay, Tabby," Marc said. "So you're *not* having *my* baby," he mocked. "Congratulations. I'm . . . happy for you. Really." Marc reached for my hand and took it in his. "I've gotta admit, I'm relieved as hell. I thought that you were going to come with something entirely different. But this, I'm glad you told me." Finally, I felt like it was safe to smile. "So now," he continued, "tell me about this donor . . . and wait, when did you decide to implant the embryo?"

These felt like much easier questions than the ones Marc had introduced earlier, and they had answers. The other questions—"how will you . . ." and "what will you . . ." and "who will . . ."—those did not. At least, not yet.

BRUNCH WITH MARC WAS HARDER THAN I'D THOUGHT IT WOULD be. It left me wondering why I had bothered to tell him at all, especially so early into my pregnancy. Ever since my diagnosis, any news related to my fertility felt like waiting for the other shoe to drop. The waiting game that came along with this baby was even worse. When I went to freeze my eggs, the doctor told me that my reserves were so low that there was no guarantee I'd get another good result. The safest bet was to find a donor, make embryos, and freeze them. So I scrambled into the most unfamiliar online shopping experience ever and bought the most expensive thing that I'd ever bought over the internet. Frozen sperm.

Without any counsel from my friends or any of my family members, who I feared would try to talk me out of it, I did my best to pick someone who had donated because of needs that were more schoolbook than desperation-related, and who my kid could maybe meet someday in the future, hopefully with minimal trauma. That didn't seem to be asking too much.

Ironically, the whole selection process contained way more information and analysis than most married couples probably go through—school grades by subject, entire family medical histories going back two generations, plus detailed STI and genetic disorder tests. And they even provided essay questions with the donor's responses so you could check his thought process and—low key—his grammar as well. With all this overwhelming information and the impossible decisions I had to make, I just did the best that I could in the moment. It was nothing I'd planned for, but it happened fast enough to ignore the part of me screaming for more caution.

In the safety of my car on the way home, I thought back to the most critical moment nearly nine weeks prior—the one in my doctor's office, sitting across from Dr. Young in his neutral-toned room. He was supposed to give me an update over the phone on the third day of my embryo development, but he called me in to see him instead. His face looked stern and serious as I mentally prepared myself for bad news.

"Tabitha, I know this is a lot of information coming all at once. A lot of decisions," Dr. Young said. "And I'm sorry to add one more choice for you, but you must decide." I leaned forward with heavy anticipation of his next words. *Was something wrong with my embryos?* Dr. Young continued solemnly. "Your embryos are developing . . . but slowly, all but one. We think the best chance is to implant now instead of test and freeze on day five. Best time is today, but we can wait until tomorrow latest." *Implant? Did that mean I'd be pregnant?* It was all so overwhelming. My Granny Tab had passed away less than a year prior, and the pain that still lingered was a constant reminder that time is promised to no one. But was I ready to be *pregnant?* I wasn't. I didn't have a nursery ready in my new house or a childcare plan or even any thoughts beyond making sure that I preserved my options. If I said no, I stood to lose everything. But still, I hesitated. I waited, deciding to do the testing anyway. When we got to day five, there was only one embryo. Just one. And when the testing cleared, confirming that it, that *he,* in the miracle of the genetic lottery was deemed "normal," it didn't seem right to wait. All I had was a small amount of money left over from Granny Tab and enough faith to muster the courage to tell Dr. Young to move forward with a transfer, but that was enough.

Weeks later, I got my first positive pregnancy test. And where I thought the questions would end, a whole new universe of worries and anxiety opened up. There were so many more tests to be scheduled and risks to be aware of and the notorious first-trimester wait that felt like spending every second of every day walking on the most delicate of eggshells. And I still had to wonder if my body could handle this new life that was growing inside it. I still had to wonder if my heart, mind, and finances could handle all that came along with it. I didn't have time to consider the questions that Marc threw at me from across the table, the *how will yous, what will yous,* and the *whos* of it all. I just knew that I wanted a family more than anything, and at least as far as my own fertility was concerned, that one chance was the most certain thing I had. So I took it. And I hadn't slept a full night since.

2

FACING THE WORKWEEK AFTER MY MEETING WITH MARC, I WALKED into KVTV carrying more than just the weight of my shoulder bag. Not much had changed, besides the addition of an extra bathroom break to my morning routine. But that was the thing about pregnancy, as I was learning: changes could be sudden. The silence surrounding me in the KVTV restroom felt like a winning lottery ticket on a Monday morning. Better yet, it felt like a guilty win, like I had gotten away with a very poorly executed heist. As my first trimester progressed, I started to think that morning sickness was a myth. That is, until it showed up with a vengeance that seemed to intensify with every passing day. At first, I thought that queasy feeling meant that I'd simply eaten something disagreeable the night before. But then, like a nag that wouldn't go away—it sat at the back of my throat until I finally gave in and ran for the confines of the nearest toilet stall.

Every day since, I'd found myself sneaking like a fugitive—

peeking around corners, tiptoeing past offices, carrying empty coffee mugs and pretending like I was heading to the kitchen, only to stalk that restroom door, waiting for the last occupant to exit so that I could swoop in and make the most silent barf that anyone has ever known. *If only my mother could see me now . . . A puking princess, how lovely.* Well, to be more precise, I was a pregnant puking princess, holed up in the stall, thankful for the moment of relief, and hoping that I could escape before anyone noticed.

Now that I'd won the battle for the senior reporter role at KVTV, the next step would soon be weekend anchor. With new responsibilities to consider, being up for another promotion meant the last thing I wanted the swirling vultures I worked with to know was that I was pregnant. They'd start doing their own math, warming up their hatchets to try to make the most of my maternity leave. Nope. If I could have it my way, I'd be nine months along, having still said nothing, leaving people to simply wonder if I'd swallowed a beach ball.

Just before my stealthy exit from the bathroom, I examined myself in the mirror, took a swish of the alcohol-free mouthwash I had in my pocket, and reapplied my lipstick. A sideways glance was all the reminder I needed to straighten my shoulders and pull in my gut. Even though I wasn't showing, I was starting to look bloated. I rectified that with my last glimpse in the mirror before my heels hit the hallway.

Rounding the corner to my office door, I could hear my cell phone ringing. I picked up the pace. *Ugh, that ringer is so loud and annoying,* I thought as I chased my phone's insistent melody. I managed to pick up just before the last note sounded, glimpsing the words *Alexis Carter* flashing on the screen. I barely got out my hello before my best friend started talking at an unusually frantic speed—even for her.

"Tabby? Tabby, can you hear me?"

"Lexi, of course I can hear you—girl, you're shouting."

"Sorry, Tab, I'm in a hurry, late to show a house in the Valley, and I need to ask you a favor. Can you please pick up your godson from school?"

"Sure, Lexi." I relaxed a little, hearing the nature of Alexis's emergency. It seemed easy enough to manage. I allowed myself a small exhale before asking for the rest of the details. "Just pick him up at the usual place after school?"

"Oh no, Tab, not after school. Like, in the next hour, maybe two? Sorry, it's going to take me a minute to explain, but the short version is that Lexington was fighting at school! His little butt is in the principal's office right now. My parents are away on a jazz cruise, and Rob can't do 'daddy duty' because he's at work and can't leave until later. I just don't know what to do with that little boy!" The exasperation in Alexis's voice was unmistakable. It was rare to hear her this way.

"Oh, Lex, I'm so sorry. Fighting? That doesn't even sound like him!"

"That's the thing, Tab—it's not. Not at all. This is new. I think my baby is acting out because of . . . well, because of the separation between Rob and me. He hasn't said anything, but this behavior . . . I just know it. I don't know what to do, but I've got to work." Alexis sighed heavily. "So, can you do it?" I had to bring my free hand up to cradle my head. My stomach had just started to settle, and here was this crisis to start things back in motion. Even worse, of course this would be the morning that Chris Perkins asked to see me in his office.

"Um, Lex, you know I'm a default yes. It's only that right now I'm on my way in to see my news director. Lord knows what he wants, but it shouldn't take longer than thirty minutes for him to crush my soul. After that, I'll probably be thankful to leave the office. If I can get there closer to noon, then count me as a definite."

"Tab, I'm in a bind, so I'll take what I can get. Plus, it serves Lexington right to have to sit there and think about what he did. You know we did not raise him like that! Fighting?" I could hear her desperation mounting. Knowing Alexis, somehow she'd have already found a way to blame herself, just like she always did—even for Rob's indiscretions. "I'll see you this evening, Tab. If you just take him to your place, I'll pick him up there after work."

"No problem. It actually works out perfectly because I'm having a first meeting with that doula you recommended."

"Oh, that's great—you're going to love Andouele. Everyone swears by her. Just remember to keep an open mind. I heard that she's . . . not what you'd expect at first."

"Lexi, I just did another morning sickness covert op in a public restroom. Nothing in my life is as I expected."

The call with Alexis left me with a few minutes before I was scheduled to see Chris. I tried to stop my mind from obsessing over the unknown reason for the meeting. Chris never scheduled one-on-ones unless the ratings were in and they were either really good or really bad. Ever since my Emmy-winning news story on the Daequan Jenkins shooting, my popularity seemed to be growing in our market. It would have been great to finally get some workplace recognition. If only it were *ever* that simple.

"HEY, CHRIS," I SAID AS I KNOCKED ON HIS OFFICE DOORFRAME to announce myself. "You wanted to see me?" Chris barely lifted his pasty bald head from his iPad screen, which he was frantically stabbing with his stubby index finger.

"Damn, KTLA just scooped us on the . . . How are they getting their news?" Caught up in a mental battlefield, Chris slammed his fist down on his desk before finally looking up at me distractedly. "Tabby." He said my name as if it were an entire mood, and not a good one. It sounded like a Monday-morning, the-coffee-shop-just-ran-out-of-light-roast-as-I-got-to-the-register kind of mood. *Shit.* I stiffened a bit by automatic response, and my hand reflexively went up to my head to twirl on one of my springy, kinky curls for comfort. It was a habit I'd developed since going natural. As I'd learned, evidently everyone *did* want to touch kinky hair. At least my touch target was my own head.

"Please come in," Chris said in response to my hesitation. He seemed to think for just a moment before adding, "Shut the door behind you, will you?" I nodded and moved forward into the office, even as I felt my eyebrow rise. Chris Perkins never shut his door with a woman in his office.

I meant to sit in the chair in the perfect projection of confidence, but that was not how things "went down," so to speak. My heel slipped as I positioned my body to drop gracefully into the seat facing Chris's desk. The landing itself was less like an elegant raindrop and more like a clumsy flop, braced by my arms at either side. I had to stop myself from allowing my hands to travel reflexively to my belly. "So, Chris," I said with forced, cheery nonchalance, "what can I do for you?"

Chris looked up at me over his glasses with his head still hovering over his device. His eyes lingered on my hair and then finally came down to meet my own. This time, he shifted uncomfortably and cleared his throat.

"Tabby, I don't know how to say this exactly. And I'm not usually at a loss for words. Just that . . . the station has been receiving some less than favorable messages lately . . . about your . . . appearance on air." *Wait, what?* The entire discussion had just instantly veered into unbelievable and unfamiliar territory. While my internal ornery girlfriend was cursing to high heaven, I was trying to control my assumptions.

As the news director, Chris had an annoying politically correct way of saying things without really saying them, leaving me to read between the lines for the real story. The only visible change I'd made lately was above my eyebrows—to my hair. Just a couple of weeks before, I found the courage to do my first broadcast with my natural hair texture. Prior to that, even after my "big chop," I'd been wearing wigs that closely mimicked my previous shoulder-length, straightened (and largely heat-damaged) style.

People say that the death of a loved one changes you in unknowable ways. After Granny Tab's funeral, I went to Denisha's salon one Saturday and simply said, "Cut it off . . . all of it." And I felt free in a new way. When I first wore my curls, I thought that viewers might have to make an adjustment to my new look, similar to a color change or haircut for a non-Black anchor, but I never imagined that there would be hate mail. *Hate mail for a hairstyle?* Who had the time?

"I'm sorry, Chris, I don't understand. What is it about my appearance that the viewers don't like?" He took a deep breath. Oh, no way. This couldn't be what I started to think it was.

"Tabby, I'm just going to be frank and candid, because we both know that I don't know how to be anything different." I sat still as stone, waiting for him to continue. After an almost visible selection of his next words, he continued, wringing his hands together on top of his desk in the process. "Viewers are complaining about your hair. I could read you some of the letters and email messages that have come into the station, but I'd rather spare you that. They are not kind, and the details are unnecessary." I pushed my hands down into the cushion of the seat and propped myself upward as far as I could, trying as much as possible to straighten my neck. I wanted to be looking Chris squarely in the face to see what he would say next. When the pause had lingered long enough, I took it as my turn to speak. I hoped it would be Tabby speaking, and not a takeover by my internal ornery girlfriend that the circumstance truly called for.

"Chris . . ." I spoke slowly in the hope that I could swallow my anger. "I'm not sure why you're telling me this unless you simply want me to feel bad, or you expect me to do something about it. Which one is it?"

"Tabby," Chris said quickly, seemingly back in his comfort zone, "I'm not in the business of feelings. I'm in the business of ratings. You have to decide what you're going to do."

"And what if I do nothing, Chris?" In spite of my best efforts, I could feel my eyes narrowing and body tensing.

"Then we see what the ratings say and go from there." I opened my mouth to speak and then shut it again. A thousand retorts flew through my mind, each one slightly more inappropriate than the last. If I hadn't had a child to worry about, I might have quit just on principle and figured out what other jobs my resume afforded me later. The thought of children reminded me of Lexington—I had more important things to deal with this afternoon than this.

"I guess we'll see, then, Chris." Without waiting for a response, I got up and was halfway out the door before concluding the meeting with a jab I couldn't resist. "If you don't mind me excusing myself, me and my *appearance* have some news to produce."

I was halfway down the hallway back to my office when I heard him call after me, "Don't shoot the messenger, Tabby!"

3

I WAS STILL FUMING ALMOST FORTY-FIVE MINUTES LATER WHEN I walked into Lexington's elementary school in search of the principal's office. I'd been there for plays and recitals, but not for disciplinary infractions. I sincerely hoped this wasn't practice for my own impending motherhood. In any event, today I'd get my first true test as a disciplinarian. A few turns and a lot of clacking of my heels across tiled floors, and I arrived at the forbidding deep brown wooden door of the principal's office. Even though I wasn't the one in trouble, as my fingers circled the brass doorknob, the brief pang of anticipation in my gut felt strangely familiar, as if I was a still a kid. Through the window, I could see little Lexington with his backpack on, sitting slouched in an adult-sized chair next to the receptionist. His whole body swayed with the motion of his swinging feet a full few inches above the ground. Even the dulling effects of the fluorescent lighting couldn't mask the megawatt boyish charm that he exuded. I could feel a smile breaking through my otherwise stern expression. I didn't want the usual beaming amusement he brought to my face to make him think he was off the hook. The way Alexis sounded on the phone, that boy was in a world of trouble—and the school discipline was just the beginning.

"Auntie Tab!" Lexington shrieked when he saw me, and he made a move like he was going to rush toward me, his grin growing by the second. And then suddenly, as if he'd remembered something, he sat back in his seat and turned to the receptionist, who still hadn't looked up at me coming in the door. "Ms. Fwanklin said I'm not allowed to move until *she* says so," Lexington tattled with his distinctive pouty voice. I'd heard him enunciate better when he was five years old. I reminded myself to toughen up and not let him see his antics working.

"Well then, Lexington," I said to him as sternly as I could muster, "you better sit there while I go and speak to your principal. I heard that you did some very naughty things today." I gave him my best "Black momma" look and tried even harder not to smile. He sank backward in his chair with a pout. I turned my attention to the receptionist who, based on the nameplate on her desk, was evidently Ms. Franklin and who had yet to look up at me from her computer screen, her fingers flying across the keyboard. I cleared my throat to get her attention.

"Ms. Franklin?" I said in my best "don't you see me standing here?" voice. She finally brought her eyes up to meet mine, still saying nothing, so I continued. "I'm here to pick up Lexington Carter. I'm his godmother. I understand that I'm supposed to speak with the principal as well." She squinted her eyes at me, and then softened her gaze and finally stopped typing.

"Wait, aren't you on the news? KVTV? Walker, right? Teresa Walker?" I sighed. I could not get out of there fast enough.

"Yes, I'm *Tabitha* Walker. Thanks so much for watching." Still bristling on the inside, I gave her my practiced smile. "Is the principal available now to see me?"

"Let me just get him. It's so nice to meet you—I really do like watching you on the news. And, I have to say, I love your hair. I never imagined I'd see natural hair on the news, but look at you!" With that, she gave me a big smile and got up to lean into the slightly ajar office door behind her. After a few words directed toward the entry, she turned back to me. "Principal Miller can see you now—just head right in."

I wanted to ask her to use all that typing time to send a viewer note to Chris Perkins, but she had already turned her attention back to her screen. Plus, I needed to put full focus into this conversation with Principal Miller because there was no way Lexington's mother wasn't going to ask me for each and every detail when she came to pick him up.

I FINALLY GOT LEXINGTON LOADED INTO THE CAR AFTER WALKING him from the principal's office in the cutest seven-year-old solo shame parade imaginable. The insanity of my workday now seemed like a distant memory, replaced in my consciousness with the level of attention the child in front of me required. My visit with the principal confirmed that Lexington was indeed fighting with one of the other kids, who was also sent home, and was now looking at a three-day suspension.

Lexington's superhero backpack was bigger than he was and hung low, pulling down the collar of his already rumpled and dusty white polo shirt in the back. He had his head down as he shuffled in front of me, alternating between pulling his thumb toward the opening of his mouth, then pouting more and putting it back down again. It was so adorable, I really tried not to chuckle while I followed behind him. We walked in relative silence until just before we reached the car. He turned around abruptly to look at me, and I stiffened.

"Am I in twouble, Auntie Tab?" Lexington asked, still using his pouty voice. I paused, wondering what Alexis would want me to say in the moment. I realized that I had very little experience doling out kiddie discipline. I honestly had no idea what Lexi would say, or what I should in her place. In this moment, perhaps my first test of acting motherly, I was worried about making a misstep of bad parenting.

"Lexington, your mother is very upset," I said, hoping that I could stay neutral.

"But it wasn't my fault!" He balled up his hands for emphasis.

According to Principal Miller's narrative, that fact was debatable.

"Well, whose fault was it, Lexington?"

"I already told Principal Miller," Lexington pleaded. "Noah started it! Making fun of the new shoes that my daddy bought me."

I looked down at Lexington's shoes. If they'd been brand-new before, they were noticeably dirty and scuffed now. I wondered why they were so important to him, but decided to save the real questions for Alexis. I opened the car door for him and ushered him into the back seat and strapped him into the booster seat I kept for him in my trunk.

"Lexington, Principal Miller had a different story about what happened. But, I'm sure you know that, right?" I gave him a stern look. He just stuck his lip out, pouting, arms folded, with no answer.

It wasn't until I started the car engine that I realized Lexington and I were stuck alone together until the end of Alexis's workday, with no way for me to entertain him. And I had my first appointment with Andouele in just a couple of hours. He was still pouting behind me when I decided to make an emergency beeline for the three-in-one miracle cure for all upset tiny humans: fast food. Once his hands were full of fries and crispy nuggets, he reanimated into an entirely different person.

"Auntie Tab, can I ask you a question?" I heard his high mini voice drifting forward from the back seat. I looked in the rearview mirror to see ketchup stains on his shirt and just hoped whatever mess he created would eventually come out if I took my car over to Crenshaw for a deep cleaning.

"Sure, sweetie," I said, signaling the end of my jailhouse bailiff role.

"My mommy said that you have a baby in your stomach, but I don't see it. Maybe it looks like you ate too many nuggets—just like me!" He smiled at me with a still somewhat snaggletooth grin. *Of course*, my mind whined, now I have to improvise a birds-and-bees conversation for a seven-year-old in the car on the way to meet *my doula*.

"Well, Lexington, babies grow over time, just like you did when you were in your mommy's belly." I congratulated myself on a response that I hoped would close the conversation. But when I heard him take in a long breath. I braced for the follow-up.

"How do they get in there, anyway?" he squeaked back at me. My mind went blank, flashing the warning lights of, *Oh no. Not this question.* How does this little boy pick the day that he gets suspended from school to be the day that he is most interested in learning where babies come from? *But of course.*

"What did your mommy tell you about how babies get in their mommies' tummies? You know what? Let's ask her when she comes to pick you up!" I grinned enthusiastically, playing up my suggestion.

"Oh, Auntie Tabby, I know how babies get made!" *Oh, gracious.* I prayed for mercy and braced myself for his explanation. Who knew that Lexi and Rob were such progressive parents? He continued, "Well, first a deliveryman comes . . ." At this, my eyebrow rose so high it almost met my hairline.

"A deliveryman, Lexington?"

"Yes, first a deliveryman comes . . . and he's sent by the daddy, or the guy who wants to be the daddy. And the deliveryman comes with a package that the daddy sent." He paused and smiled, seemingly very satisfied with himself. "And then," he continued, "if the lady, the mommy-lady, likes the package, then the deliveryman can come in and leave the package and the lady will open it."

I was afraid to ask, but I couldn't resist hearing the rest of Rob and Lexi's wild explanation of human reproduction.

"And what happens when the mommy-lady opens the package, Lexington?" At my question, he got even more animated.

Excitedly, he rambled on. "Inside the package for the mommy-lady there are candies—like jellybeans we get at Easter. And the mommy-lady eats the candies and they go into her belly and hatch and then she has a baby in there!" He concluded smugly, with as much pride as if he had just presented a paper at a major medical conference. I tried to stifle my laughter.

"Well, Lexington," I said once I had regained my composure, "for a seven-year-old, that's surprisingly accurate." The way I came to be pregnant, it took me thirty-four years to understand.

4

I ARRIVED AT MY HOUSE WITH A VERY MESSY LEXINGTON, WHO had created a watercolor art piece of his already dirty school shirt well before we made it to the driveway. I tried to navigate us toward homework duty, but Lexington had more questions for me about seemingly everything in my home, as if this was his first time visiting and not his fiftieth—about my kitchen, and how furniture gets made and who invented the television. By the time my highly recommended prospective doula arrived, Lexington was finally bored with me and well settled in watching kid-friendly programming on Netflix in the den. I'd managed to find a stash of popcorn to keep him continually occupied during my meeting. I had a lot of questions, and I needed a few minutes to quell the bubbling nervousness that this meeting awakened. It was unusually early in a pregnancy to be picking up a doula, but Dr. Young's office had advised me as a single mother—"By choice," as they liked to call it—to afford myself as much support as possible, and that included a "mother's helper" if I could manage the cost of having one. I needed all the help I could get.

Alexis told me that all of the women in her mommy circle group swore by this one woman, even if she was a bit unconventional. Because of the emergency school pickup today, we didn't get a chance to do a full briefing call before I heard the doorbell. When I opened the door, I was shocked—to put it mildly.

"Andouele," she said, holding out her hand. I tried not to let my mouth drop open as a dreadlocked woman stood in front of me in bright African print parachute pants, with beautiful beaded bracelets garnishing her very light arms. The contrast was striking. I tried not to let confusion show in my face. I knew just as well as anyone that the African diaspora came in all shades, even paler than my Granny Tab, who was as zero percent Motherland as someone could be. I wished that Lexi had given me some kind of warning. Clutching on to composure, I let my reporter professionalism take over and lead the way.

"I'm Tabitha, or Tabby, whichever you'd like. Why don't you come on in?" I used my most inviting tone to mask what surprise still lingered and pushed the heavy wooden front door further open to accommodate Andouele's relatively slight frame and much bigger presence. "Can I get you anything?"

"Oh no, I'm fine," her voice sang softly to me. She did have a soothing presence, even with few words. I could see why women felt at ease with her. *Give it a chance, Tabby.*

"Oh-kayyy!" *Crap.* I hadn't meant to say any of my awkward thoughts out loud, even if it was under my breath. I tried to recover on the fly. "Okay!" I said even more cheerfully.

"I'm just glad you're here, Andouele. Am I saying your name correctly?" Still slightly unsure, I pronounced her name for the first time carefully, as I'd heard her say it and as I'd remembered it spoken by Alexis. She must have heard the hesitation in my voice.

"Yes, it's Andouele," she said slowly, enunciating each syllable with calming patience, sounding out *and-way-lay*. I felt a slight pang of panic hearing a pronunciation slightly different than the one I'd used reflected back to me as she continued. "It's traditionally a boy's name and means 'God brings me.' My parents gave me my own spelling when they found out I was a girl."

"Ah, *Andouele*, that's beautiful." I smiled quickly, hoping that she didn't notice or mind my fumble or, worse, think the worst of me already and not want to take on my mess of a charge. "You'll have to forgive me—I'm babysitting my godson today, so I'm just a little more frazzled than usual." I sat on the sofa across from the large plush chair that she had chosen in my living room and tried not to wring my hands in my lap.

Andouele smiled at me gently. She reached for one of my hands, enveloped it in the warm softness of both of her own, and looked at me intently, waiting for me to settle. "You're nervous. It's okay. It's a scary thing being a new mom. I understand." For some reason, I felt the pressure of tears welling in my eyes. So quickly, she'd pierced my truth. I gave a slight smile and a nod of agreement while struggling not to cry. "You're not alone," she continued. "You just have to remember that. Your body was made to do this, and you'll have the benefit of the wisdom of our ancestors if you just

allow yourself to be open to it." I stopped my mind from in-
quiring which of our ancestors Andouele and I had in common. Somehow, it didn't matter, anyway. I resigned myself
to the assumption that Andouele was invited to the picnic
and made a mental note to ask Alexis about the details later.
I finally found the words to speak.

"Honestly, none of this has been easy. Not any part of it.
I didn't even think I'd be able to have children—*this* was a
miracle . . . and I've lost a lot along the way." I felt the first tear
stream down my face. Andouele didn't change her demeanor
or appear that she was made uncomfortable by my instant
emotion. I supposed she'd been desensitized by the hordes of
hormonal pregnant women who swore by her services. She
loosened her hold on my hand just slightly to reach for my
other one.

"For any woman who wants children," she said, as softly
as if reciting a love poem, "she has to be ready to face her
greatest fears and the uprooting of any lies and delusions she
holds about herself. She must be ready to fail . . . and hurt.
It's life's way of making you face necessary resolutions. That
beautiful baby growing inside of you will demand that of you.
And the purpose and blessing, at least in part, is to become
more aware of who you are and the strength you have access
to as a woman." Her words caused me to draw a sharp, stuttered breath. I wanted to burst into ugly tears, but more than
that, I wanted to hear more. It was the first bit of pure encouragement I'd heard. Her words sounded like foreign thoughts,
but also like wisdom. "Tabby, *if* you decide that I'm a good
match for you as your doula, I will be there with you along
the way. If we decide that we're a good match for each other,

my only job is to make sure that you get everything you want in your experience. We'd work together so that *your* birth plan and *your* wishes hold weight, and that you are respected. You're in good hands, my sister. And do you have a partner, a significant other?"

My mind slipped quickly to that last conversation with Marc, bringing a feeling of mild disappointment. Once again, I'd allowed him to break into the beauty of what was meant to be my moment. I pushed him out of my mind, speaking my next words only as an affirmation. "No, no partner. I'm a single mother by choice." Andouele stiffened at my words.

"Sister, all that are blessed to be mothers are mothers by some choice," she said to me firmly. "There is no separation between you and my married sister or my single sister who became pregnant by surprise. The journey is an equal blessing for each of you. The mantle of motherhood alone is a high honor." She spoke to me sternly with intention in her eyes. I understood my error.

"I should have said that I'm a single mother by my own choice entirely," I said, making a quick correction. "There was . . . There *is* no partner involved."

"Single motherhood is a path of courage, Tabby. In so many ways, the road will rise to meet your feet and you will find your magic. Congratulations on your journey." I couldn't help but smile at her words, which I could feel inflating my chest slightly. I had forgotten all about trying to place her culturally in favor of knowing that I had found my doula.

A thought occurred that made me laugh lightly to myself. "Hmmm . . . a single mother by *courage*," I said with a smile. "I like the sound of that." Anyway, it was true. I would *need* courage and my own brand of magic to face the uncertainty to come.

ANDOUELE AND I WRAPPED UP OUR MEETING WITH A WARM HUG. As soon as she left, I delivered a fresh round of snacks to Lexington, which he was still eating through yawns and giggles when Alexis showed up at my door. We lived in the same neighborhood since I exchanged my downtown condo for a house.

Alexis breezed her way through the door with the clamor of her gold bracelets as she marched her stilettos across the living room toward the kitchen. "Girl! Thank you so much!" she said breathlessly. "I had no idea what I was gonna do. I can't believe that little boy. Where is he?" Alexis turned around frenetically and headed toward the den at the back of the house where Lexington could be heard giggling.

"He's in the back. He's all right—watching TV with some snacks. That boy can eat! I've been worried about overfeeding him, but it's like his stomach is a bottomless pit!"

Alexis paused her mission to laugh. "Girl!"

"Lex, why don't you sit for a second and have a glass of wine?" I knew she was close to her tipping point, and Lexington would do much better with a calm mama than the fire-breathing bestie who had started hurtling through my living room. "I have a bottle of that rosé you like in the fridge."

"In the fridge?" Alexis whipped around to look at me. "Tabby, I *know* you haven't been drinking?"

"Girl, no! I just put it in there when I got home because I figured *you'd* need a drink. And after what the principal said, it might save my godson's life." Alexis conceded and switched direction to head with me toward the kitchen. I couldn't help but notice how slim she had gotten over the past year during her and Rob's separation. She said that she was turning herself into a MILF, and everything about her current presentation, from the pants to the blouse to the heels, was screaming her old high school moniker, Sexy Lexi.

After more than a few sips of wine, a noticeably looser Alexis circled back to the topic of her youngest son's discipline. "Okay, Tab, I'm ready. Tell me what the principal said." Alexis gave me the "come on" gesture with her free hand, while the other held the now half-empty wineglass that had slightly shifted her temperament.

So much had already happened that day. It took me a minute and a sip of lukewarm chamomile tea to even recall my relatively brief time with the principal. It was amazing how taking care of a child could completely change the focus of the entire day—away from Chris's ridiculous conversation about my hair and even the mounting anxiety I was feeling about my next and most crucial doctor's appointment. Lexington, even the badly behaved version of him, had brought me to exactly where I needed to be.

"Girl, *your son* got riled up on the playground with another kid. Next thing, the teacher was pulling the two of them off of each other and both are suspended for three days."

"Three days!" Alexis brought her heavily jeweled arm up to her face and placed an exquisitely manicured hand on her forehead. She must have had to look expensive to sell people expensive homes.

"I asked him, and he said it wasn't his fault."

At that, Alexis raised an eyebrow.

"Oh really? What else did he say?" Alexis asked.

"He said a kid was making fun of the shoes that Rob bought him. So, it's going to be up to you to determine what really happened. I don't envy you one bit."

"Good Lord, that boy." She looked at me, exasperated. "Tabby, you know it's getting harder every day to believe that my and Rob's separation isn't causing all this."

"Lexi, don't blame yourself. You didn't cause Rob to cheat. You didn't cause Lexington to fight on the playground. And you're not wrong for trying to put your own life back together."

"Yeah, but I can't help thinking that this is my fault, that I'm being selfish."

"It's not your fault, Lexi." I tried to look her in her eyes and give the same comfort that Andouele had offered me earlier. "Being a mother takes a lot of courage. That's what Andouele said to me today."

"Oh! Tab, I forgot all about that! How did that go? She's great, right?" Alexis quickly shed the air of heaviness from the prior moment. She seemed to want to move on, so I decided it was best to let things flow into the new topic.

"She's . . . interesting. She definitely came looking like a soul sista. Heavier on the soul than the sista, though. I wasn't exactly sure how to place her?"

Alexis dropped her head with laughter, confusing me further. "Ohmygosh, Tabby!" she garbled through chuckles. "Andouele is *Black*. She's Creole, and with an African name! Girl, I hope you didn't say anything to her!" She could barely talk for laughing at my ignorance.

"Lex, I'm going to be honest, I did think that we were possibly in a *transracial* situation, and I totally mispronounced her name." Reflexively, my hand came to meet my forehead as I remembered my faux pas. "But she's amazing. I don't care what she is, she won me over as a person, seriously. I just felt . . . *seen*. I can only hope I made enough of a positive impression with her as well. Everything I've been worried about, she knew—it was like she could read my mind. Somehow, she managed to give me confidence. And honestly, after everything that's been happening lately, it was right on time. She was like a breath of fresh air when I didn't even know I was suffocating."

"Tab, I heard she's busy, but I don't think it's a competition. She's just great in providing supportive care with an awareness of the needs of Black mothers. I wish I'd had her when I was pregnant with the boys. All the women in my mother's group swear by her. So, overall your meeting went well?"

"I think so. Sometimes it takes that feeling of focused support, even just for a second, to realize how much weight you've been carrying." A cloud of concern crossed Alexis's face.

"Did something else happen?"

Reflexively, my hand went to the comfort of the curls on my head, reminding me of the earlier conversation with Chris at the station. I took a deep breath and decided to share. "Well, in my meeting at work, the news director told me viewers were complaining about me switching my hair to a natural style, *and* Marc was giving me static over the weekend about having this baby as a single mom . . . so now I have all these doubts, and—" Alexis cut me off.

"Tabitha Walker, did you just say 'Marc'? Your *ex*? What does Marc know about you being pregnant? Wasn't the whole point of using a donor to leave him out of it?" Alexis's eyes were wide with disbelief. She did have a point. And the way that Alexis felt about Marc, it would have been so much easier if we were talking about my hair instead.

"I don't know why I told him. I guess I wanted to show him, and maybe myself too, that I could be happy without him, you know? Lexi, every step of this has felt so unpredictable. I mean, I don't know how this next doctor's appointment is going to go. I'm praying that everything will be fine, but what if it isn't? I just needed to take that moment for myself while I had it . . . not that I'm not paying for it. Leave it to Marc Brown to make me question myself, even when he's *not* involved."

Lexi's expression softened as she reached out to touch my hand. "Tab, I see you. I love you. I acknowledge your struggle." I smiled as she very soberly echoed the words taken from our therapy sessions that had followed our friend Laila's hospitalization. But like Laila's presence lately, a piece was missing.

"Wait, you missed a part! You don't think I'm beautiful? Good thing Laila didn't hear you!" I teased Alexis, who'd left off the last part of our often-used affirmation.

"Girl, Laila is in a full-blown, all-consuming romance with her business startup, and I was just trying to get to the main point." With a dramatic flourish, Alexis waved away my critique. "Seriously, Tab, don't let that fool get you down. You were smart. You made the best decision in front of you. And you're going to be the best mother, I just know it. Plus, you won't have any of the problems that I do."

"At least you have Rob's support and some kind of effort. Marc had me thinking of all of the *whos* and the *whats* and the *how-will-yous*, and I can't shake it. Well, I couldn't. Thank you for recommending Andouele. And thank you for letting me borrow your baby and play mom for a bit . . . Even if I did overfeed him."

"Tab, you keep saying that! He's not a goldfish!" Lexi said, standing up and shaking her head. "It is impossible to over-feed those boys; I have to sell two houses a month just to buy enough groceries!" Alexis threw her hands up in exclamation like a human emoji. Her wineglass sat empty on the counter as she started to get up from her seat at the kitchen island. "Speaking of boys, I'm too tired to spank that child tonight, so let me go get my son and put his little bad ass to bed. Followed shortly by me. Girl, I'm exhausted." I put my mug on the counter, then placed both hands on her shoulders and looked Alexis squarely in her eyes.

"Evidently, having courage is exhausting, Lex."

"Yep, exhausting . . ." Alexis sighed heavily. As she turned to walk toward the den to collect my godson for the evening, one last thought popped into my mind—something I couldn't believe I'd forgotten.

"Lexi, one day, you're going to have to explain to me about the deliveryman . . . and the jellybeans?" I pointed to my belly with a teasing smile. She broke into a grin.

"Girl, bye. That story was Rob's idea." And with that, she disappeared down the hallway in the direction of the giggles.

5

"Looking good, girl!" Ms. Gretchen called out to me from the large open recreation room behind the sign-in counter at Crestmire. I had managed to maintain my commitment to weekly, and at worst biweekly, visits with Granny Tab's bestie. I would not soon forget the look in Ms. Gretchen's eyes at the service; it seemed to threaten a loss of the spunk and energy that this woman delivered daily. It was enough to ensure I paid her as many visits as I could. She was no longer the icing on the cake of my visits with my grandmother. Ms. Gretchen was now the whole cake, plus the icing, the ice cream, and the cherry on top.

Just hearing Ms. Gretchen's voice triggered a big smile to break out on my face. My hand reflexively went upward, toward my curls, but I caught myself . . . *No need to be self-conscious here, Tabby.*

I crossed the floor in quick strides, my Saturday flip-flops squeaking the whole way, and joined Ms. Gretchen at a table with some other women finishing what looked like lunch. "Come on and take a seat," she said with more energy than I could muster on even my best day. "Bessie, move your chair over so Tabby can sit down. You remember Tabby, doncha?" Ms. Bessie looked up at me through her glasses, her wavy silver hair wobbling a bit with her unsteady neck, and a faint smile started to peek through.

"Hi, Tabby," Ms. Bessie said quietly, continuing to focus on her meal. "We're supposed to have ice cream today," she said to me as much as to herself. As I adjusted in my seat, I looked over to Ms. Gretchen. Surprisingly, it seemed like she was getting up.

"Come on, honey, I've already finished." Ms. Gretchen motioned to me insistently. "No need for us to sit here—we can go somewhere more comfortable." Even before I was fully standing, she had my hand in hers and was pulling me toward the large armchairs near the window. As we walked, she whispered to me, "Sitting with those old ladies is downright depressing! I'm not dead yet, but there are times I get so bored I've got to check my pulse!" We both shared a generous laugh and claimed two seats providing a luscious view of the trees outside. Sitting down, I noticed that I had inadvertently started fidgeting with my hair again. Irritated with myself, I brought my hand back down to my lap. Ms. Gretchen briefly showed a slight frown and then said, "That haircut is just what you needed! It's opened up your face, and you look younger. Plus . . ." She smiled knowingly. "It sets off that little glow of yours you've got going." Following her last words, her eyes drifted down to my belly. I felt embarrassed by my own misgivings.

"Thanks, Ms. Gretchen. I do love it, but people out here are trying to give me all kinds of second thoughts."

"Second thoughts? Whatcha mean, *second thoughts?*" Ms. Gretchen challenged.

"Well, my news director, Chris, sat me down the other day and told me that viewers were complaining about my hair," I said sheepishly. Part of me felt like I was complaining or tattling. Things like this seemed like they should be my problem to solve, not to burden Ms. Gretchen with. But she appeared interested, and the words flowed naturally.

"What viewers are complaining? With everything going on in the world right now, honey, your hair seems like the last thing they should be worried about." Ms. Gretchen waved her hand in the air loosely. "Seems like they ought to mind their own affairs," she added with a raise of her eyebrow.

"Yeah, Chris didn't go into specifics, but I have all this pressure to deliver ratings with my new position, and soon, I could be up for another promotion. Sometimes I think it'd be easier just to slap on a wig again and be done with it." I finished with a sigh that was more dramatic than I intended.

"Honey, let me tell you this, and I wish I had learned it sooner than it took me to figure out in my ninety-three years of livin' . . . but, you have to just be *you*. That's all you're responsible for. Let everyone else sort out their own mess. And believe me—half the stuff they try to put on you, that's their mess they're dealing with," she said with a long blink and a flip of her perfectly dyed, shoulder-grazing blond hair.

I couldn't help but smile. This was so much like the times we used to share with my Granny Tab, the three of us just chatting, sometimes even at the same place near the window. I felt the pang of missing her that had only just slightly started to dull. "Ms. Gretchen," I said, smiling, "you're going to make the best glam-maw!"

At my words, Ms. Gretchen's face lit up brighter than I had ever seen it. "Glam-maw . . . I like the sound of that," she said before she turned to look out of the window. After a pause, she added wistfully, "You know, I always thought I'd lived my life without regrets. I never believed I'd get the chance to have a grandchild . . . and I never knew it would matter . . . until . . ." I waited for her to finish, but she just kept looking out of the window.

"Do you regret not having children, Ms. Gretchen?" She turned to look at me, almost as if she'd forgotten for a moment that I was sitting there with her.

"Oh Lord, no! I got enough of that teaching, honey, you can believe that! But . . . well . . ." Ms. Gretchen seemed to be searching for words, an unusual moment if I'd ever seen one. But eventually, she continued. "Well, you," she said, turning to me, "you're the greatest gift my best friend ever gave me." As she spoke, I could see her eyes welling with tears, triggering the familiar twinge in my own. "And it makes me wonder," she paused, turning to face the trees, "what I'm going to leave the world when I'm gone . . . who it's all for." Turning back to me, she took my hand and looked me in my eyes. "Thank you, honey. You know I'm honored and tickled splendid to be that baby's glam-maw, or whatever you want me to be." I got up and hugged her.

"Oh, we know there's gonna have to be some glam in there if it's you, Ms. Gretchen," I said, gesturing with my eyes to her neon-yellow painted fingernails. We both shared a welcome chuckle. I knew that somewhere, Granny Tab had to be laughing with us.

"So now tell me again, honey, when does this baby boy of ours arrive?"

"Well, Ms. Gretchen," I said, suddenly remembering my upcoming doctor's appointment with apprehension, "my so-called 'graduation' appointment is next week. If everything checks out, I'm out of the danger zone. So I'm just hoping and praying every single day that everything is okay."

"Everything is going to be just fine, honey, you'll see," she said, patting my hand. And while I wanted to believe her, something in the back of my mind was still waiting for the other shoe to drop.

6

On a Tuesday afternoon, in my ninth week of pregnancy, Lisa Sinclair sat across from me at a small coffee shop table with her eyes closed, soaking in the last bits of sunshine during our usual midmorning beverage break. She shook her immaculately highlighted blond hair across her shoulders as she tilted her head back and released a loud sigh.

"Tabby, don't you just wish we could stay out here all day? Who needs to sit inside that station anyway, with that terrible coffee and *no straws*!" Lisa shook the cascading wave of her flaxen tresses and flashed her perfectly straight, perfectly white teeth in a smile before she brought her own coffee cup to her perfectly lined and glossed lips. She took a sip through the narrow white straw. "So, what's up with you? Did you talk to Chris yet about weekend anchor?" *Ugh*. I appreciated the push from Lisa but wished that Chris Perkins could stay out of my hair, figuratively and literally, at least during my coffee breaks.

"Lisa, you know I love you and I appreciate the nudge,

but I don't want to talk to Chris about anything right now. I didn't tell you what he said to me about my hair?"

"No, what?" Lisa asked innocently, leaning forward out of her sunlit reverie.

I shook my head, not wanting to repeat the words I'd been trying unsuccessfully to push out of my mind. "He said . . . there were viewer complaints."

"Viewer complaints?" Lisa sputtered, seeming to choke on her sip of coffee. "About . . . about what?" she managed to croak the words out through a coughing spell. I patted her on the back, but she waved me away with her hand.

"Girl, my hair! Evidently, some viewers don't like that I'm wearing my hair natural now."

"No way!" Lisa said, patting down her own silky style. "I *love* your hair. It looks so good on you like that—and I love the curls . . ." As she finished speaking, she reached forward with her hand toward my head. I backed away with a smile. She seemed to remember quickly. "Oh, sorry, that's right. Don't touch." She recoiled sheepishly.

"Thank you." I forced a bigger smile than came naturally. "Lisa, you may like the curls, but some viewers do not."

"Didn't we just report on the new CROWN Act that was passed in California?" Lisa's voice hit a higher pitch. "I can't believe Chris sometimes. He's not threatening you, is he?" She leaned forward in a mama bear stance. Lisa was the evening anchor, and effectively the queen bee of our station. She and I had, thankfully, made friends a while ago, creating a hybrid relationship of mentorship and mutual support that I really cherished. "You know what, Tabby, I have an idea." My eyebrows rose reflexively.

"I'm all ears because, honestly, I'm at a loss for what to do. Chris didn't threaten me—he put it back on me like he usually does and just said 'ratings, ratings, ratings.'" I gave my best imitation of his common refrain.

"You should bring this up with the women's issues group. This is an ideal topic for us to address collectively. There's no way that anybody should be told by viewers what hairstyles to wear. Everyone should be outraged!" Lisa brought her French-manicured fingertips down onto the tabletop with a quiet thump of her palm. "I'm pissed. Aren't you pissed?" she said, looking at me incredulously.

"Of course I'm pissed, Lisa." This time, I couldn't help but roll my eyes. She simply didn't understand. "I just don't know what to do about it."

"I get it—it's the 'every battle' thing, right?" I nodded back at her with a small smile. Lisa Sinclair was a quick learner. "Tab, we're going to fight this one out with you. You should be able to wear your hair the way you want to, and if viewers complain, so what? Not everyone loves going to the art museum, but that doesn't mean that we shouldn't keep all the pictures there." I gave Lisa a puzzled look. "Well, you know what I mean," she said sheepishly.

I smiled. "Maybe I will bring it up to the group. I just don't want to deal with the added stress at the moment."

"Yeah, seriously, you've been through a lot in this past year with your grandmother, a new house, and that boyfriend of yours, and of course, the serious stress of that egg freezing series you did . . ." Lisa paused to smile knowingly at me. "So, when do you think you'll start working on that family you've been wanting?" I felt a brief shock of guilt in my gut. *She'll know soon enough*, I reassured myself, forcing the corners of my lips to rise.

"Good question!" I managed to force out. "I guess we'll have to see." I looked down at my phone. "Time to head back, no?" I started to get up, hopefully signaling to Lisa that our conversation was finished for now. After a pause that caused me a moment of doubt, she finally pushed her chair back with a loud buzz against the floor.

I'd tell Lisa another day, if there was even going to be something to tell. I would have been relieved for the reprieve, except for the reminder that popped up on my phone. Just one week until my appointment with Dr. Young. Even with two degrees under my belt, I'd never felt so uncertain about a graduation. I said a silent prayer for my son and took one last sip of my chamomile tea before heading behind Lisa back into the office.

7

IF YOU COUNTED THE TIME THAT HAD PASSED UNTIL MY TEN-WEEK appointment in anxiety, tears, pacing, or sleeplessness, I'd have been a Crestmire resident by the time I made it back to Dr. Young's waiting room. It was in this same place that I'd had to explain to my mother that sperm donors were more likely to need money for books than for a burrito. The irony wasn't lost on me that I still took that same ridiculous conversation to heart when it eventually came time to select my own. I had searched and searched the database of available donors, some with "specimen," as they liked to generically refer to it, that had been frozen for thirty years. It all felt like a very science-fiction way to be starting a family, but in a land of no options, the choice in front of you wears the king's crown.

I'd carefully picked someone with a similar education to my own who seemed, at least based on his profile, like we might have just as easily met at a bar one night, and maybe even happened upon a one-night stand. Except, all of this was so much more deliberate and orchestrated than that and, let's not forget, expensive. All of the money and injections, and waiting, and testing, then all of the procedures and more waiting, and more testing, and more procedures, and then even more waiting led, finally, up to this day. Today, the doctor would tell me if my baby boy was healthy and well formed enough to "graduate" to a regular obstetrics practice. We'd be official, if we could just make it through the final gauntlet.

I had already started nervously shuffling my right foot when the nurse took mercy on me, calling my name to come in.

She smiled at me as we walked together. "You must be really excited; this is a big day." I swallowed hard.

"Yep, supposed to *graduate* . . . Um, can I ask you a question?" I bit my lip. The nurse nodded. I willed my mouth to move and ask what it was I really wanted to know. "Is it common to, um, *not* graduate? Like if everything's fine now, it should be fine later, right?" The nurse turned and looked at me, slowing down her stride. We came to a stop in the hallway, facing each other just shy of the examination room door.

"Ms. Walker, I'm sure you'll be fine. For many of our patients, this is their best day with us. Don't worry." She opened the door to the examination room in front of us. "You're in very good hands." She cleared the entryway, delivering me to the waiting ultrasound technician who had the big screen and probe rig already set up. Next to the machine stood an uninviting arrangement of stirrups latched to a paper-covered examination bed. The paper crumpled under me as I took a seat, and the technician explained the drill, allowing me to undress before she returned.

Two knocks, some positioning, and some cold and squishy lube later, we were deep (and I do mean deep) into my exam. I was holding my breath for any sound or sign coming from the technician.

"Is everything there?" I asked. "All the fingers and toes? Is he still in there?" I tried to peek around to the screen. Meanwhile, the pacing of the exam seemed to pick up. The technician started to move the probe around more aggressively.

"I'm just looking for . . . should be right . . ." she said while turning the knob. After a pause, she looked up at me and asked, "And you said you had the early genetic testing, right?"

I nodded. "Yes, the pre-implantation PGD test and then the noninvasive DNA test. I'm supposed to get those results today. Is everything all right?" I could feel my heart rate start to pick up. The technician didn't answer me but instead started to murmur something to herself.

"Um . . ." She paused. "Um . . ." She pulled the probe out of me and placed it back in the holder. She touched my leg to speak to me. "Ms. Walker, I . . . I need to go get the doctor. I'll be . . . I mean, he'll be in to see you shortly." I felt the tears welling up. Something was wrong. I knew something had to be wrong.

"Is there something wrong with my baby? Please just tell me," I begged.

"Don't worry, Ms. Walker—I'll send Dr. Young right in." She kept trying to reassure me as she inched her way back toward the door. But she gave me no information. I knew what that had to mean. *Oh no, this can't be good.*

Less than thirty seconds later, the technician burst back through the door, followed closely by Dr. Young.

"Dr. Young, is my baby okay?" I pleaded again. He looked at me.

"Tabitha, we're going to see right now. It seems that the technician is having a hard time finding . . ." Dr. Young stopped speaking and switched his concentration over to the screen in front of him, continuing my exam. This time, instead of the technician, it was him seated at the console. "Okay . . . right there is where we should see it . . . Do you have the chart? Ask Noreen to bring the chart." The technician bolted up and out of the room almost before his last word was out. I was barely breathing. I wanted with everything in me to ask again, but I knew I shouldn't break his concentration. If there was something wrong, maybe he could fix it on that screen.

Noreen rushed in through the door holding a manila folder out to Dr. Young. He pulled the probe out of me, threw off his gloves, and flipped open the folder. He held up a single sheet of paper in front of him. "Impossible," he said quietly. *Impossible? What was impossible?* "Ms. Walker," he continued, "did you follow all of my instructions following your embryo transfer?" My mouth dropped open; I was speechless. I had followed every instruction. All the instructions . . . well, all of the instructions except maybe a little harmless one.

"Yes, Dr. Young, to the letter."

"Well, Ms. Walker, I have bad news for you and good news for you. Which one do you want first?" Anger flashed in my brain, and I couldn't think straight. I snapped.

"Don't play games with me, Dr. Young. I want to know right now, is there something wrong with my baby? Nobody is telling me anything, but I can tell something is wrong!"

I could hear myself yelling, and it felt like my temples were about to pop.

"Okay, Ms. Walker, we'll start with the good news. You are having a genetically perfect, healthy baby girl."

"What?" I could hear myself say. My mind spiraled. *What was the bad news? Did he say a girl?* And all of a sudden, the room started to spin around me and went to black.

8

"Ms. Walker . . . Ms. Walker . . . Ms. Walker."

I could hear the increasingly insistent voice prodding me forward into consciousness. I remembered groggily that I'd had been having the most unbelievable and ridiculous dream taking place in a doctor's office. I was grateful to wake up to a completely different reality, in time for my actual appointment. Except, opening my eyes with a slow flutter, I could see the medical gown draping my body . . . and the stirrups my feet were still in . . . and the ultrasound screening equipment to my right. *Oh no.* It was all real.

"Ms. Walker, how do you feel?" the nurse standing next to me asked. She held a paper cup out to me tentatively. The look on her face was one that I imagined she'd have if she saw a lost puppy.

"I . . . I . . . don't know," I managed to stammer.

"It's normal to feel a bit confused and groggy. Ms. Walker, you fainted while Dr. Young was in the room. Would you like some water?" I nodded with gratitude, and the nurse helped me pull forward to a seated position. I accepted the paper cup from her hands, but thirst wasn't my most pressing concern.

"Is . . . is . . . my baby all right?" This was all I could think about and all that mattered to me in that moment.

"Yes, Ms. Walker. You and your baby are perfectly fine. Dr. Young is waiting to speak to you in his office, once you feel comfortable enough to get dressed. I can stay here and help you, if you like?" I finished the entire cup of water and steadied myself with one hand on either side of the examination table. I looked down at my swinging feet just to collect my thoughts.

"I . . . I think I'll be okay. I can get dressed on my own." I forced the words out while my mind was racing at the speed of a bullet train. The nurse hesitated for a bit before making any move toward the door. I didn't blame her. I wouldn't have believed me either. Still, I wanted desperately to be alone. Well, as alone as a pregnant woman could be.

"Okay, Ms. Walker. I'll be just outside the door if you need anything." I nodded and exhaled deeply when the door shut behind her. My mind whirred with the same thought over and over: *baby girl . . . baby girl . . . baby girl.* Oh my God, what happened?

All I could think to do was embrace my stomach. "Hello, baby," I said. "I'm still your mommy, and I want you here more than anything. It doesn't matter to me if you're a boy or a girl, as long as you grow healthy in there." I rubbed my belly, hoping *she* could hear me. "Maybe all the doctors were wrong about you all along, but what do they know, anyway? You just grow in there . . . strong and healthy, okay? I'll be out here doing everything I can to protect you . . . and me too. I promise, you're gonna have the best life. We are. We're gonna have the best life, no matter what." I wiped my tears and got up slowly enough to steady myself and find my clothes. I got dressed, said my own silent prayer, and then headed out of the room to meet with Dr. Young. I needed to find out exactly what in the hell happened that made the male embryo they supposedly transferred suddenly turn into a female one.

"PLEASE, HAVE A SEAT, MS. WALKER." DR. YOUNG GESTURED toward one of the chairs sitting across from his desk. I walked over slowly, still a bit unsure of my grounding after fainting, but at the same time, wanting to get there as quickly as possible to retrieve the answer waiting for me. Dr. Young didn't waste any time. "So, you know that it is impossible for an embryo to spontaneously change its genetic sex, Ms. Walker?"

"Yes, Dr. Young." I nodded vigorously in agreement. "That's what I would have thought. So how do we explain what happened?"

"Do you recall when I asked you if you had followed *all* of the post embryo transfer instructions?"

"Yes, I recall . . ." I shifted nervously.

"Well then, let me just cut to the chase." He leaned forward. "The only situations where we observe the phenomenon of this morning is if another embryo implanted, other than the one we placed there. Do you know how that could possibly happen, Ms. Walker?" I could feel the flush come to my face, and all of a sudden, Marc flashed in my mind, with his proclamations and questions at our brunch a few weeks prior. All I wanted to do was sink into the chair and disappear into the muted colors of the fabric. And so much for fainting; I already did that.

I didn't need Dr. Young to say anything else; I already understood. *That damn Marc*, my mind protested. But I knew he wasn't the only one to blame. "Yes, Dr. Young, I think I understand pretty well how that could have happened. I mean, I understand *how*, but I didn't know it was possible."

"Ms. Walker, if you have sex, it is *always* possible to make a baby. We talked about that on appointment one." *Oh dammit*, my mind replied. "Listen," he said, leaning forward across his desk, his expression seeming to soften, "this could be rare good luck for you. One embryo failed to implant, but at the same time, you made another very healthy one. Maybe not what you intended, but some would call that fortune. You're still pregnant with a healthy baby, just not by your donor. I assume you know who the father is?" I felt the warm flush return to my face again. What did he think, that I was just having drunken one-night trysts as follow-ups to my embryo transfer procedures?

"Yes, Dr. Young. I know who the father is. He's . . . a long-term partner." I couldn't pinpoint why I felt the need to explain. For some reason, I felt like I was falling into a stereotype that maybe I deserved but wasn't entirely fair. Maybe it wasn't fair for any woman.

"Well, it looks like you might have a phone call to make, Ms. Walker. Some very lucky man is going to be very surprised." *Surprised . . . or livid . . . or homicidal . . . what was I thinking?* I could just hear Alexis's and Laila's voices in my mind, admonishing me for slipping back to Marc when I had made so many plans and taken so many steps to take my life into my own hands.

But what was done was done, and now it needed to be dealt with.

I gathered myself and traced a shaky path back to my car. At a time like this, there was only one thing left to do. I pulled out my cell phone and composed a text message to Alexis and Laila.

> 911—MY HOUSE ASAP—BRING WINE, YOU'LL
> NEED IT.

Alexis responded right away.

> OMG! Everything ok?

And this was the question that had no answer. I had a healthy baby, but would we have a healthy life now that Marc was involved? Marc, the man with all the questions and none of the answers? I texted back:

> Baby is healthy, just found out other news. About
> to start driving. Pls come soon.

Please come soon, and since I can't drink, bring Jesus with you. My son is now my daughter; my donor is now Marc. If I can't have a bottle of "Jesus Juice," then I'm going to just have to take the Jesus and leave the juice part out of it. Lord knows we, my *daughter* and I, need Him now.

9

BY THE TIME I REACHED THE FOOT OF MY DRIVEWAY, LAILA WAS already sitting on the steps of my porch with a brown grocery bag sitting next to her. A text arrived from Alexis that said she was five minutes away.

Laila stood up to meet me as I walked toward my front door. I was really glad to see her and hugged her close and tight.

"Girl, you can't send a 911 like that and then not explain what is going on!" she scolded. "You know I'm caught up in this startup. If you're not giving me regular in-person updates, this is a level-ten emergency. Better not be a friend fire drill."

"Laila, once I explain, you'll understand. I wish it were only a test," I warned. She had no idea what she was in for. Part of me was aching to blurt everything out. But I managed to hold it all in. I was too shocked to cry, too disappointed in myself to be surprised, and too overwhelmed to even start thinking of the repercussions. *Now, even after everything, I*

have a baby daddy . . . and it's Marc? Way to go, Tabitha; some-
how, you made it worse than it already was.

Trying to silence my racing thoughts, I decided to take
up other topics with Laila. "While we're waiting on Lexi," I
added, "how's your new website going? Last I heard, you were
starting to get some real traffic!" I tried to sound excited.

"Tab, I can't believe you'd resort to small talk after a 911
text. But whatever it is, I know you don't want to tell it twice,
so I'm not that mad . . . yet. Girl, this better be good." *Oh, you*
have no idea. To my surprise, Laila continued, her whole sun-
kissed, caramel face lighting up as she spoke, the ringlets of
curls on her head bouncing with her physical animations.

"Girl, who would have thought that site traffic would
pick up so quickly?" She waved her arms in exclamation.
"I'm making more than I did at the newspaper, and I got a
call from a literary agent who wants to explore getting me a
book deal! It didn't seem like it at the time, but getting laid
off from my job might have been the best thing that ever
happened to me." Laila's words buried deep in my body and
hugged my soul warmly. It wasn't so long ago that I thought
that I was going to lose her. It was comforting to have that
feeling pushed aside by something much more hopeful.

"Laila, you're so much braver than I am. Sometimes I
want to walk into work and tell everyone, especially our news
director, to kiss my entire ass. I dream of making an exit, but
now that I'm a baby momma, I'm stuck."

"Girl, sometimes you become brave by necessity. And believe me, looking back on it . . . after my *incident*, I realized
if I was willing to go to that extreme, then there wasn't any
other thing that could hurt me. Might as well make it count.

Girl, we're living out our dreams. Sometimes it's just happening in slow motion, so you don't notice until you hit a milestone or look back on everything."

Just as I was getting ready to respond, Alexis's white Mercedes screeched up to the curb in front of my house. She didn't even take the time to park straight before she was out of the car, her heels clacking up my driveway as she pulled her oversized handbag up her arm. "Tabby, what is going on? I knew I should have made you let me come to that appointment!" Alexis screamed at me with a look of deep concern on her face. She continued her march up my walkway to meet Laila and me on the front step. I dug out my keys to let us all in. "I didn't even stop to pick up wine because you can't drink anyway. You better spill it. What happened? Is everything okay with the baby? Are you having twins?"

I took a deep breath and dropped my head. I knew what this news was going to mean when I told my best friends. I'd sworn that things were over with Marc, and even believed it myself, but I hadn't made it true. In fact, I'd caused the opposite result. This was my fault, so there was no avoiding the consequences. I opened the front door for us and then turned around to face both of the women making their way in from the porch.

"So . . ." I dragged out the easiest word as long as I could. My racing thoughts were hard to form into sentences. "I'm pretty sure that Marc is my baby's father." The silence that followed was as if a needle had scratched on all of human existence. It seemed like even the birds stopped chirping. Alexis's and Laila's faces were frozen in a condition of shock like I'd never seen. Their mouths had dropped wide open, and the only sign of life was the blinking of their eyes. My hand reflexively found its way to cover my own mouth as I observed them for any type of reaction and, specifically, to find the disappointment that I was looking for. This went on for seconds that felt like minutes that could turn into hours.

Eventually, I heard small attempts from Alexis to speak. She finally managed to push out a "Whhhhaaaatttt" with an accentuated ending. Both friends stayed suspended at my doorway, as did I, locked in a moment that was heavy with the weight of disbelief and realization.

"Marc's your baby daddy?" Alexis challenged quietly. "How, Tab? How is that possible? You told us you had a donor."

I scrambled for an explanation that would match the doctor's. "Well, what happened was . . . I did have a donor. I did the whole thing, including the embryo transfer. And I followed all the rules—well, almost all of them . . ." And then I hung my head, realizing that "almost" didn't count in my case. "All except one . . . I had sex with Marc after the transfer." And just like that, with my head hanging, the tears started to fall. I fumbled through the rest of the words that came pouring out of my mouth like nonsense. "And . . . I just wanted . . . andhewasthere . . . andIthoughtitwouldn't . . ." By this time, both Alexis and Laila stepped inside to encircle me in a hug, although I was bracing myself for a slap across the back of the head by one or both of them at any moment. "I was supposed to already be prrreeegnnnaaaant!!" I bawled loudly at the end, finally collapsing into a cascade of real, guttural sobbing shame. I'd held it together on my own as long as I could. Finally, overwhelmed by the circumstances, Alexis and Laila held me up.

"Come on, Tabby, let's go inside," Alexis said, her motherly instincts taking over. She ushered all of us to the seating area in the living room.

"I don't even drink anymore, and I'm about to go find a bottle of wine," Laila said, breaking away from us and heading toward my kitchen. "I might even drink it myself."

"Bring two glasses please, Laila," Alexis sang from the sofa, where she sat with her arms around me.

"Glasses? Who said anything about glasses?" Laila called back. "One bottle for you, one bottle for me. It's that kind of night."

Alexis rolled her eyes. "Do you want some tea or something, Tab?" she said, leaning back into our embrace. I shook my head no on her shoulder. "Laila, can you put the kettle on just in case?" Alexis called out. "Well," she said softly to me, "I guess you're going to get some of those answers you didn't have the other day."

At this, I looked up. "Oh no!" I pulled away from Alexis, feeling the panic rise in my throat. "This means . . . Lexi, how I am going to tell Marc?" I dropped my head into my hands. Marc was so clear in what he said. He didn't want to be a father. He was relieved that I'd moved on without him.

"Marc's ass has no choice but to understand," Laila yelled from the kitchen. "He better not give you any static, Tabby. You aren't the only one to blame here. He's old enough to know that. Even if he is a man-baby."

"You're calling him a man-child, Lah?" Alexis gave a half laugh.

"Lexi, Rob is a man-child, I'm sure you'd agree. And Tabby knows. Marc, he's a man-baby." Alexis and I both laughed.

"Yeah, they all need to do some growing up," Alexis said with a sigh.

"So, what am I going to do?" I asked them, finally regaining my composure and focus.

"See? This is why I don't even date anymore," Laila said, walking over to Alexis and me. To my surprise, she really was holding two open bottles of wine. She handed Alexis one and looked at me with an apologetic look. "I'm just focused on my business," she continued. "I solve those problems, I make money. Man problems just cost me . . . in time, happiness, *and* bottles of liquor." Alexis and I both shook our heads. Not even so deep down, I knew she had at least some kind of a point.

"Maybe I'm just too much of a sucker for a comfort animal," I admitted.

"More like a wounded animal," Laila shot back. I looked at Alexis for backup, but she just shrugged her shoulders.

"Maybe you have a point," I said, finally.

"Maybe Marc will be excited to have a son," Alexis offered. *Oh crap, I hadn't even told them that part.*

"Oh, that's the other part of my news." I looked at both of them in the pause. They leaned forward, and I hoped they wouldn't spill their wine. "This baby is a girl, not a boy."

"Wait, the baby changed sex and daddies?" Laila questioned.

"No, it seems that at some point, two embryos were in my womb at the same time. The one that the doctors implanted and then, a little later, one that I evidently made with Marc after the fact. The one that was a boy was tested before they transferred it. The girl, well, she came along and surprised us all. And it was her that showed up on the test results. That's how the doctors knew that we had a whole new situation here."

"Wow, whole new situation for real," Alexis said quietly before taking a swig from her bottle.

Just then, the teakettle started to whistle. Thankful for a moment to breathe lighter air, I jumped up to tend to it with an eager "I've got it!" and did my best to outpace Laila and Alexis, who both moved to get up after me. "You guys just stay there, I'll get it."

"Girl, if you weren't my friend, this would be the perfect story for my blog site . . . I would pay money to be able to film Marc's face when you tell him. Talk about a social media meme going viral, that one's a definite," Laila said, shaking her head before taking another swallow of wine.

"Well, Tabby," Alexis said tentatively, "I'm actually not even worried about you telling Marc. What I want to know is, what are you going to tell *your mother?*"

10

"BABY GIRL, DON'T YOU WORRY ABOUT THIS AT ALL. SOUNDS LIKE a pure and simple blessing to me." Ms. Gretchen pulled her teakettle off the stove and poured the steaming water into two mugs on the counter of her kitchen at Crestmire. Only a week had passed since my prior visit, but that was enough time for my world to flip on its axis. "That Marc, he can't make a decision to save his life. Looks like the Good Lord decided for him. He better be glad he's even gonna have a baby before his testicles shrivel up," she said flippantly. "Seems like men these days, for all of their money and jobs and walking around thinking they're the prize to be captured, need to come here and talk to some of these old raisins that live at Crestmire, popping those little blue pills like they're candy! What's it called again, Vinagra, Vi-gara . . ."

"Viagra, Ms. Gretchen?"

"Yes, that's it. Viagra, I can never get that right, vi-ag-ra. Anyway, whatever it is, it just makes 'em go crazy! They don't realize that their little pokey poke is gonna stop working, and what then?" She looked up at me as if waiting for a response. I wouldn't have been able to say anything, even if I wanted to. All I could do was laugh. She walked over to the table with both mugs in hand. I stayed put. I knew she liked to be able to do for herself much more than she liked the polite offer of assistance that she never took. "Honey, it takes two people to make a baby. Well, at least it didn't for you at first, but it seems like fate went on and changed its mind. Sometimes two people need each other and fate just finds the glue. Maybe you need him . . . and maybe he needs you too. Or, I should say, you two, Two." She winked at me, gesturing with her eyes down to my belly. I felt comforted by her use of the nickname my grandmother had for me. It brought me the warmth of her presence, even though I still missed her terribly, especially now. In any tough situation, Granny Tab always knew exactly what to say, even when that right thing was nothing at all. I smiled at Ms. Gretchen.

"Well, maybe this means that there will be a Three," I teased.

"Oh goodness, I don't know if the world can handle a third Tabitha Walker," Ms. Gretchen said.

"Well, watch out, world!" I said with a smile. "But now that Marc's in the picture, she wouldn't be just Tabitha Walker, she'd be Tabitha Walker Brown."

"No matter, even if she were named Carolyn, your grandmother would have been so happy, Tabby. You know she'd be proud of you, no matter what." She patted my hand as she took a sip of her tea. "A baby is a blessing, however they manage to get here. I've lived long enough to know that everything, and I do mean everything, happens for a good reason."

"I want to believe that, Ms. Gretchen. I really do. I just haven't even told Marc yet, or my mother for that matter, and I don't know how they're going to take it. I know Marc is going to be so mad, and my mother, well, best case is that she's going to be disappointed, but I can't even imagine what she's going to think." I dropped my forehead into the cradle of my hands.

"Now, you listen to me." Ms. Gretchen put down her mug, lifted my chin, and grabbed both of my hands, flashing her periwinkle-blue nails. "It doesn't matter what either one of them thinks or says. That baby is coming, and she's *your* child. She's the family that you wanted. What you could control, you did, and what you can't control should be the least of your concern. When there's something in front of you to figure out, you'll do it, just like you always have. Tabby, you're stronger than you think, remember that. And plus, you have love *and* support coming from all directions. I'll make sure of that." She came around the table to embrace me. I allowed myself to sink into the comfort of her arms.

"Ms. Gretchen, you're the best fairy glam-maw anyone could ask for."

"I'll say this, honey. If that Marc acts up"—she broke away to wave a slender finger at me—"you let him know that I'm going to turn him into a frog. And your mother, well, you can handle her, I just know it."

"Thanks, Ms. Gretchen. At least one of us is confident." And as I sipped my tea, I let my mind drift to the phone call I had been dreading for days.

BY THE TIME I LEFT MY VISIT WITH MS. GRETCHEN AT CRESTMIRE, the sky was already washed with the pinks and purples of the Saturday evening sunset. Los Angeles traffic was merciful heading back down to View Park from Glendale. I scrolled to my mother's number several times through the Bluetooth connection in my car but always managed to find some other distraction to stop me from calling. So far on the ride, I'd scanned through five of my playlists, made six voice notes, and even tried calling Laila, who sent me an immediate text back telling me she was on deadline for her site and she'd call me later. Alexis's admonition was so right. Compared to dropping this news on my mother, Mrs. Jeanie Walker-Williams, Marc was going to be a sunny beachside walk on holiday.

I'd only just gotten my mother acclimated to the idea of me as a single mom by courage—as I had now learned to call it—and as a follow-up development, I was going to have to break it to her that instead of just a single mama, I would become a "baby mama"—Marc's baby mama, on top of it. There'd be no greater insult to her traditional mindset than me deliberately having a child out of wedlock with the very man who she just knew was supposed to be her son-in-law. Not that she had ever met him, living across the country, but on paper, he was perfect—Stanford-educated, professional, handsome, financially well-off, and Black, of course. He was everything she'd imagined for her only child, and her dream for me involved a giant diamond and a wedding dress. How could I explain that fitting into a stereotype didn't automatically make me one, especially if it meant my life wasn't "over, but only just beginning in an unexpected way"?

Knowing I couldn't hide this forever, or even all the way to my house, I took a deep breath and said the words, "Call Mom."

"Calling Mom," my car speakers echoed back to me in exaggerated pleasantness. Even as the phone rang, my mind searched for excuses to opt out of the inevitable. Thoughts of *are you sure you want to do this, Tabitha?* challenged me to hang up, but it was too late.

"Tabby Cat!" my mother answered cheerfully. "Just give me one second, this is Tabby calling. Sweetheart, can you load up the car, and I'll be right out?" Through the phone, I could hear her interrupt her greeting to shout instructions to my stepfather, Nathaniel Williams, who we all still called by his previous title: the general. "How are you this lovely Saturday?" she chirped. Oh boy, I was going to really hate to ruin her good mood.

"Hi, Mom." I tried with all my abilities to sound cheerful and to hide the shaking in my voice. "Um, I'm good."

"Oh no, Tabby. No, you are not. I can hear it in your voice." *Crap, how does she always know?* I sat silently for a split second to gather my thoughts. With no good way to say something, I figured the only option was to get it out as quickly as possible. So I took a deep breath, braced myself, and went for it—speed-demon style.

"MomIwenttothedoctorandthedoctorsaidthebabyis-Marc'sandI'mfinebut—"

"Hold up one minute, Tabby." I could hear my mom's voice deepening. "Did you just say that the *doctor* said that the baby is Marc's? Didn't the doctor implant an embryo? Doesn't he know you used a donor? Didn't his lab make the embryo?"

"Well, Mom, that's just it. Um . . . I don't know how to say this, but, well, see . . ."

"Are you trying to tell me that you used Marc as your donor and the doctor found out?"

"Not exactly, Mom . . ."

"I don't understand."

"I'm a baby mama, Mom. And I already know you're going to be disappointed in me, and I'm disappointed in myself, but it just happened."

"Tabby, what are you telling me? Why would I be disappointed?"

"Mom!" I heard myself sounding almost as exasperated as I felt. "They implanted the embryo that I thought I was pregnant with this whole time, but then I saw Marc . . . and . . . and . . ." I pushed to get out the words that had gotten stuck in my mind and in my throat because, no matter your age, there's simply no good way to tell a parent you're having sex. I continued, "And it's Marc's baby that I'm pregnant with . . . and I've been pregnant with *her* this whole time."

"Her? Tabby? What?" I heard my mother shift the phone from her ear. "Nate! You have to wait one second, seriously! I'm talking with Tabby. Leave without me if you have to." My mother's voice was terse in a way I'd never heard her speak to my stepfather before. I felt guilt rise and intertwine with the shame flushing my face. "Tabby, I'm going to have to sit down for this. You're meaning to tell me that you and Marc are still together?"

"Mom, out of everything I said, that's your takeaway?"

"Well, Tabby, I'm just surprised. I thought you two broke up."

"But aren't you upset that—" My mother cut me off quickly.

"Upset that what? What's there to be upset about? Your second chance at a fairy tale? I didn't even start buying baby clothes, so now I just get pink instead of blue!" she said cheerily. "I just love little girls! Tabby, you were the cutest baby. I had all of the best little outfits for you . . . I wish that I had kept them . . . I bet I could still find—"

"MOM!" I yelled back, to try to get her attention. She must not have understood what I was trying to say. "Mom, I'm trying to tell you that Marc and I were together after they implanted the boy embryo, and because of that, somehow I got pregnant again, but with a different baby. With Marc's baby."

"So are you saying there are twins?" My mom sounded downright giddy. I was more confused than ever. In every scenario I'd thought of, my mother turned out upset.

"Mom, not twins, just one baby. Marc's baby. Not the donor's. Not the doctor's embryo. Everything I'd planned is out the window. Now I'm having a baby with Marc."

"Well, Tabby Cat," my mom said, following a sigh. "You know what they say, we make plans, God laughs." She ended with a small chuckle of her own.

"So . . . you're not upset?" I asked timidly.

"Upset? Why would I be upset? It sounds like a miracle happened. Are you upset?"

"I'm not exactly upset, but until now, I thought I'd be a single mom, and not like this . . . I didn't have any plans with Marc."

"Tabby, you know how to fix this, don't you?" My mom asked the question as if the answer was the most obvious in the world. I couldn't believe that she'd even propose it.

"Mom!" I was so mad, my brown knuckles turned nearly white around the steering wheel. "You can't be suggesting . . ."

"That you and Marc get back together and make it official? Of course, Tab, that's exactly what I'm suggesting. What a wonderful turn of events! And a happy surprise for the both of you." At that, I didn't know whether to laugh or to cry. My mother was cluelessly ecstatic over the news that I thought would devastate her. And here I was trying to convince her otherwise. I guess sometimes you need to know when you've won. I forced myself to take a very, very deep breath.

"That wasn't quite what I had in mind."

"You and Marc have plenty of time to figure things out. And I have plenty of time to plan your baby shower! Oooh, we can have it right here at the house. It'll be decorated so nice. Maybe it will be an engagement party also, you never know!"

Things had gone so differently than what I'd expected that I couldn't muster the energy to contain her imagination. There wasn't a shot for Marc and me; he'd made it clear over brunch. I just hoped that when he found out, he didn't hate me for ruining his life. This would be the truest test of our friendship, if we ever even had one at all.

11

THE LARGE POT ON MY STOVE GURGLED LOUDLY WITH BOILING water, announcing it was time to add the pasta I'd placed nearby. Next to it, a sauté pan simmered with fragrant garlic steam, rising over a bubbling cream sauce that teemed with freshly cooked, pink shrimp. I felt more tired than usual but was putting extra effort into this meal because Marc was coming over for dinner. I hoped a good meal would soften the blow of the unexpected revelations of the evening. The news alone would be hard to swallow, so the least I could do was make it taste good.

All the effort triggered muscle memory of the meals I'd made before, trying to pretend for dates that I could cook, hoping that they'd make some man or another like me more—maybe even love me one day. This time, it was a hopeful effort to prevent Marc from hating me, and even more importantly, from hating this surprise entry into fatherhood—unexpected, unwanted, and unplanned.

I had just barely had time to freshen up, do a quick fluff

on my twist-out, and spritz on what I'd long stopped wearing but would never forget as his favorite perfume. I started to put on a dress, but I didn't want him to think that I was trying to seduce him. This was a sales pitch. *That's it.* I would sell him on the wonderful benefits of having this child with me. He wouldn't even have to do that much, I'd tell him. I'd planned to be a single mom all along. This, for him, was just a heads-up. He'd never have any baby mama drama coming from me. Although even the thought of Marc moving on with his life and a new and unknown woman being around my child made me sick to my stomach.

The doorbell broke into my thoughts, announcing Marc's arrival. My palms started to sweat. I wiped them down the front of my jeans and headed over to answer the door barefoot, with my ivory-toned pedicure leading the way.

"Hey," Marc said softly when the door opened. In his hand was a bouquet of yellow roses. "I knew I couldn't bring wine, so I figured this might be something you'd enjoy." He held the flowers out to me. I wasn't sure if that yellow color meant apology or friendship, but they definitely weren't red. As intentional as Marc was, that was almost certainly a message to pay attention to.

"Hey, come in," I said, opening the door wider for him to pass by me. "Marc, thanks so much for these, they're gorgeous."

"The neighborhood Joe's always has a brotha's back!" Marc gave a big smile and a small chuckle, rubbing his hands together. "It smells great in here, Tab. You never *used* to cook like this!" It did smell great. He'd know why soon enough. Marc looked casual and well put together. His fresh haircut accentuated his features. Together or not, I still loved it when he had a fresh haircut. Even though I knew what needed to be done, for a second, I thought that maybe the difficult part of our conversation could wait—just a little longer.

"Thanks for making the stop and snagging some flowers for the pregnant lady," I added with a smile of my own. A big smile—actually, bigger than it needed to be. Marc still had a way of making me nervous. "Here, come have a seat with me in the kitchen, I'll pour you some wine." I led the way to my kitchen island, where I'd start him off with a glass of my best wine, followed by the best meal I'd ever cooked in my life. I'd save the news for dessert.

FULLY CAUGHT UP AND MOSTLY FULL, IT CAME TIME FOR THE MOL-ten chocolate soufflé that was purchased frozen but finished in my oven. I brought the sweet, rich treat to the table and carefully set it between Marc and myself, along with vanilla ice cream and some extra sauce on the side, just in case.

"Tabby, you really went all out. What, you trying to get some tonight?" Marc gave me a wink. *Here's your chance.* I paused for a long time; all the words I'd practiced dissolved in my mind as fast as the sugar crystals swirled in a steaming cup of tea.

"Well . . . actually, Marc . . . um, about that . . . about *that*, specifically."

"If you're really trying to get some . . . you can just say so," Marc teased sexily, his long eyelashes lowering as he leaned in closer to me. *Oh Lord, please help me,* I pleaded silently. If I were any less Paul and Jeanie Walker's child or Granny Tab's grandchild, I would have pushed this conversation to another day and claimed what my hormones were screaming out for. I took a deep breath.

"That's just it, Marc, we already did that, and . . ."

"And what, Tabby?"

"And, well . . . and, now I'm pregnant." Marc recoiled with a puzzled look on his face. His hand flew up to his goatee.

"Right, yep, you told me that a few weeks ago. Does that mean you can't have sex anymore?"

"I'm saying something a little different, Marc. The last time we had sex, that's actually *how* I got pregnant."

Marc leaned forward again. "But weren't you already pregnant before the last time we were together? Tab, I don't get it. You can't get pregnant once you're pregnant, so, girl, what are you talking about?" Marc laughed, and his body seemed to relax a bit. "Tab, those pregnancy hormones might be going to your head."

"I wish," I muttered softly.

"What'd you say?"

"I said, I wish," I repeated louder and more deliberately. At this, I got up and pulled my chair closer to him. I was sitting so close to his face that I could almost feel his breath. Close enough to kiss him, or close enough to be in the line of fire. I'd soon find out. He looked puzzled. "Marc." I took his hand in mine; he let me, with only slight hesitation. "On my last visit to the doctor, the genetic test . . . showed that . . ." Marc's chocolate skin started to burn redder, and his mouth dropped a bit. "It showed that there's no way that the donor-created embryo is the embryo I'm pregnant with. Marc, we made a baby."

"Oh, hell naw!" Marc yanked his hand from mine so hard that his chair pushed back with a loud noise against the floor. "Are you fucking kidding me?" He started looking around wildly. "Is this a hidden camera moment? Is this some kind of joke video for my birthday or something?" His own explanations seemed to bring another wave of slight ease. His voice quieted a bit. "This is a joke, right?" His question sounded like a plea if I'd ever heard one.

"It's not a joke, Marc."

"Well . . . well, couldn't it be from another leftover donor . . . donor . . ." Marc waved his arms in the air as if he could grasp the right word and push it into his mouth. "Donor thing— whatever it is that you did before?" It was getting harder to stay calm, but I knew I needed to . . . for all three of us.

"No, Marc, it doesn't work like that," I said as gently as possible. "If you just give me a chance, I can explain." Marc scooted his chair farther back and stood up.

"Tabby, honestly, sometimes I wonder about you, but this right here is some bullshit." He started patting his pockets until the jingle of his keys could be heard. Then he swiveled, headed toward the door. I stood up to follow him, feeling the tears welling up in my eyes. I knew that somehow I had blown it.

"Marc, please just give me a second and let me explain."

"What is there to explain, Tabby? How a few weeks ago you're asking me to be in some kind of a village for the child that you decided to have, and then all of a sudden I'm the father? How is that even possible? When you were already pregnant? Nah, man. You're crazy, and I'm out of here." Marc crossed the distance to the door faster than an Olympic sprinter. He struggled with the doorknob in frustration and finally yanked the door open.

"Marc, please, I didn't mean for this to happen this way," I begged, this time with tears streaming down my face and sobs forcing their way up my chest. "Please, please let me explain!" He turned and looked at me, eyes narrowed, a cloud over his expression that radiated the hurt of anger and betrayal, and that was the last thing I saw before the door slammed behind him.

1 2

MOONLIGHT MADE A BEAM THROUGH THE BEDROOM WINDOW AS I curled myself on my bed. My earlier sobs had quieted to a soft whimpering. On any other night like this, I would have driven straight to Granny Tab and found my way into her bed and her arms for comfort. It was too late to even call my mother, so I resolved to just lie there, replaying the night in my mind.

I looked over at my phone and saw that I had missed a text message. It was from Alexis.

How'd it go?

I weighed the downside of giving an honest answer that would require an explanation. I typed back:

Didn't go well. Will fill you in tomorrow. Exhausted, need to sleep.

I saw the dots on Alexis's end signaling that she was composing a message. The Alexis I knew was probably composing and deleting in search of the right words. Eventually, another message popped up on the screen.

Don't worry, you don't need Marc to be happy. Trust me.

When I didn't respond, there were more dots on Alexis's end. The text scrolled upward again with yet another message.

Love you, girl. It's going to be alright.

I sent her back a heart to let her off the hook and let the phone slip from my hand onto the bed beside me.

IT WAS THE INSISTENCE OF THE DOORBELL THAT PULLED ME OUT OF whatever restless sleep I had cried myself into. I patted at my side in the darkness for the phone that I had seemingly just been holding. Once it met my hand, I pulled it forward to my face and waited for the screen to flicker. It took a moment longer for my eyes to adjust to the brightness. *Is it really three-thirty in the morning?* The ding-dong of the doorbell again broke into my thoughts. Someone really was at the door. I started to text Alexis back again but decided that if she was worried enough to come over, I'd better just go ahead and answer the door.

I shuffled quickly to the front of the house and yelled at the door, "Okay! I'm coming! Lexi! I swear, I'm fine!"

"It's not Lexi," the deep voice answered from behind the door. "Tab, let me in, it's Marc." *Marc?* I moved more swiftly to the door and pulled it open.

"Marc, are you *crazy?*" I whispered loudly. "It's three a.m.! You're lucky none of my neighbors called the police!" Marc just looked at me silently as he walked past me into the house. I closed the door, leaning my back against it while I said a silent prayer of thanks for protecting him.

Standing in the middle of the living room, Marc turned to face me, his eyes bloodshot and wild, his hand holding and waving a small stack of paper at me. "I'm sorry, Tab, I . . . I had to get home, and then I got home and I started thinking and I realized, what was I doing?" He looked up at me, pausing his gush of words that was almost too fast to follow.

"What, Marc, slow down, please—I'm sorry, I'm just waking up."

"Tabby, that's what I'm saying. I'm sorry I left like that. I'm *sorry*. I . . . I just . . ." He waved the papers at me again. "I have a plan. I got home, I started thinking about it—okay, neither one of us meant for this to happen, right?" I nodded back at him, and he stepped closer to me. "But it happened. So I wrote out a plan."

"A plan?" This man had me so confused.

"Yes, a plan. I've got it figured out—how this can work. Tab, we're going to make this work." He put both hands on my shoulders and looked into my eyes. "You and I are going to make this work. Okay?" I nodded again. He took my hand and led me over to the sofa, gesturing for us both to sit. I sat down next to him, close enough to read some of the hand-writing on the papers . . . *daycare* . . . *school* . . . *college* . . . *clothes*. I could see the words and dollar signs and figures on the page.

"Marc, did you seriously just go home and make a baby business plan?" Marc looked at me for a long pause, his serious expression answering the question better than any words ever could. Suddenly, he let out a laugh big enough for the both of us. Then he looked at me sheepishly.

"Yeah," he said, lowering his head to look at the papers. "I guess I did."

"Seems like we won't have to worry about our baby's analytical ability," I offered, trying to double down on the levity.

"Oh, you know *she's* going to Stanford, right? Am I right, that's how you found out? Because *he* is actually a *she*?"

"That's what happened at the doctor's office. And you know you're the only one I've been . . ."

Marc took my hand and offered the richness of his deep brown eyes to me, making me catch my breath. "Tabby, you don't have to explain. I get it. I get how babies are made . . . by *two* people. And this baby, this one that *we* made right here." He took one hand to pat my slightly rounded belly. "This young lady is going to Stanford, like her dad."

"I need a drink," I said to Marc, half teasing. "These days that means chamomile tea. You want something?"

"Sure, we have a lot to discuss." Marc started to stand like he was going to follow me, then sat back down on the sofa, but then got up again, came over, and sat at the kitchen island.

"Tabby, there's something else that's very important to me." I looked up from filling the kettle. "Look, the reality is,

I mean . . . What I'm trying to say is . . . I know you're probably not feeling me right now, but . . ." He got up off the stool
and came over to where I was standing by the stove. God,
he smelled good. Like wood chips and sweet spice, mixed
with musk and manliness. His body was close enough that I
could feel the heat emanating from him, just like the stove.
He leaned down. "I'm sayin', I know you're not feeling me
right now, but . . ."

"I don't know if . . ." I tried to break out of the moment by
moving away. Marc caught my hand and pulled me in, closer
to him. He searched my face until our eyes met and locked.

"Here's what *I* know," he said firmly. "Everything I was
uncertain about, it seems like there's no point now. Was I
ready to be a dad? No, I wasn't, but honestly, Tab, deep down I
was a little bit hopeful when I asked you at brunch . . . and . . ."

"But . . . you said you didn't want to . . . that you were relieved to . . ." Marc pulled me even closer, further intoxicating
me with his smell . . . I loved that smell. I forgot the rest of
my words.

"I'll be honest, Tabby. Truthfully, I was a little disappointed when you said no."

"Marc," I whispered, "what are you saying?"

"It's a lot easier to choose when there's not really a choice,
I guess."

"Wow," I said, turning away. "How romantic." He pulled
me close to him again.

"Tab, maybe I'm saying it wrong, but I can see it. I can see
us. The *three* of us." He interlaced his fingers with mine. *No
better time to just go with the flow*, my mind said. Well, most of
my mind at least. The other part, in a tiny, tiny voice, asked

timidly, *Are you sure you can trust him? Is this what you want?* But who questions their fairy-tale ending, right?

"Marc." I tried pulling away from him again. He held me tighter. "You're confusing me. I wasn't trying to get us back together. I just had to tell you the truth. This isn't a trap."

"I know, Tab." He brought his face closer to mine. My heart was pounding. I couldn't think. The combination of fear and arousal clouded my thoughts. I wanted to protect myself. Marc had just walked out on me, and now it seemed like he wanted to kiss me. I pulled back.

"But do you, Marc? Because just a few hours ago, you . . ." Marc's lips connecting with mine stopped me from speaking. His fingers wrapped around the small of my back, pressing me closer to him. In spite of myself, I reached for him. My hands connected with the firmness of the flesh underneath his shoulder blades. We were locked in an embrace, connected through touch, through lips, through a penetrating desire that seemed to make sense and that suddenly felt guiltless.

The teakettle whistled its siren. Reluctantly, I backed away from him to turn off the flame beneath it. "Do you still want tea?"

Marc reached for me again to draw me closer and then lifted my hand up toward his lips. He pressed them softly against my fingertips, one by one by one. "Tabby, what I want is you."

THE WARM BODY NEXT TO ME FELT FAMILIAR AND UNFAMILIAR AT the same time. It was Marc on the outside, yet a completely different person seemed to have taken over at the controls.

In the bed, we were a mess of limbs in all directions—his leg was over mine, my arm draped across the ripples of his torso while the other was caught up behind his neck. Morning could no longer be denied, and I slowly blinked my aching eyes open. I'd earned my fatigue. We'd spent a very long night traversing the entire range of human emotions. I was exhausted but exhilarated all at the same time. I wanted to stay in this moment forever.

Marc stirred next to me. The sunlight had grown brighter, insisting its way into the bedroom fully, making it near impossible to fall back asleep. I felt Marc move again, and even though he was there next to me, uncertainty trickled through my consciousness, making me question what about that night had been real at all. Maybe I'd imagined what I needed to, heard what I wanted to; the good parts seemed too good. I managed to pull myself away a little and studied him.

There, stretched out before me, was the vivid and irresistible brown of his skin that seemed to glisten in the sun like a billion tiny diamonds. I gazed at his shoulder, thick with muscle, and then up, letting my eyes caress the curvature of his neck that pulsated ever so slightly. I looked at his angular jawline, accentuated with a trimmed, full beard that had just a sprinkling of salt and pepper hairs, enough to let me know that I was looking at a grown man, at least, in appearance. And then to his full lips, slightly parted, giving me a glimpse of his straight white teeth that looked strong and perfect. This was the face that our daughter would recognize. She would see herself somewhere, maybe in his strong nose or long eyelashes, or the thick eyebrows that could show a million expressions, or maybe the full, kinky curls that graced the crown of his head, giving him an extra inch on a good day. This man, this man would be my daughter's father . . . and, if he kept all of the promises he made last night, maybe he'd finally be my own dream come true too.

I traced his lips softly with my finger, causing each side to slide upward into a faint smile. "So, we're really doing this?" I heard myself finally echo my thoughts aloud.

Marc tightened his arms around me and blinked his eyes open slowly to meet my gaze. "Yes, Tabby. *We're* doing this." The rasp in his voice only made his words sound more intentional. I believed him. With our eyes still connected, we allowed our lips to meet, sweetly at first, and then fully. The promise of everything to come and the energy of passion between us had kept us in orbit. It had also, without our knowledge, created the life I carried. I allowed myself to be swept away and let the familiar feeling of ecstasy that he brought to each cell of my body erase all the traces of doubt and pain and resentment, just for that moment.

It was my alarm that woke me up the second time, still in the sprawl of limbs, but no longer believing this was just a dream. It was real.

1 3

Marc had given me both the evening of my nightmares and the morning of my dreams. Finally heading into work, I looked like hell on the outside. On the inside, though, I felt like heaven. So much had happened that I'd almost forgotten about my early meeting with our women's issues group. As promised, Lisa had put me on the agenda to discuss viewers' responses to my natural hair and the lack of support that I was receiving from the station management. I wasn't thinking about my hair. I was thinking about Marc. Things were finally looking up. And I really didn't feel like adding another concern to my plate. I wasn't worried about viewers; I was planning the perfect family life.

I made myself a cup of tea and forcibly bypassed the crumb-topped, Marie Antoinette–esque pastries that sat in our kitchen, beckoning to unsuspecting waist-watchers. My stomach still looked more like pudge than pregnancy, and I didn't want to contribute to the expansion. Plus, the terms "gestational diabetes" and "high blood pressure" loomed in the back of my mind from an earlier report I had pitched on the troubling statistics of Black maternal health outcomes.

When I walked into the meeting, Lisa and another woman were huddled toward the front of the conference room. I settled into a seat near the end of the conference table. Others filed in quickly after me.

"Here, Tabby, take one and pass it down." My neighbor pushed a stack of papers at me, with *Agenda* labeled on the top. I complied and studied the list of topics that we'd be covering.

Number one on the agenda was *Equal Pay*, followed by *#MeToo Support*, then *Flexible Work Arrangements and Extended Maternity Leave*, then *Appearance Bias*. I assumed that my topic would fall under Appearance Bias, but I had to admit, in comparison to the big-ticket items that preceded it, and with my mind in another universe, I wasn't feeling the same conviction that I had felt earlier. Compared to the others, mine started to look more like an issue of one within our group, rather than something anyone else would care about. I imagined the embarrassment I'd feel looking at the blank expressions in front of me—women who probably never thought twice about their hair texture or could even imagine receiving a viewer complaint about it. It was exhausting to be constantly swimming against the current. I wanted to simply float along, to enjoy the bliss of just one thing in my life going right. After a few moments of trying to think of what to say, I felt the heat rising in my face. *It's not too late*, my mind offered. *Just go over to Lisa and tell her to take you off the agenda. Easy.* My body felt like it was ready to go in two directions. Automatically, my hand went to my head to finger a few of my curls, but instead found the neat pinned-up style that I had resorted to after the long night and early morning with Marc. I looked around the table, and sure enough, there was nobody else with a hairstyle like mine, nobody else that needed protection in that way except me. These ladies weren't going to sacrifice what was actually important to them just for my problem. I knew what I needed to do. But the hesitation cost me. As soon as I started to get up to leave, Lisa cleared her throat and started the meeting.

It was too late, but what would I do? I couldn't even find the words to explain what had made the issue so significant to me in the first place. So a few viewers complained. Couldn't I just wear a wig or find a different hairstyle?

As the agenda progressed, I talked myself further and further out of stating my case. I was pregnant, my hair would grow like a weed, right? So what if I wore a wig for these few months until my maternity leave. When I came back, my hair would be much longer and more versatile. Then what I would really want was a flexible work schedule, right? *That's right, Tabby. Don't make this a big issue. You're pregnant, now you have Marc, don't take on more than you can handle at once.* The palms of my hands started to sweat, and I felt the heat flush to my face. All that thinking, and I had lost track of the conversation.

"Tabby," I heard Lisa say in the quieted room. "Tabby, you're up on the agenda—it's your topic, Appearance Bias." I felt my head swivel around to meet some of the many sets of eyes that were fixated on me, some centered in puzzled facial expressions, some filled with curiosity, and a few that squinted with what looked like disdain. I could taste the bile of fear in my throat. Still, on shaky legs, I stood up.

"Um . . . thanks, Lisa," I stammered. I looked around again, still holding the single-page agenda in my hand. I started looking for the closest verbal off-ramp. "Some viewers, in response to my . . . my natural hairstyle, um . . . sent messages to the station about it." *Don't become a victim, Tabby, remember your promotion . . . and your competition.* I paused for a beat to gather my thoughts before continuing. "And . . . I . . . I . . . just wanted to offer my support to the group, in case any others of you have experienced something similar." And with that, I sat back down. Lisa had a puzzled look on her face.

"Tabby, the messages were disparaging, right? Was there something that you wanted the group to do to support you? Anything that you'd like to bring forward to consider?" she prompted.

I stiffened and tried to meet her eyes. "Thanks, Lisa, but no," I replied firmly. "It's just a minor issue—but if anybody else has had this experience"—I surveyed the room of blank faces registering zero relation to my words—"I just wanted to . . . to offer my support. Anytime." I tried to sound very sure of myself and hoped that Lisa would catch the hint.

"Well then," Lisa said, looking at me with a confused expression. She quickly masked it with reporter-like professionalism. "Thank you for that, Tabby, and I'm sure the group appreciates your *generous* offer." She paused to look at me for more than a moment before, thankfully, she moved on to the final agenda item—a fundraiser that one of the other anchors wanted donations for. I breathed a sigh of relief to myself and pulled out my phone, scrolling through my contacts. I quickly found *Denisha* and started composing a text.

> Hey Denisha—I need help, can you make a wig
> for me?

Moments later, before I had a chance to stand up from the table, my phone signaled a message reply.

> Girl, yes. Come in on Saturday at 11. I got you—
> just need an hour or so for the braid down.

And just like that, every problem in my life had a solution, even if just for a moment.

OTHER THAN THE REGULAR TRIMS THAT I'D COMMITTED TO WITH Denisha, I hadn't been keeping my usual weekly appointments as I had in the past. If I added up all the time away from the salon having gone natural, I'd probably added an extra five years to my life. That time would come in handy, especially with a child on the way.

In some odd way, the disrepair of Denisha's salon off Slauson Boulevard felt comforting. It was like a well-worn sweatshirt that, in spite of the holes, still provided a comfort that couldn't be newly purchased. Even though I'd moved back into the neighborhood that Alexis and I had grown up in, the historically Black professional makeup of the families had been dramatically shifting. In fact, in some ways, I was part of the gentrification. I paid far more for my home than my parents had paid for theirs years ago, contributing to the price inflation. Everything around us was changing faster than I would have liked, erasing memories tied to locations that seemed to disappear each day.

But Denisha's salon, with the dusty front window, the crass old-school signage, cracked tile on the floor that should have long been replaced, and the too-old television up front that stayed on free broadcast channels throughout the day, somehow it was the visual equivalent of chicken soup. Denisha was too.

"Hey, girl!" she called out to me as I walked through the door. "I'm just finishing up this press and curl, but you can go straight to the bowl." I looked toward the shampoo bowls in the back of the salon, and there was yet another assistant that I'd never seen before. Even when I came weekly, it seemed as if there was always someone new at the washbowls, and they never stayed long enough for me to remember anyone's name. I just hoped for a long and vigorous shampoo, especially since I wouldn't be able to directly access my scalp until my next appointment.

The shampooing felt sumptuous, and I was grateful for the acrylic nail tips that contributed to the kneading, scratching, and scrubbing that was so oddly relaxing. I made a mental note to give this assistant a tip and make a comment to Denisha that might help her stay around a little longer. Goodness knows I'd need another refresh when I came back in two weeks to have my hair rebound under the wig I'd be wearing.

Nearly an hour later, I finally returned to Denisha's chair.

She pulled out a limp arrangement of hair that looked like a dead animal and showed it to me as if it was a fine garment. "Girl, look. This is your unit. I made it special to look just like your old style. For real, once I melt those edges and blend it all in, nobody will even be able to tell it isn't growing out of your scalp." Denisha was *almost* right. Nobody would be able to tell, except me. I'd know from the familiar itching of the innumerable weaves and wigs I'd worn over the years. As Denisha started to manipulate my hair, I wondered again if it was all worth it. She seemed to read my mind. "I'm sure you'll be glad to get a break for a minute. I bet you didn't know natural hair was so much work, right?"

"Hmm . . . it wasn't so bad. I just need a break from the friction at the station."

"What happened? They told you that you couldn't wear your hair natural? Isn't that against the law now?" Denisha had her own way of expressing her views, but no one could ever say she wasn't up to date. In the salon all day, they never missed a local news broadcast.

"It's supposed to be, but that doesn't help so much when you're on television. We've got a long way to go, Denisha. A long way." Denisha tugged at my hair by the roots, tightening her grip as she started to braid my hair into cornrows. I winced.

"Sorry, girl, I know it's tight, but it'll loosen up by tomorrow. I'll put some oil on it too before I sew the wig on. You want an aspirin or something?"

All I could do was sigh. "No, I'll be fine."

"Girl, you are gonna love this wig, and your hair is gonna grow so fast, you won't believe it. Your hair will be at your shoulders just in time to win your next Emmy." Denisha beamed. I gave a halfhearted laugh. Denisha and I continued to make small talk while she finished my hair. When she'd secured the wig and finished the cut and styling, she walked around me to admire her handiwork. "See, Tabby? It looks just like your regular style! Can't even tell the difference." She spun me around to face the mirror. She was right; it looked like the old style, and the old me. And I didn't recognize her at all.

14

It had been almost a week since the women's issues group meeting and I still hadn't seen or spoken with Lisa, so it was a not-so-unexpected-surprise when I saw her head poke into my office door while I was typing up notes for my latest story assignment.

"Hey, got a second?" she asked tentatively as her blond hair brushed against my doorframe. It was a debriefing that I wasn't looking forward to, but there was nowhere to run, and I couldn't disappear.

"Hey, Lisa," I said back, trying to force a casual, cheery tone. "Come on in."

"Whoa, nice hair. You decided to go back to straight?"

"It's a wig," I said tersely.

"Oh, okay. Well, I brought you some . . . tea." She extended her hand out to me, the other holding her usual coffee with a straw. I looked at her with a puzzled expression, and after an awkward pause, Lisa continued, "I noticed that you've been drinking a lot of tea lately . . . rather than coffee . . ." As she spoke, her eyes quickly flashed down to my stomach and back up to my face. I let out a small laugh.

"Okay, so clearly that's not all you've noticed." I smiled.

"I wasn't going to say anything until you did . . . or until you do," Lisa stammered, still standing. I shook my head, widening my smile. I should have known that Lisa of all people would figure things out.

"You can have a seat, you know," I said, gesturing to the chair in front of me. She was unusually timid in her approach but pulled the seat out and sat down, bringing the straw in her cup up to her perfectly tinted lips.

"I like the new hair." I knew that she meant her words as a compliment, even if I still thought of it as my own failure. The attention prompted me to bring my hand reflexively to the back side of my head and smooth down the straight hair that covered the lumpy understructure of protective cornrows and wig tracks.

"You do? Really, Lisa? Better than my natural look?" I could feel my face flushing as I asked.

"Oh no," Lisa said quickly. "It's not better necessarily . . . just, different." I could see Lisa studying me. "I will say, Tabby, I figured when you changed directions at the meeting, that maybe you'd changed your mind. But I was definitely surprised that you didn't speak up . . . Is everything okay?" I watched the mild look of concern contort Lisa's otherwise beautifully chiseled face. I sighed heavily and leaned back in my chair. I had gone to Denisha's salon and gotten a wig. Problem solved, right? No more viewer complaints for Chris, no more headache for me.

"Everything is great!" I forced my voice upward in pitch,

hoping that it didn't sound as noticeably fake to Lisa as it did to me. "You know . . . that meeting, everything else on the agenda was such a big deal to everyone in the room. The thing about my hair, it just felt so . . . so small in comparison. I mean, who else has that issue other than me, right?"

Lisa shifted uncomfortably, with an expression I couldn't read. I didn't know if it was my friend's Botox kicking in, or something else. She leaned toward me with her elbows on her knees. "Look, I get it. Believe me, when you've been working in this business as long as I have . . ." She gave a loud sigh. "Tabby, I will never forget when you told me after your grandmother died that you couldn't fight every battle. It gave me a lot to think about, and like I said, I get it. You're pregnant, you're up for another promotion, and this business is already cutthroat. But I want you to know, if you want to tackle this, I'll have your back, just like I said I would. I can't speak for the others, but your issue is just as important as any other—at least it should be." She slapped her free hand down on my desk. "It is to me." Lisa stood up. "I've gotta go for makeup. But seriously, Tabby, as long as I'm in the room, you'll never have an issue of one. Just let me know if you ever want it on the agenda again."

I smiled. "Thanks, Lisa, I appreciate it, really."

She headed out the door and then stopped, came back in, and shut the door behind her quickly.

"Listen," she whispered as if she was telling me a secret recipe, "I know you didn't ask for my advice on this, but don't tell Chris about the baby until you have to, okay?" She surprised me, but I nodded my agreement. Lisa continued, even more quietly, "And don't let up. Keep your focus on the assignments you want, and make sure you get that promotion. The newsroom isn't kind," she warned.

"Thanks, Lisa. All right, this stays between us."

"Yep, between us." And with that, she slipped out of my door into the bustle of the office space outside.

15

IN THE BLISSFUL BLUR OF DAYS AND NIGHTS WITH MARC THAT LED into my second trimester, weekends with my younger half sisters, Danielle and Dixie, began to become time I most looked forward to. Through the regular schedule of doctor's appointments and baby preparations, and the settling-in of nesting, Marc's belongings could be found scattered throughout my home, marking his comfort and presence there, even when he was not actually present. We'd reached an equilibrium that brought neither excitement nor unbearable resignation. For the first time, we were on the same page about what we were doing, and even what "we" were. We were starting to look like a family. Later in the weekend, as with most weekends, it seemed, we'd be continuing our routine of baby shopping and preparations. The countdown to delivery day seemed to be accelerating in its growing proximity.

As much as my relationship with Marc had developed, it was my relationship with my sisters that had evolved into another dimension. It seemed like my pregnancy brought us closer. My sisters, who I no longer called "Diane's kids," had already started to spend more time at my house after our Granny Tab died. Before, at her insistence, I'd made an effort to suffer through labored appearances at awkward dinners hosted by my father and stepmother, solely so my grandmother could delight in having all her grandchildren in one place. But death isn't a transition only for those who've passed. You never know who or what it will change for the living. In the case of the Walkers, Granny Tab's death seemed to change everything. My relationship with their mother wasn't perfect, not by a long shot, but it became an easy conversation between the two of us to coordinate my sisters coming in from Calabasas to spend bonding weekends with me. When they found out that I was pregnant, they really delighted in the idea of becoming aunts, especially at the ages of ten and fifteen. That they could be somebody's aunt seemed to inflate them with pride, and they monitored my growing belly like it was their own science experiment.

On this particular weekend, we gathered in our usual places in my kitchen for breakfast. It was easy to feed them cereal. I couldn't touch it. With a pregnant woman's appetite, one bowl of cereal for me could have just as easily turned into seven. I stuck with the basics of eggs, toast, and tea. Leaning over the kitchen island and watching the girls happily crunching over their bowls, I wrapped my hands around my tea mug and prepared to break some difficult news.

Before I could speak, my thoughts were interrupted by my youngest sister's voice. "Two?" Dixie looked up at me, having addressed me by my rarely used family nickname. "What do you have to do to be a good auntie?" She and her older sister looked at me intently as if they'd been thinking about this for a while. An opening made, I felt only slightly guilty for what I was about to do.

"Well, Dix, I hate to break it to you guys, but the first duty you'll have as aunties is to redecorate your room for the baby!" I mustered as much enthusiasm as I could. "We're going to turn it into the nursery! Won't that be fun?" My heart broke a bit watching both of their faces fall. I continued quickly, "I'm sure your niece will love knowing one day that we did it together."

Danielle, the older of the two, broke her silent observation. "If we do that, where will we sleep?" She looked disappointed, more than I'd expected. Dixie too. I didn't want them to think that they weren't welcome, or that they were being replaced. We'd just started spending time together. Our relationship was still fragile, and in many ways, my sisters were all I had left of our grandmother. Every time I looked in Dixie's blue eyes, I could see her. The worst would be to push them away.

"How about we also redecorate the guest room? You can make it exactly the way you like it." I started to laugh, thinking about what horrific directions my offer could take, leaving those girls to their own devices. They looked at each other with a reaction I did not expect. I waited for at least a smile from either of them, but time passed without one. Not even a giggle. The silence was unusual. Their gaze had gone from each other to the soggy mess developing in their cereal bowls.

"What? What'd I say?" I looked quizzically back and forth between Danielle and Dixie, "What?" I asked again with a broad gesture of my hands. "Is somebody going to tell me what's going on?"

It was Dixie that spoke up first.

"Well . . ." she said. Her usual animated cadence turned into a slower and more somber tone. "Mom and Dad . . ." She paused and opened and closed her mouth a couple of times without saying anything. Danielle came in quickly in what seemed like a rescue attempt.

"It's not a big deal," Danielle said in a quiet voice. "Mom and Dad have been fighting more than usual, that's all."

"Yeah, but Dad is gone a lot too!" Dixie chimed in finally.

I felt a pang in my gut at the familiar setting being described. The nine-year-old me hidden away behind the doors of adulthood started to poke her head out with panic. *Just before my dad left my mom for Diane . . . he was gone a lot too.* My mind offered the words I wouldn't dare speak out loud to my sisters. But now I understood what was hiding underneath the smiles they offered. It was the same thing causing the unusual silences and Diane's seemingly gracious concession in "allowing" the girls to stay with me on weekends. Maybe before Granny Tab died, I would have thought it better to mind my business. Now these girls weren't just *Diane's kids*, they were family—my sisters. I shifted my position on the counter just to give good thought to what I would say next. I wondered what I wished someone had said to my nine-year-old self when my dad started being gone a lot.

"You both know that you're welcome here anytime, right? And that none of what's happening at home is your fault?" I searched until I was able to meet each pair of eyes in front of me. I not only needed them to hear my words, but I also needed a confirmation that they understood. Hearing nothing, I followed up more intently. "Right? Danielle? Dixie?"

"Yeah, we know," Danielle said softly, without a hint of her usual teenage defiance.

"Yes, Two, we know," Dixie followed. She had taken to using our grandmother's nickname for me after the funeral. She didn't use it often, just like she wasn't usually clingy but held my hand the entire day of Granny Tab's services. Dixie came around the counter and nestled herself next to me, placing her head into the space between my growing belly and my expanding breasts with a hug.

"Danielle, you want some of this sister hug too?" I offered the biggest smile I could muster, extending my left arm, while still holding on to Dixie on my right side. I watched Danielle hesitate for a moment, seeing her eyes well up with water. She stiffened and turned in the opposite direction.

"I'm all right," she said as she made her way toward the hallway. "I'm just going to go watch TV."

Dixie and I looked at each other and held on. In her, I saw myself in similar circumstances. I knew far too well what fear and uncertainty looked like at that age.

Dixie spoke first. "Sorry, she just gets like that sometimes." I rubbed her tiny back and held her tighter. Her head rested on top of my belly.

"It's okay, Dix. Everything is going to be just fine." I just hoped silently that Dixie was still at the age of believing the stories that adults tell for comfort—stories that often exchange hope for truth. Adults know that some of the best stories are really just the most elaborate lies.

16

"Now that you finally have a bump, Tab, this would look so cute on you!" Alexis held up a colorful maxi dress secured on a wooden hanger. The sudden motion caused the bracelets decorating her arm to twinkle. We were in the bright and airy interior of BABE, the trendy maternity wear store in West Hollywood that Alexis swore she'd seen tagged on Instagram by every pregnant celebrity. Our outing was to celebrate the six-month mark in my pregnancy. Supposedly, the idea was to make you feel like you were still hot even as your body started to change beyond recognition.

The sand-colored wooden floors hosted well-crafted table displays of sparkling accessories, and along the perimeter were sparsely populated racks of select clothing items in mostly soft grays and pastels, with a lot of black. Alexis had found what seemed to be the only print in the entire store.

"Well, what do you think?"

"Hmm . . . it's nice, I guess. I mean, Lex, do I really want to emphasize the fact that my round parts are on a growth spurt?" I reached out my fingers to examine the low-cut neck-line.

"Tab, what's wrong? You look beautiful. This is your time to celebrate. Every woman gets excited when she starts to see her bump! Aren't you?"

I paused a moment to think about her question. Part of me was beyond excited. And the other part of me was just starting to comprehend all of the other changes at hand.

"I'm sorry Lex, it's just that I'm a little distracted," I admitted. I was distracted. In just a few hours, I would be meeting up with Marc for a doctor's appointment. At least, I was supposed to. He hadn't confirmed. Work was busy, and he had a meeting that he couldn't cancel, but he was going to try to come anyway.

"Marc is supposed to come with me to my doctor's appointment today, but I'm worried that he's not going to be able to make it." At my words, Alexis frowned. She turned to put the dress she was holding back on the rack and turned to me, putting her arm soothingly on my shoulder.

"Tab, try not to worry about that. You know you have his support. And I would go with you if I didn't have school pickup today," she said, rubbing my arm. "Why don't you see if Andouele can go with you? That's one of the benefits of having a doula. You don't have to do any of this alone." Alexis was right. Even though I'd started this journey expecting that I'd be able to navigate the experience solo, I'd become much more dependent on others than I'd ever expected. Part of me didn't like the feeling, like it was confirmation my original plan was wrong.

"I don't know, Lex. I have *something* from him, I'm just not sure what that is. It's like he's all for the big moments, but the little ones, the ones in between, there's always something more important. I understand he has to work, but—" Alexis caught me off guard as she rushed me with a strong hug.

"I get it, believe me, I get it. But nothing's perfect. I know that better than anyone." As she pulled back, I could see her face tighten up, her mouth drawing into a straighter line. Right away, I knew what thought was animating her expression.

"Are you still feeling guilty, Lex?" I asked softly.

"Girl, every day." She sighed heavily and then continued. "Trust me, at least you know what you're getting with Marc. He doesn't come with surprises." Seemingly as if on cue, the ping of my phone announced a new message. I knew it had to be Marc.

> Tried to get free, but can't make it today. Just routine apptmt right?

Marc's words hit me sharply. My staggered inhale and deflated exhale caught Lexi's attention.

"Is that Marc?"

"Yeah, he can't make it," I mumbled softly. "Just like I thought." Alexis hugged me again.

"I'm telling you, just ask Andouele." As I considered her suggestion, a slender saleswoman dressed in a chic soft gray dress came up to us.

"Well, aren't you gorgeous!" She said with enough cheer

to almost convince me that she was telling the truth. "Can I help you find something?" Just as I was ready to respond, Alexis cut me off with pressure on my arm.

"Actually, yes, thanks," Alexis said. "We need something that's going to make my friend feel special—like she's the most beautiful six-months-pregnant woman in the world." The look she gave me, with raised eyebrow, paused my protest.

"Oh, Mama, we have that handled." The saleswoman seemed excited to be set upon a task. "I'll just pull a few things and set you up in a dressing room." She animated into action, leaving us again to ourselves.

"Tab, you need to let go. Let someone else step in and help. Trust me, it's part of the point of having a doula. Do this for yourself."

"You're right," I said, pulling my phone up. I saw her smile build from the corner of my eye as I composed my reply to Marc.

> Should be routine. Will see if Andouele can go instead.

Just after I hit send, I looked for Andouele's name in my contacts and started a message to her.

> Hi! So sorry for the last minute request, but I have a doctor's appointment and my partner can't go.

My fingers hesitated at typing the word *partner*. I was tempted to go back and erase it, or put it in quotations, but I let it stand and continued my message.

Would you be able to come with me? It's at 3 pm today.

Andouele already had my doctor's information as part of the intake process we'd gone through. I'd never asked her how much notice she'd need for nonemergencies. I was relieved to see the three dots signaling her reply pop up almost immediately. Moments later, the screen scrolled up and her message appeared.

Hi Tabby. Good to hear from you. Yes, I will meet you there.

"She's coming!" I looked up to tell Lexi, surprised but also feeling an unexpected mixture of relief and happiness.

"See? I told you." Lexi smiled as she poked me gently in my arm. I felt the sides of my face rise into a smile in return.

"Hey, Mama!" The saleslady buzzed past us, arms full of clothes. "I pulled some things for you to try. Follow me to the dressing room?" Alexis and I both nodded.

"Let me see if I can get Laila on video," Alexis said fidgeting with her phone. "That girl is never available."

"She's working on her startup. I think it just takes a lot of time."

"Girl, not that much time." As she muttered her reply, I could hear Laila's voice coming through the phone speaker.

"Hey, girl, what's up?"

"I'm out shopping with Tab. We're dressing the bump. And we need your oh-so-very-honest opinions. You busy?"

"I'm just . . . working." I couldn't see the screen, but I

could hear the distraction in Laila's voice. I'd started to inter-rupt, telling Lexi to just forget it, when Laila went on. "But I can take a break. I can't leave the two of you to your own devices. You'll have Tab looking like a soccer mom." Lexi laughed.

"Whatever, Laila, I am officially the queen of the make-over," Lexi responded as she moved ahead of me, following the saleswoman. The ding of my phone stopped me follow-ing behind her. I worried for a moment that Andouele was canceling on me, but looking down, it was Marc's name I saw. The message said simply,

Next time, I promise.

I shook my head and put my phone back in my purse. Today, it was going to be just me and the girls, and that was all I needed. At least, for the moment.

TRUE TO HER WORD, ANDOUELE MET ME AT MY DOCTOR'S APPOINT-ment. Thankfully, it was routine, with the normal checks for blood pressure and ultrasound. There was something about the constant checkups and check-ins during pregnancy that felt like something could be proclaimed wrong or you could easily disrupt nature's process at any moment.

At her suggestion, we left the appointment to sit together at a café to debrief and speak about what to expect from the next segment of my pregnancy. To thank her for accompa-nying me on short notice, I offered to treat her and found myself in line at Café Paris, a small, quaint bistro just doors down from my doctor's Beverly Hills office building. The décor was aged and dated, with a bit of a stale Paris motif on the walls. A faded beige and white wallpaper embodied various points of attraction in the city, an easily recognizable Eiffel Tower among them. To my surprise, we were not the only people in the establishment, as I expected a place like this to be nearing its closing time.

As I approached the counter, the older woman behind it had a look of amusement as she eyed my obvious belly. Her red-stained lips formed a warm smile, and her blue eyes glistened.

"Hello, there!" she said with a surprising amount of cheer for the afternoon hour. "What can I get you?" After a brief scan of the menu, I'd made my selection. Andouele had already told me that she'd like a latte.

"I'll have a latte . . ." With my words, the woman's face fell out of its smiling demeanor. Her eyes dropped down to my bump and then looked back up at me. "And a chamomile tea," I continued, exaggerating the word *tea*.

"Why sure, dear." The warmth returned to her face, and her reply came back in the chipper singsong voice that originally greeted me. I wondered if I'd imagined her reaction. I paid and took from her a plastic numbered square, set upon a thin silver rod, to place on our table.

I made my way back over to the table that Andouele had selected for us, placing the base of the silver rod down in the center of the table.

"I think I almost got my head bitten off ordering your

coffee," I joked to Andouele. She tilted her head back at me. "I'm pretty sure the woman at the counter thought I was ordering for myself." Andouele smiled at me and placed her hand on mine.

"I'm sure you're realizing that pregnancy is the time when almost everyone will have an opinion about your body. Try not to let that add on to the stress." *Stress*. There was that word again.

"Do you think I'm stressed? Even now? The doctor said my blood pressure was good. It seems like things are going well. I have Marc and you and—" Andouele stopped me.

"You have stress, Tabby. You have support too, which is great, but you do have stress. It's in the fabric of living and in the layers of your life. It's invisible until it's not. That's why I chose this work," Andouele concluded with a serene closed-mouth smile.

"I guess I do have some support," I said. "Although, it's not what I thought it would be. And, I guess as you figured, my so-called partner isn't always available."

"No one is ever going to be as available as you'd hope. But you also have to ask. That's why it was so important for me to be with you today. So you'll know I'll be there."

"I . . . I do know that," I stuttered out, surprised by her words.

"Not just now, Tabby, not just before the birth or even during, but after. After is where it gets difficult and overwhelming. After is when you'll need to be able to ask for help. So, hopefully, we're practicing that now."

Andouele's words sounded soothing and haunting at the

same time. I had been so focused on getting through the pregnancy, I hadn't even thought about what it would be like when the baby was actually here. As our drinks arrived, I tried to push the worries from my mind. One step at a time, Tab. One step at a time.

17

"Do you know what you want to get?" Marc whispered into my ear as he opened the door for me to walk through the entrance of Baby Oh Baby.

Completely contrary to the supermom I'd planned to be, with work obligations and the extra time dedicated to my sisters and Marc, as my seventh month of pregnancy approached, I hadn't had time to properly plan anything. I was hoping that somehow, walking into that humongous superstore of all things tiny human, I'd get inspired with a flash of motherly brilliance.

"Um, not exactly." I turned to look at Marc, thankful to break my focus from the overwhelming rows and rows of bottles, pacifiers, baby clothes, strollers, and things that looked far too sophisticated to simply stock a nursery; some looked as if they could raise the entire child on their own.

"Well, Tab, if that's the case," he said, reaching into the back pocket of his dark wash jeans, "I have a little list I made." Marc fumbled for a second, opening the folded papers nervously. "I mean, it's just a little something from a few of the blogs and books I've been reading." As the paper unfolded, I saw his handwriting covering the facing page and two more pages behind it.

"Marc, that's not just a *few* things!" In spite of my state of overwhelming shock, I managed to push the words in the direction of the man standing in front of me, who seemed to be a clear impostor of my boyfriend. He looked back at me sheepishly and then down at the ground.

"Yeah, um, I . . . I guess I might have gone a little overboard." I put my hand on his arm and stepped closer to him as quickly as I could manage, maneuvering to meet his eyes.

"No, Marc, not overboard. I like that you're taking part in this." I reached up with my hands for either side of his face to pull him closer to me. "I love that you're planning. I love that you're researching. I love . . ." I brought our mouths to meet for a kiss. "I love that I'm not in this alone, and I love you for that." At my words, Marc's face broke out into a brilliant smile, almost as if he was basking in sunlight. Hiding any hints of disappointment had been worth it. I'd never seen him so . . . so happy?

"I love you too, Tab. You're a sexy momma," he said as he swatted my double-wide bottom.

Marc and I used his list as the treasure map to navigate the seemingly endless aisles of baby gear and gadgets for every circumstance of pregnancy, birth, and the first years of parenting that one could imagine. Each item triggered a new imagined experience in my mind. *Am I really going to be somebody's mother?* I thought as I traversed aisles three and seven and stood somewhere in the middle of aisle nine.

Just past the burping cloths, Marc turned to me. "Tabby, Rob and Darrell and I are having a summer barbecue at Darrell's house, and I want you to come. I want . . . and I think Rob wants . . . to make it more of a *family* day." Marc held both of my hands and looked me in the eyes. *Family?* This new parenting Marc never failed to surprise me as the complete opposite of boyfriend Marc. Darrell's backyard parties had been nothing more than a bachelor haven filled with thinly clad younger women. For a year, Alexis's estranged husband, Rob, stayed holed up in the guesthouse after getting kicked out of his own home for being a hoe-while-married. Was there any means of redemption for that defiled space? And why now?

I gave him severe side-eye. "Hold up." I returned the colorful terry cloth bib set I was holding to the shelf so that I could fully focus on the astonishing words exiting Marc's mouth. Could something so simple as a baby literally turn a man into an entirely different person? I couldn't ignore the twitch of suspicion that was starting to rise in my gut. "So you honestly expect me to believe that among you guys, someone came up with the idea to convert Darrell's bachelor retreat into a family park? And to put all that work into having a barbecue just to have big, pregnant me and Rob's wife over?"

Marc looked down sheepishly. "Tab, honestly, it's a little more than that." *Finally, some truth comes out.*

"Okay, so what is it really?"

"It was Rob's idea," Marc started to spill words like a faucet turned on high. "Rob thinks that he has a good shot at getting back together with Alexis, for real this time, if he can just show her that he really is focused on their family. He wants to prove to her—and I think to you too—that he's a changed man. Maybe all of us." I allowed my eyebrow to raise but said nothing. "He thought that if he could show her how much he's changed, even in that environment . . . Well, you know how Darrell's backyard can be . . ."

I nodded my understanding. "So you guys came up with a brilliant plan to demonstrate his changed man status?" He nodded. "What about Darrell?"

"Well . . ." Marc said sheepishly, "Darrell's always got his own agenda, but he agreed to host. Even with two or three of Darrell's *friends* making an appearance, Rob and I are calling this a family day."

As hard as I tried to stop it, my side-eye returned with a vengeance. *What are you up to, Marc?* I found another line of inquiry to get the information I wanted. "This still doesn't make sense. What's the point of it all?"

Marc looked down for a second and then back up at me with a teasing smile. "Tabby, Rob wants to get Alexis back, for real this time. It's all he talks about. So, I offered to do this family day with him to show her how much he's changed. And . . . I was hoping that maybe, just a little bit, you'd see something's changed in me too."

My insides melted. "All I know is there better be no cameras allowed. I can't be all over social media looking like a baked potato in a bikini!" Marc grabbed me to pull me in close to him. His arm draped across my lower back as I pretended to lean away.

"You," he purred at me, "look hot . . ." He kissed me. "With and without clothes." Marc accentuated every word with his lips on mine. As if to make his point, he looked me up and down. The roaming of his eyes made me feel naked in spite of wearing my favorite heather-gray, makeshift maternity dress.

It was just us two in the aisle of nursing supplies, enmeshed in a current of attraction. In that moment, the same kind of story adults tell themselves started to develop in my mind. It was my own kind of story, one about Marc and me, one with a happy ending—the kind with blurred lines between hope and lies.

18

"COME ON, TAB, LET'S GO! YOU LOOK FINE!" ALEXIS PRODDED ME from across my sunlit bedroom as I stood in front of my floor-length mirror, trying to make sense of my obviously pregnant figure in a bathing suit.

"Lex, look at this." I rubbed around my belly for emphasis. "You know good and well I have no business at anybody's pool with all this going on."

Alexis laughed and then stopped abruptly. Maybe she could see that I was serious. There were many things I'd been insecure about in my life, but my physique had never been one of them. Television gave me a ridiculous standard to adhere to, and I simply made that a part of my lifestyle. My body had to look a certain way, my face had to look a certain way, and evidently, my hair did too.

"Tabby, nobody should be worried about Darrell's young little hoochies running around that pool. We'll be chillin' in the 'Grown Folks Only' section and letting Rob, Darrell, and Marc entertain the *children*." With that, Alexis put on her sunglasses and turned to leave my bedroom, signaling for me to follow. "Come on, Tab. Let's go!"

Begrudgingly, I pulled my glance away from the mirror in front of me. I made my way toward the door, swiping the turquoise, tropical muumuu-like cover-up off the side of my bed for good measure.

"I don't know how I agreed to this," I murmured under my breath.

"Girl, it'll be fun!" She tried to sound encouraging. To me, it felt like walking into hot torture. But Marc seemed to want me there and Alexis was insistent, so there was really no point in resisting.

When we made it to Darrell's house, Rob plus the boys were already playing in Darrell's pool, along with some other brown children of various shades and progress to sunburns. Alexis shifted next to me, rustling through her giant shoulder bag. I could make out some of the words through her mumbling. "Now, I know I have the spray sunblock with me, so how . . ." She lifted her head in Rob's direction. "Rob!" She had to shout his name in progressively higher decibels before he looked up from the splash game in the pool.

"Yeah, babe, what's up?" Rob shouted back. Rob Jr. took advantage of his father's distraction and slammed a multicolored beach ball at his head. It bounced off hard with a hollow slap, and the boys laughed and kept playing. Rob looked shocked and then annoyed. I tried to keep my snicker to myself.

Alexis, on the other hand, made zero effort to conceal her amusement. She could barely speak. When she finally composed herself, her words were interjected with laughter.

"Um . . . hum . . . I just wanted . . . to give you the sunscreen . . . so you and the boys . . . don't get buuurrnt."

Her laughter was contagious. At poor Rob's expense, we all broke into belly-holding ripples of glee, including Marc, who I located at the grill, and Darrell, in the bubbling spa tub with two bikini-clad girls who looked like they still had UCLA student IDs.

The sun was shining, the rhythmic bass thumped along through a recognizable playlist of up-tempo electric-slide-worthy music, and I managed to find a comfortable seat in the shade in a lounger close to the pool. I put on my sunglasses and tried to imagine that I was the sleek and svelte version of myself, the one that I could barely remember after nearly seven months of pregnancy. Marc came over briefly to help me get situated and then went back to manning the generously covered grill, turning over veggie skewers, hot dogs, and hamburgers. This was a side of him that I could certainly get used to.

It didn't take me long to get hot and need to empty my bladder, not once, but seemingly every fifteen minutes, so I found myself again and again inside the bathroom of Darrell's pool house. Even though he'd moved on into an apartment, Rob's original crash pad was still littered with his shaving tools and cologne. I wondered how the day was going in Alexis's mind so far, given that it was basically Rob's audition to get back into their house. On one of my bathroom trips, once I moved past the guilt, I gave in to the urge to snoop and went through every single drawer and medicine cabinet shelf I could find. I figured if I stumbled across a pack of condoms or, worse, a *partially used* pack of condoms, or even an extra toothbrush, that would be information that Alexis would want to know.

Hearing the high-pitched laughter of Darrell's *friends* outside made me seriously doubt that Rob's time spent here was completely pious. Still, my extensive search came up with nothing damning or even particularly interesting, which made me all the more curious about the rest of the pool house. No one would question a pregnant lady about how long she'd been in the bathroom, right?

Making my best attempt to be inconspicuous, I tiptoed my way around the wall of the bathroom and into the living area of the studio apartment setup. Near the bed was a nightstand with a drawer in it. *That's it!* I thought, and started in that direction, after making sure the coast was clear at the door. My heart pounded in my ears. I had no idea how I'd explain if I got caught. I'd just have to make sure I didn't. Maybe there was something that Alexis needed to know. I didn't have a clear view of the entire pool area, but it didn't seem like anybody was looking for me. Marc was at the grill, Darrell was still in the spa, beer in one hand, a woman's shoulders in the other, the boys were splashing around the pool, and Alexis . . . Alexis was . . .

"There you are, Tab! I was looking for you!" Alexis was standing ten feet away from me. Her face came into my peripheral vision as I saw her step into the living room area. "Getting some air-conditioning? Girl, I understand, it's hot as hell outside. You must be miserable." Guilt tickled against my ribs as I thought about why I was really inside the pool house after all.

"Mm-hmm . . . much cooler in here," I said slowly, while

allowing my glance to survey the entire space once more. "So this is where Rob spent all his time, huh?" I let my glance linger on the neatly made-up bed and the nightstand drawer that had been my target.

"Girl." Alexis rolled her eyes as she spoke. "You know that I already went through every drawer and cabinet up in here!" My eyes widened, and my mind cheered while my body released some of its tension. I was pleasantly surprised to hear about this snooping—since high school, Alexis had believed everything that Rob told her, especially if that meant they could stay together.

"Lexi, you know I was about to head for that bed stand?" My confession easily escaped. Something that I would have never told old Lexi seemed to flow freely. Still, I braced myself for her reaction.

She stood still for a moment, shifted on her feet, and then broke into a wide smile. "Girl, you know I'd do the same for you!" Alexis brought up her hand to slap me five.

"Well, did you find anything?" I asked, more quickly than I'd meant to.

"Girl, no. Rob is dumb sometimes, but he's not stupid. I know what he's up to. He's been trying to get me to say I'll take him back. He keeps trying to tell me that what he did isn't who he is . . . and all that." Alexis waved her hand in the air, swatting at the words like fruit flies.

"Lex, are you going to? Seeing Rob with the boys . . . Now that I have this situation with Marc . . . Let's just say I understand a lot more now than I ever did." My hands floated up to my belly, rubbing around my overinflated midsection.

"Tabby." Lexi walked over to me and brought her hand up

to rub my back. "Don't ever feel like you need to choose any-thing or anyone other than yourself and your child. It's never worth it if you do. Believe me, there isn't a day that it doesn't weigh on me . . . the decisions I could make for everybody else. But, if I take Rob back, it will be for all the right reasons. And I just hope that you're with Marc . . . because you *want* to be, not because you feel like you have to be."

I turned to hug Lexi, only for her to turn away in response to a tug on her bag. It stopped me from saying what I'd been thinking—that I didn't know what I wanted, or if Marc was what I wanted, but at least it felt like the comfortable side of right, and that hope was all I had to go on. My thoughts were interrupted by the insistent tone of a familiar high-pitched voice.

"Mommy! I'm hunnnnngrry!" Lexington was standing there, hair in springing coils. His narrow body was dripping with water and shivering while he hopped back and forth from one foot to the other. "Hi Auntie Tab!" he added with a small wave. As usual, his presence pulled my biggest smile out of me and I felt it spreading wide across my face.

"You're still being a good boy at school?" I teased with faux scolding. He smiled, hiding behind his mother.

"Yes . . ." he said coyly, looking up at me with doe eyes. Alexis pursed her lips lightly and sighed.

"He knows he better be! Lexington, why don't you have a towel?" Alexis said, beginning to furiously rummage through her bag, seeming to have finally struck mommy gold. "Here, take some fruit snacks . . ." Alexis produced several small rumpled packages from her bag and handed them to her son.

"Thank you!" Lexington grabbed his stash and ran back out toward the pool.

"Don't run!" Alexis shouted after him. "And share with your brother!" She turned back to me with a roll of her eyes. "Girl, see what you have to look forward to? At least he's playing nicely today. And if not, that's his dad's problem to solve." We both laughed as we headed back to the pool area.

Not even thirty minutes later, it was me that was starving. I waddled my way over to Marc at the grill. He seemed to be enjoying himself, deep into his grill master vibe. When I got close enough, I draped my arm over his shoulder lazily to give a kiss to the chef.

"*We're* starving," I said to him with a smile.

"Let's get you something to eat, then," Marc replied, flipping some hunks of hamburger in a region of the grill shared with a couple of ribeye steaks. "Seems like some of this burned, and the kids grabbed the hot dogs. This should just be a few more minutes." Marc looked at me sheepishly. "There's some grilled corn on the side, if you want that?"

The heat and hunger had worn away at my patience. I tried to hide the disappointment from my face, but gauging from the look on Marc's, it registered anyway. "It's fine, babe." I added a reassuring kiss on his cheek. "I can wait."

Marc studied my face with his delicious-brown eyes and crinkled his forehead slightly. "You're not feeling this barbecue thing, are you?"

I shuffled my feet, trying to think of a quick answer. I looked back up at him with the only response I could think of—an honest one. "No, not really feeling this. What I feel like is a literal beached whale. Yep, a whale on the beach—out of my element, uncomfortable, and maybe a little hangry."

"Oh, so you're hangry now?" He grabbed me by my waist with a tickle and a kiss on my neck. "Okay, *Hangry*. Let me wrap this up quick and then I'll get you a real meal."

Satisfied with his answer, I glanced back at the pool over my shoulder, relieved that we'd soon be making our exit. "At least I won't have to fight Darrell's *friends* for any of the good stuff—those girls look like they haven't eaten this week." I looked down at my own large protruding stomach for comparison. "I can't help feeling like . . ."

Marc pulled me in tighter. "You look beautiful." He studied me closely, biting his lip. "You should take this turquoise thing off and get some sun on that bun of yours . . . of *ours*." He smiled at me with that irresistible look.

"Marc Brown, if I didn't know better, I'd think that you were looking at me like I was one of those steaks over there."

He narrowed his eyes slyly. "A smart lady knows what she sees." I smiled back at him and rubbed around my belly for emphasis. A small gasp escaped as his hand made contact with my backside in a brisk and tight squeeze. It sent an electric jolt through the center of my body. At least some of me was still holding its shape.

"Careful, your eyes might be bigger than your appetite." I pulled away from him with a sly smile of my own.

"Come on now, Tabby," he called after me as I walked back toward Alexis and the shade, "you already know *exactly* how big my appetite is."

Marc was right. That I did know—and the thought of it made me start to get impatient for dessert.

MARC SMILED ACROSS THE TABLE AT ME AS I LIFTED A CHEESE-laden French fry to my mouth. His hands were folded in front of him with the untouched menu sitting off to the side.

"Mmm . . . this . . . is the good stuff," I mused after swallowing, savoring the salty, buttery, crunchy texture of my latest indulgence. "You're sure you don't want some? You're just going to watch me eat and make me self-conscious?"

Marc laughed. "Girl, you've been pregnant for almost seven full months. I've seen you eat much worse than some late-night cheese fries. Plus, after being in front of that grill all day, if I don't see another piece of food . . . I'll be good for a week."

Just thinking about the day spent at Darrell's pool in the hot sun made a section of my scalp start to itch. I reached for the space between my cornrows underneath the sewn-on wig that Denisha had replaced the week prior. I imagined what it would have felt like to be fully comfortable, pregnant belly and all, jumping and splashing in the pool like Lexington, without a care in the world about messing up my hair. I got lost momentarily in that fleeting feeling of imagined freedom.

"What're you thinking about over there that's got you smiling like that?" Marc gave me a wink. "You thinking about dessert? Because I definitely am . . ."

As I started to give him a word to keep him encouraged until we could get home, a middle-aged white man came up to our table. He was dressed conservatively, so I assumed he was a colleague of Marc's, especially given the familiarity of his approach.

"Hey, man!" the guy said, holding out his hand to Marc. Marc looked as surprised as I was. He said nothing but tilted his head and gave the guy a once-over. The guy continued enthusiastically, "I saw you pull in with the USC plates. Nice car, man! Did you play at SC? You still playing somewhere now?"

Marc, who was certainly fit, but without the physique of any sort of professional athlete, allowed his face to scrunch up completely with furrowed brows. I braced myself for his reply. It seemed like forever passed before he actually spoke. "Nah, man, you got the wrong guy. I went to Stanford." With that, he turned back to me and gave me "the look" that I immediately understood.

"Aww cool, my bad, man. You played at Stanford?" The shadow across Marc's face deepened. I saw his body tense up. The baby kicked me, causing me to jump a little.

Marc took a deep breath and then turned slowly to the stranger standing in front of us. Again, it seemed like he was carefully considering his words. "Nope, I only graduated Phi Beta Kappa undergrad, got great GMAT scores, and was at the top of my investment banking class. No sports stats. I guess they had to just let me in on merit."

The stranger shifted nervously. He held his hand out again to shake Marc's. "Aww, man, I'm sorry, dude. I didn't mean to imply . . ."

Marc smiled back, took the guy's hand to shake it, and cut him off. "Yeah, man, you did. But it's all good. I think we're on the same page now, right?" The guy nodded his head, seeming to have fallen into a state of shock. Marc took advantage of the silence to continue. "So, sorry to disappoint.

I'm not famous, but my lady here is, and . . ." Marc stood up and brought his other hand around to pat the stranger on the shoulder. "And let's just say she needs my full attention. So you have a nice night, okay?"

The guy's face turned bright red. He looked at me directly, waving his hand in my direction, then turning from Marc to offer it to me. "I'm so sorry, I didn't mean to disturb you guys."

"Nothing to worry about," I said, smiling at him and then looking back at my neglected fries.

"So, are you an actress or something?" he continued, causing my eyebrow to raise and my mouth to drop open slightly. *This guy!* The baby kicked me again. I turned to Marc with my own version of "the look." He sprang into action.

"Hey, man, she's the absolute best at what she does, but we're just trying to grab a bite and not draw attention. Cool?" Marc used his body to block the table. I turned back down to my fries and tried to continue my hard-earned enjoyment before the mass of gooey cheese solidified on me.

Finally, at least two fries later, the guy seemed to get the hint. "Hey, dude, my bad. I'm sorry. Can I get you guys a round of drinks or something?"

Marc answered for both of us. "Naw, thanks for the offer, but we're good. You have a good night, though, man."

The man lingered for a bit with a few stuttered turnaways, until he finally started walking away from our table. Marc and I looked at each other, both stifling laughter until he was out of earshot.

"I can't believe that guy even had the nerve to come over

here," I said, half laughing with my mouth full of the tail end of my fries.

"Right?" Marc said with a wave of his hand. "Did I *play* at USC law school? I mean, come on, dude. Read the plates and apply common sense. I'm tired of having to explain everything about my existence." Marc's shoulders slumped. I reached for his hand.

"I'm sorry, Marc. I guess when people see USC plates on a Porsche and *us* getting out, the automatic assumption is not only that are you an athlete, but that we're on display. It sometimes makes me wonder what kind of world we're bringing our daughter into."

Marc gave a hard sigh. "Tabby, as long as I'm around, she isn't going to have to worry about that . . . and neither are you." Then his demeanor shifted. His eyelids lowered at me. I knew that expression well. Maybe the intrusion hadn't ruined the rest of our plans for the evening.

IT MUST HAVE BEEN THE HORMONES BECAUSE CHEESE FRIES HAD never been on my list of turn-ons before. But by the time Marc and I reached my house and walked in together, my body was turned on and on fire.

The door closed; my shoes came off. My mouth was on Marc's, and all of a sudden my insides were dancing from the warm, wet heat between our faces and the synchronized acrobatics of kissing.

He grabbed at the back of my head, briefly yanking at my consciousness as well. "Ohh, babe," I whispered, "not the hair. Watch the hair."

"Sorry," he panted back at me, "I got caught up."

His hands searched elsewhere, pulling my expanded frame closer to him—my belly tapped up against his pelvis while his hands encapsulated both sides of my rear, giving a very firm tug that traveled all the way to the front of my body, tickling me against the swimsuit that I was still wearing.

He slid the cover-up off of me in one single motion and bent down to kiss my neck, moving down toward my chest.

I started to forget myself. The heaviness, the weight, the protrusion of my stomach. I just wanted him in that moment and to stop thinking about anything, really. Marc and I . . . we *always* got this part right.

"You okay?" he stopped to ask. I didn't want him to stop, not then, not ever.

"Yes, yes, please don't stop," I begged back at him. From then on, Marc was insatiable.

And just like that, still in the doorway, my body shuddered and released all of its tension in a wave of sensual delight, like being carried on a wave of silken sheets. I flowed into a moonlit pool of warmth and relaxation like I'd never known or experienced.

Holding his face to mine, he whispered softly, "Round two in the bedroom?"

There'd need to be a round two and three and maybe four before I could exhaust all of the heat that had been building inside of me. It was as if I couldn't get enough of him that night. Of my entire pregnancy, this was the best time that we would have—fueled by honest desire for one another with no idea what was to come.

19

DAYLIGHT BROKE INTO MY KITCHEN AS I STARTED THE COFFEE AND placed two mugs on the counter. Marc was still sleeping, and my body was still happily vibrating from the incredible night that we spent together. By day, I felt overwhelmingly clumsy, large, protruding, and slightly awkward. But last night, I felt sexy, powerful, beautiful, and so full of life that I could completely understand how such a miracle could be growing inside of me.

I said a silent prayer that my daughter would remember nothing of what her parents exposed her to in the bedtime hours and reached over for my phone to turn on my Sunday morning gospel playlist. I made another note to head to church next week, as I was overdue for some in-person blessing.

Before the coffee finished brewing, a yawning Marc appeared shirtless across the kitchen. Professional athlete he was not, but his body had enough ridges to hold my attention. He leaned over the cream-colored marble in my direction.

"Hey," he said with a broadening smile. "Good morning."
I leaned in to kiss him.

"Good morning to you too." As I spoke, I felt a slight flush
coming to my face as fleeting salacious thoughts of the night
before entered my mind. "Coffee?"

"You made some just for me?" Marc asked with a raised
eyebrow.

"Coffee for you, tea for me," I said, as I pulled the coffee-
pot toward one of the mugs on the counter and watched the
fragrant steam rise. I handed him a full cup and then picked
up my phone to turn down the music.

Marc set the mug on the island with both hands and
leaned forward again. "Tabby . . ." he said in a low voice that
made my full body stiffen. I walked over to face him.

"Yes, Marc? You have my *complete* attention," I teased.

Marc looked uncomfortable; he wasn't meeting my eyes
like he usually did. And in spite of what seemed like a casual
moment together in the kitchen, when he spoke again, he
was looking at his feet. "Tabby, there's . . . something . . .
something that I've been meaning, well, that I've been wanting to do, and if you're free this morning, I'd like you to take
a little trip with me."

Involuntarily, I raised an eyebrow. "A trip? Like a day trip?"

Marc laughed, this time looking down briefly at his
mug. "Naw, not a real trip. Just an errand. You down to roll
with me?"

"It's a little late to be asking me to be your *ride or die*, don't
you think?" I tried to lighten the mood, laughing at my own
joke and pulling over my own mug of overbrewed tea. Marc
didn't flinch.

"Babe, if you're about to rob a bank or something, I need to know ahead of time." I smiled over this new mystery. Knowing Marc, he had his own list of baby stuff that I hadn't even considered yet, and he probably wanted my opinion on colors or something.

"Woman, how about you stop asking me so many questions? I'm bringing my wallet *and you*, if you'll indulge me with a little bit of your valuable time?"

I nodded and gave him the kiss that he'd leaned in for. "Okay, Marc Brown. Yes, I will go on your mystery errand . . . as long as . . ."

"As long as what?" he said with a quizzical look. I smiled slowly, savoring his curiosity.

"As long as . . . there's some more of that dessert from last night."

At that, Marc got up from the seat and swiftly moved close to wrap his arms around me.

"There's a lot more of that to come." His gravelly morning voice awaked my body and my imagination.

"Well then," I said, pulling him along in the direction of the hallway, "you have a deal."

OVER AN HOUR LATER, FINALLY COMPOSED, SHOWERED, FED, AND in the car, I still had no idea where Marc wanted to take me. Even after nearly seven months of pregnancy, I was still getting used to this new Marc. It didn't take me long to realize that we were headed in the direction of downtown and, once we got there, that we were going to an unmistakable landmark on an easily identifiable block: the Los Angeles Jewelry Mart.

Spanning blocks, the Jewelry Mart was an institution in LA. Akin to the rows of side-by-side jewelry shops in Manhattan and other cities, the Los Angeles version was a unique incarnation of our own brand of "over the top." Stores with large and inviting windows lined the streets, beckoning with glistening displays, selling everything shiny from elegant watches to loose gemstones, and gold chains by the ounce. There were also name necklaces, bamboo earrings, and places that you could get anything gold-plated and diamond-encrusted, from your teeth to your nails and whatever else in between.

When I was young, my dad would bring me here every year to find a present for my mother. Each time, we'd walk the booths, and my father would ask me, "Do you like this one?" It made me feel important, as if my opinion held the key to some kind of magic that could make him do something just because I wanted it so. And, if we were lucky in our efforts, I could find at least one way to make my mother smile.

Marc brought the car to a stop in a parking lot near the main entrance, confirming my guess. It definitely wasn't the baby gear stop that I'd first thought. "So, is this the big secret destination? The Jewelry Mart?" Perplexed, I shot the question in Marc's direction as he exited his side of the car and came around to mine.

His response, after opening my car door, was a wide smile and a grab of my hand to help pull me forward out of the passenger seat. The effort to move positions almost made me forget the line of questioning. Who knew being almost seven months pregnant was its own form of exercise?

"Come on, girl, and stop asking so many questions," Marc said, maintaining that big smile, more boyish than I'd seen from him in a long time. "Today is your day off, Miss Reporter. Just let me handle things for a minute." I felt a slight flush come to my face and decided to ease off just a bit. I couldn't help my curiosity. It was, after all, such a strange and impromptu errand. And, even though the answer was around the corner, I didn't have just one question, I had a million. Marc had never been one for surprises and was nothing if not predictable. I hoped he appreciated my trust on this occasion. He said he had a plan, and even though it wasn't easy, I'd try to take my hands off the steering wheel and my foot off the gas.

Marc led me down the sidewalk and then skillfully maneuvered his way to the street side, making himself a physical barrier between the cars that passed us on the left and big pregnant me, ambling along on his right. His firm grasp and slight pull on my hand was the tugboat I needed to squeeze through the surprisingly populated squares of sidewalk between the parking lot and the Jewelry Mart entrance. It was hard to stay focused and not get lost in the distractions of glistening multicolored baubles and egregiously large diamonds strategically set in display windows. I tried not to let my gaze linger in any one direction, so Marc wouldn't think that I was trying to hijack or ruin his mission. Or drop a hint toward something neither of us was ready for.

Once we finally made our way into the Jewelry Mart, it was surprisingly quiet and a welcome contrast to the busy street outside. It was full of numbered stalls, each with a completely unsuspecting appearance that belied the hundreds of thousands of dollars of value that sat in cases and safes in the meager ten-by-ten spaces. The only clue to the true nature of the place was the armed security guards stationed at the front and strolling around the floor space. I hastily made eye contact and nodded a hello to the brotha in the security uniform as we walked in. I couldn't help but wonder if he found us suspicious just as two Black people wandering their way around. I tried my best to look purposeful.

"Marc," I whispered as I pulled down on his hand, "where are we going?" He turned to me, laughing.

"What, you think that I'm bringing your pregnant behind here on a jewelry heist?" He smiled bigger, making me laugh at my own paranoid thinking.

"No, but that security guard over there is eyeing us like we're about to steal something." At my words, Marc shifted his attention and his smile disappeared.

"Oh yeah, well, you know how that goes. Anywhere we go, we're suspicious." He pulled my hand closer to his body. "Don't worry, where we're headed—it's just over here."

Marc led us to a nondescript stall, among the many other nondescript stalls that made me wonder how he even knew to come to this particular one. Maybe he was planning to impress me with a new fancy watch purchase. But, to my surprise, in the glass case he was pointing to were brilliant, sparkling ring settings and a smattering of singleton diamonds scattered about. I could feel my pulse start to increase.

"Marc, wh-what is all of this?"

While the store owner languished disinterestedly behind the counter, looking at something on his phone, Marc turned to me, his eyes and expression as soft as I'd seen in maybe all of our years of dating, and not dating.

"Tabby." His eyes dropped down to my belly and then came back up to meet mine directly. "We're about to become parents. We're . . . about to . . . become a family. I wanted to bring you here so that we can both start thinking about . . . what's next for us. We're here so you can show me what you like."

His words made me speechless. I blinked, trying to reconnect to reality. I tried to say something, anything at all, but the flood of memories, of moments both good and bad, swamped my thinking—the breakups, the (sex-induced) makeups, the rejections, the heartbreak—and all of it culminated in this moment of me standing here in a dusty jewelry mart with Marc, my hair itching under a wig with swollen ankles and a whole mess of confusion. *But what is there to be confused about?* I asked myself. *This is the happy ending we wanted, right?* I started to sweat.

"Marc, this . . . is a lot to process." Somehow, *this* wasn't all that I'd imagined it would be, or even close to what I'd wanted. Nature and circumstances had taken me off the path of traditional so long ago. It seemed like that option had ended, and I had to make do with where I found myself. And I was starting to believe that maybe there could be a new kind of perfect, since I never got the version I was told to believe in. To find myself so suddenly staring my old dreams in the face brought on a light-headed feeling.

"I . . . I think I might need to sit down."

"There's a chair right there, miss," the disinterested shopkeeper said without even a glance away from his phone. Sure enough, there was a chair to the right of the stall at the end of the glass display. I beelined for it.

"Tabby." Marc spoke urgently to me, holding my elbow and endeavoring to meet my eyes. "Don't take this the wrong way. I mean, we're just here to look for ideas. I just want to get a gauge of what you like. I want to let you know how serious I am about this. Plus . . . there's something else."

"What else, Marc?" I looked at him wide-eyed.

"Well, my parents. They're coming next weekend, and I want us to all go to dinner. They're looking forward to meeting you."

"You said that I wouldn't like your parents. I thought that's why you hadn't introduced us."

By now he was kneeling in front of me. I held my head in my hands and let my belly fall forward between my legs, while my elbows dug wells into the space above my knees. It was almost the only place below my waist that wasn't yet swollen. Meanwhile, none of this made sense—neither the timing, nor the suddenness. And then it clicked.

"Marc, are you saying that you want to rush an engagement before your parents come to meet me?"

"I'm not saying that, Tabby!" Marc shook his head vigorously. "No, not at all! I'm just saying that . . . that . . . this is where I see us heading. I want you to know it, and I want my parents to know it too."

Somehow, this felt all wrong, and I couldn't place it. Images flashed through my mind of my mother crying at the kitchen table the night my dad left. Of Granny Tab's hands as she held mine when she spoke of my grandfather leaving. I imagined Diane sitting at the window, waiting for my dad to come home, and the looks on my little sisters' faces as they told me that the family cycles were repeating. But they wouldn't repeat for my child. I made the silent promise to myself.

"Marc." I spoke to him as gently as I could, taking his hands. "We don't have to get married if you're not sure or if I'm not sure. We don't have to do it for your parents, or my parents, or for anyone but ourselves. And that's if we do it at all." *What are you saying, Tabby? Isn't this "it" what you always wanted?* But I couldn't stop myself from speaking what I knew to be true. Somehow, between the baby and my house, and even Granny Tab passing away, the things I wanted had already started to shift. I did love Marc, but at the same time, I was only just starting to learn to love myself. "Where's this coming from, anyway?"

"Tabby, I don't want you to be just my baby mama. You know that. I was raised to know that a man steps up to his responsibilities. I'm going to do what I'm supposed . . ."

I raised my hand to cut him off, gently touching his lips. "Marc, you already are doing what you're supposed to."

He straightened up, as he had been leaning over so far toward me that he was almost lying in my lap. For a while, we both sat in silence. *You don't have to make everything so serious, Tabby. It's just looking at rings, not buying one. It's not a proposal.* I felt some of the tension drain out of my body, but the discomfort remained. In what I had always thought would be a scenario of my dreams, something felt hollow. Surrounded by a million sparkling jewels, here I was, facing a man who wanted to marry me, who loved me, certainly, but who clearly wasn't *in* love. I wanted to be more than a responsibility.

"Look," I said, finally finding words, "we don't have to decide anything today. If you want to look at rings or gemstones, or whatever, that's fine."

"Tabby, I'm serious about this," Marc protested.

"I know. We can look. No harm at all in looking."

I made it a point to stand up and walk over to make an exaggerated show of examining the shiny objects in the glass case. The image before me looked like a constellation of twinkling multicolored stars. *Is this what it's all about?* I wanted to want this. This was how it was supposed to go. Except in my fantasies, "I can't have a baby mama" wasn't the guy's rationale for proposing to me. I wanted to be *wanted*. I wanted to be claimed as his choice, not treated as the consolation prize.

"See anything you like?" Marc was peering over my shoulder with great interest, trying to follow where my eyes landed.

"Umm," I fumbled. "I think that one is nice." I pointed to an eraser-sized solitaire diamond shaped like a heart.

"Ohhh, that's a very nice, classy selection." The salesperson sprang to life, dropped his phone, and came over to join us. "Would you like me to show it to you?"

"Oh, um, no, I think . . . I think we're just looking," I stammered.

"Tabby, if you really like it, I think we should take a closer look at it." Marc had sincerity in his eyes that I appreciated, even if the circumstances left a lot to be desired. All I could think about was escape. I needed to talk to somebody. I needed Ms. Gretchen. She'd know what to do.

"Uhh . . . okaayyy," I managed to say. This wasn't what I'd dreamed of. This wasn't how I wanted this. I didn't even know if this was best for the baby. Marc's excitement seemed to escalate.

"Do you want to try on a setting?" The clerk pushed the velvet stand in my direction. I started to feel the rush of warmth rise up through my chest into my neck. I felt suffocated and faint. My breath quickened.

"I . . . I think I need to sit down again," I whispered. Marc took hold of my elbow to hold me up. My knees wobbled as if they were going to buckle. In an unsteady combination, Marc escorted the two of us back to the seat on the other side of the glass counter. Away from the rings and all that they meant and didn't mean, an increased state of calm immediately started to set in.

Marc's face showed concern as he studied me closely. I avoided his eyes for fear of looking at him too long. I didn't know if the mixture of guilt and shame swirling about my insides would force me into a bad decision. I wanted to stay and play along. I also very badly wanted to leave. Being teammates in our child's life was one thing. Trying to make things work between us was reasonable. But a forced marriage?

"Tabby, are you okay?" Marc's words were all I needed to start the flow of tears streaming down my cheeks. I could feel them making their way into pools at my chin line and starting to drip onto my wrists. I felt betrayed by crying, ashamed that my emotions could be piqued so easily and for all the wrong reasons in a moment that the old me would have celebrated.

"I'm sorry, I'm so sorry," I pleaded. "I can't do this. I can't do this today. I appreciate what you're trying to do—I do. But we don't have to do this. We don't. Let's give ourselves some time, okay?" I felt like the words spilled from my mouth faster than my mind could think them. I watched Marc's face fall. His disappointment was easy to read. "I mean, what's the rush?" I offered, trying to inject some hope.

"Tabby, I'm sorry. I just wanted to let you know I'm making a commitment to be there for you and our daughter. I didn't mean to upset you." I took the tissue he held out to me, handed to him by the salesclerk, who was pretending to ignore us with his face back in his phone.

"I appreciate that, but—" Marc cut me off.

"And my parents are coming. You know that. I'd like them to know I'm serious too. If my mother knew . . ." *Your mother?* And then I realized there was much more to this trip than Marc was letting on. It wasn't about making a new Mrs. Brown; this was about appeasing the original.

THE WIND COMING IN THROUGH MY CAR WINDOWS WHIPPED through the venting in my sewn-on hairstyle as I sped to Crestmire. For the first time since I was three months pregnant, I felt sick on an empty stomach. I was overdue to see Ms. Gretchen anyway, but more than anything, I hoped she could help me make sense of what currently made no sense at all.

My mind cycled through the same questions of earlier. *Marc wants to propose? Why now?* As much as I wanted to, I couldn't come up with an answer that didn't revolve around his fear of having a "baby momma," as he put it, or more fundamentally, his apparent fear of his actual momma. Weren't we doing fine as things were? What was the rush, after all?

I thought back to my conversation with Andouele and the offense she took at the term "single mother by choice." Not everyone had choices, but I *did* choose this. I chose to be a mother, and when Marc didn't choose me, I didn't choose him as my only means. I looked beyond him. Marc was a piece in my puzzle, but the picture I thought we were making wasn't so clear anymore. Maybe it never was. I thought about Alexis and how difficult it must have been to fight for her independence, especially in the confines of the world we knew, which penalized her for it.

I did once have it all planned out with certainty. I gave Marc the chance to get married, try for a family, and live out the so-called dream. When I did that, he told me that he had other options that he wanted to pursue. He told me that he wasn't even sure that he ever wanted to get married or have children. Was I supposed to forget that all of that ever happened just because the scraps of him I held on to produced a child? This didn't feel like a fairy tale to me. It felt like a story that Marc wanted to tell people because he wasn't strong enough to face the truth. But maybe I could be, for the both of us.

I pulled into Crestmire close to the end of visiting hours. Ms. Gretchen was expecting me. I hadn't made my usual Saturday trip because of the "family day" at Darrell's. Ms. Gretchen stayed busy, with nail appointments, classes, and even a new volunteer project she was working on, but she always seemed to make time to see me, and that I appreciated. The front desk clerk directed me to her apartment near the back of the building, which was a rather long waddle this time. When Ms. Gretchen finally opened the door, she beamed like a ray of sunshine, perhaps even brighter than her vibrant orange-polished nails.

"Well hello, there, honey!" She wrapped her thin arms around my shoulders and pulled me in as close as my belly would allow. "Look at you! You're round from the front, but I bet you can't see nothin' from the back. The rest of you is just as tiny as you ever were!" Given how I felt at the pool party, this was about the best compliment that anyone could give me.

I smiled back at her and did a little twirl around so that she could see the back of me after all. When I faced her again, her smile had turned into a slight frown with furrowed eyebrows.

"What's going on with your hair?" she asked me seriously. I felt my hand float up to touch my sewn-on hairstyle. I patted all around. Feeling the tangles, my face flushed on its own.

"It's a mess, isn't it? I had the windows down in the car and forgot to smooth it all out. This hair was supposed to be easy, but most of the time, it's more work than it's worth."

Ms. Gretchen patted and smoothed down the chaos on top of my head. I closed my eyes for just a brief moment and allowed myself to be soothed. "Now there, that's better," she said, stepping back to admire her work. "Don't worry about it, honey, we all need shelter sometimes. Who am I to judge if your place is underneath a wig? If you don't like it, when you're ready for a change, you'll change it."

"Ms. Gretchen, after the viewer letters, and with the pregnancy and everything, I just . . ." I stammered, trying to find the words to express why I allowed Denisha to hide away my God-given curls under an itchy performance of straight hair.

"I understand," she said with a wink, patting my hand and pulling me toward her sofa where we both took a seat.

I was happy to drop the subject of my wig. It was on my head, but not on my mind at that moment. "Ms. Gretchen, Marc took me ring shopping today," I blurted out.

"He did?" Ms. Gretchen sat wide-eyed for a moment before she continued with a puzzled expression. "Now, isn't this the same man who was concerned about his options just about a year ago?"

"Yes, that's true . . . he was . . . and then he said today that he wanted to get married."

"Well, do you?"

"That's just it, Ms. Gretchen. I don't if it's for the wrong reasons. I don't want to wind up like my grandmother, or even my mother. I just feel like it needs to be right, because I've already seen enough wrong."

"Well, sweetheart, I can tell you because I've done it. Being married isn't always all it's made out to be. It's work. It's two imperfect people trying to fit together like pieces in a puzzle that doesn't match the picture on the box. And every generation has an opportunity to walk a different path. Your mother and grandmother tried it their ways—in your life, you get to try yours."

"I thought I knew what that was, Ms. Gretchen, until it all changed."

"Tabby, you don't have to do anything you don't really, truly want to do. What we can't control always comes along to throw a wrench in our plans just when we think we know where we're going. But that's when you have to stay focused on where you want to wind up."

"I thought I wanted to wind up with Marc, but not like this. I want the real thing, not what looks like the real thing. Not some kind of temporary thing."

"Like that hair you're wearing?"

"Well, yes, Ms. Gretchen, like this hair." I couldn't help but laugh. She gave me a playful pinch. "And he wants me to meet his mother."

"Oh, well, finally. I can't see how you'd be talking about marriage and you hadn't met his momma! Honey, I can tell you for sure, after two marriages—if you marry the man, you marry his mother also. I found that out the hard way." Ms. Gretchen shook her head. "Tabby, this is your life, so it's up to you to live it. At the end of the day, you are the one who is going to have to deal with the consequences of your decisions. So make them for you and nobody else. If you stay true to yourself, there's no way that it won't work out."

I leaned over to give Ms. Gretchen a hug and let my head linger on her shoulder for a second. I hoped the faith she had in me would rub off. I was going to need it.

20

I SAT ALONE IN CHRIS'S OFFICE, FEELING MYSELF SINK DEEPLY INTO the chair across from his desk. The white stacks of paper that were always there seemed to be growing rather than shrinking. He was still old school in that way, printing out everything, writing notes by hand, reading ratings reports and viewer letters, all while paying almost zero attention to social media. I couldn't help but wonder if following his lead was the truest way forward into a future of higher ratings. Maybe things did need to change, but who was I to take that on? I could barely stay on his good side as it was.

Chris hadn't given me a clear directive, but essentially implied what he wanted, and I'd done it. Yet still, every time I was called to his office, there was a lead-up of dread. For distraction, I buried myself in scrolling through my phone. The five minutes that passed felt like fifty before Chris finally pushed the door open and walked in. His stocky frame and huffing presence elevated the stress of the environment, even in relative silence. He seemed to carry the weight of our entire staff on his sloping, meaty shoulders. Chris exhaled deeply, taking a seat behind his desk, and leaned forward to look at me over his circular wire-rimmed glasses.

"So," he said, studying me from the top of my wig-covered head to my protruding stomach, "let's talk about your maternity leave situation."

"Well, I didn't exactly know it was a *situation*, Chris." The words escaped my mouth before I really had a chance to consider what I was saying.

"Oh." Chris laughed uncomfortably. "I didn't mean it *that* way." He shifted in his seat. "We just need . . . to prepare the viewers for your leave. I want to have your pregnancy mean something for them. I mean . . ." I watched as his eyes shifted to my empty left hand that rested on the side of the armchair. "Once again, Tabby, you have a *unique* situation, so I'm saying, let's share that perspective."

At his words, I felt the same all-too-familiar throb in my gut. It was the same feeling in the grocery store every time people took their own look at my protruding stomach and then at my *ringless* left hand. I knew that look; I knew that judgment, and I didn't like it. I thought back to Marc's unromantic offer at the Jewelry Mart. In that moment, a lesser part of me pleaded for us to take the deal. *We all need shelter sometimes* . . . Ms. Gretchen's words echoed in my mind.

"Chris, I'm not sure what you're talking about, but I'm open to hearing your idea." I tried to soften my voice into an airy professional friendliness and hoped it sounded at least halfway believable.

"Oh, come on, Tabby!" he bellowed enthusiastically. "You know you're on the cutting edge of a new trend. I've been reading about it, it's called 'single mothers by choice.' Evidently, it's all about women redefining the rules of reproduction on their own terms. You did it, now let's talk about it."

I took in a sharp breath, trying to process what I was being presented with. Never before had I been asked to dive into something so personal at work.

"Chris," I said carefully, considering my next words with a mixture of intent and trepidation, "I think I view my job as reporting the news, not to *be* the news. I don't want to make my personal life the center of a report like this."

"Again, Tabby, I have to say, who better than you?" He looked at me with a raised eyebrow.

I turned to the window to gather my thoughts. *Why does Chris always keep his blinds closed?* I would have loved to see the sun just for a moment to be sure I wasn't in some sort of extended nightmare. *Do I even want to talk about my pregnancy?* No, I didn't. I also had started to form an idea of what I actually did want to talk about. Maybe it had been right in front of me all along.

"Chris, to be honest, I'm not sure I even believe in the term 'single mother by choice'—so that really has *nothing* to do with me or my personal choices." I watched the surprise that took over his face fade into a look of disappointment, but I continued anyway. "I know what I do want to talk about on air, and it's something that's important to me."

"Well, I don't know what could be more important than a baby story, Tabitha. Everybody loves a good baby story— perfect human-interest angle—" I cut him off.

"Chris, what I want to talk about . . . is the CROWN Act. It's timely, it's important, and given the viewer letters about my natural hair, if I'm going to go personal, I think it's time that we start a different kind of conversation."

Chris blinked slowly behind his glasses. The color drained out of his knuckles as he gripped the pen on his desk. I braced for the blowback but wasn't sorry. I said what I said.

"The CROWN Act? Is this the thing about the hair? Tabby, how is this news? And how does this affect you? You don't even wear your hair . . ." He gestured toward me as if he couldn't find the right word. "Natural . . . naturally curly . . . whatever you call it. You wear your hair as straight as I do."

I winced. Whether I liked it or not, Chris was right. Somewhere along the way, I had lost my credibility and my courage. I let it slip away so easily because maybe I wasn't ready to risk it all with no reason to put everything on the line. I'd worked so hard for my career. I'd fought hard to get to this place. And to keep it, all I had to do was slap on this wig and wait. But what exactly was I waiting for? Another conversation just like this in Chris's office, perhaps?

I shifted in my seat, silently praying that I could disappear. But, in reality, this was a moment of my own creation. I needed to make a choice. Resentment smoldered inside me in a twisted mixture of my own shame and disappointment.

"Chris," I finally managed after a too-long pause, "that's just it. This . . . this hair that I'm wearing isn't me. It isn't my hair. It isn't my choice either."

Chris leaned back deep into his rolling chair. His quiet consideration turned up the dial on my already bubbling nerves. His eyes stayed fixed on me until he finally shook his head slowly.

"I thought you liked your hairstyle. I told you I liked your hairstyle—*this* style. It's how you've always looked. This is the same Tabitha Walker we hired."

"Yes, Chris, that's correct. And when I simply stopped doing the physically and psychologically damaging things it took to look that way, you said that my natural hair was . . . *interesting*." At my words, the color drained from his face. I was not only playing with fire, I was dancing in it. My heart thumped so loudly in my ears, I was sure that Chris could hear it too. He seemed to slouch more, looking like his chair could swallow him at any moment. After a long pause and an exaggerated sigh, he continued.

"Tabby, what you carry around in your mind, I will never understand. I told you before; you're the one that has to fight your way into the career you want. Because, at the end of the day, what you believe . . . about yourself and about others here, is going to be all that you see reflecting back at you. I can't change that. You're going to have to be the one who decides. It's *your* hair."

In that big chair, across from that big desk, I felt like a little girl. I wished for someone to rescue me, to call time-out so I could regroup and recompose myself. I needed for it all to stop swirling in my mind. But in that moment, all I had was me. Somehow that was going to have to be enough.

"Chris." My voice belied the fragility of my courage. I took a breath and pulled myself upward, steeling my core against the uncertainty that threated to show in my tone. I started again, steadier. "I . . . I'm not going to speak about my pregnancy. Leading up to my maternity leave, I plan to work on a comprehensive story about the CROWN Act. And, I want that to be the first big piece I do when I'm back. If you really mean what you just said, then you'll let this be my call to make."

I'd said my piece, even though I instantly regretted it. I started making a mental list of other stations that might be hiring. The sound of Chris clearing his throat broke through my thoughts. He leaned toward me.

"All right, Tabby. It's your call."

As I got up to leave Chris's office, the weight of my decision landed on me with the full force of gravity. Why didn't a battle won ever feel like more of a victory? Because it just wasn't that simple. And it never is.

I headed back to my office, furiously texting Laila.

Tabby:
Help! I just had it out with my news director.

Laila:
You still have a job?

I think so, but my hands are still shaking.

What offensive thing did he do this time?

He wanted me to take on a story about "single mothers." I said no. I wanted to do CROWN Act.

Good for you! Haven't you seen all the NABJ folks taking a stand on their hair on social media?

Girl no, you know I'm not on social like that.

Maybe you need to check your feed.

Just then, I heard a familiar voice all too close to me, right before I felt the impact of another body. I had run straight into Lisa.

"Hey, Tabby!" Lisa effused, grabbing me before the force of our collision tipped me over. I looked up at her, half in thought about Laila's response and half engulfed with the full-on worry about what I had just brought upon myself in Chris's office. What if nobody actually cared about the CROWN Act? That would be even worse than having never covered it at all. The look of concern built in Lisa's eyes as her gaze moved across my face. She wasn't my first choice of confidant, but she was what fate had produced in the moment.

"Tabby, are you okay?" Lisa held my shoulders tighter and made an effort to meet my eyes with her own. I couldn't lie, even if I wanted to.

"Honestly, Lisa, I'm not okay." I was determined to fight back the tears this time, even though they'd already started to well, blurring my vision. I took a deep breath and rolled my gaze upward toward the ceiling.

"Here, step into my office." Lisa swiftly ushered us a few paces down the hall and into her expansive office, overflowing with bright sunlight. Its size was a reminder of who and what was important at KVTV. Lisa was our big-time anchor, but I was counting on her today to just be my friend.

"What is it? What's wrong?" Lisa asked me intently.

I shook my head slowly, searching for the words. In that moment, it was obvious how accustomed I had gotten to hiding, not just my hair but my feelings and true thoughts—all in the name of being professional. I decided to take the risk.

"Lisa, I'm honestly just so tired." I allowed the words to

flow out of me freely, reflecting the exasperation that flowed through my veins.

Lisa perked up with concern. "Oh, Tabby, pregnancy will do that to you! You just have to take it easy." Her sentiment sounded sincere, and I wished for the simplicity of physical exhaustion. Physical exhaustion you could rest from.

"I wish I could take it easy, Lisa. That's just it—I can never just take it easy."

"You can—"

Without meaning to, I cut Lisa off. "No, I cannot." I worried about speaking too sharply but continued anyway. "Lisa, do you know what Chris wanted me to report about? Being a 'single mother by choice.' As if this is the biggest issue that I'm confronted with. As if I hadn't noticed that I'm not married to the father of my child. As if it matters!" I searched Lisa's face for a glimmer of understanding. "Chris wants to talk about me being a single mother but doesn't want to talk about the disparity in Black maternal health outcomes? He doesn't want to talk about why I'm wearing this itchy-ass wig all day instead of my own hair? He wants to talk about me being a single mother, but he doesn't want to talk about why I'm the only Black on-air talent at this station? Nobody wants to talk about it!" I felt the tears fall in small streams down my cheeks. I'd lost the battle to control my emotions; now I was officially crying at work—big, heaving sobs this time. Lisa moved closer to give me a hug as I braced myself for a tone-deaf response.

"Oh, Tabby, I know it must be hard. I was so excited when I saw you wearing your hair with all of its amazing curls, but when you changed it, and then after the meeting, I thought that maybe you just wanted it that way. I had no idea this was weighing so . . ."

"How could it not? My hair became such an important issue that viewers took the time to send complaints. Not compliments, complaints. Can you imagine? Enough that Chris pulled me into his office yet another time to tell me about them? Because that's what happened. And so I tried to make it easier on myself. I did. I just decided to conform. But I shouldn't have had to.

"And then, when I told him that I wanted to report on the CROWN Act that protects natural hairstyles, he told me that I didn't even have one and couldn't connect authentically to the story! I'm sorry, Lisa, this isn't your fault. I'm just . . ." I buried my face in my palms. I didn't expect Lisa to understand the weight of anything that I was saying, but I needed to vent. I needed to let this out somewhere, even if it was in perfect Lisa Sinclair's perfect office.

"Tabby, I had no idea that it affected you so deeply. That's nothing for you to be sorry about. You know I support you one hundred percent. And you're right. This industry has been in need of change for a while now. Chris told you that he wanted you to bring your perspective, right?"

I nodded.

"Then he's just going to have to trust your decisions. But maybe the hardest part is that you're going to have to trust yourself."

I let myself melt into Lisa's awkward embrace, trying not to get my makeup on the shoulder of her immaculate cream silk blouse. I wished in the moment I could have just absorbed the sureness and certainty she promised. But that wasn't how life worked, because so far, I'd learned that nothing was sure or certain.

The high-pitched noise of my phone's text notification broke up our moment. Laila had sent a chain of back-to-back messages, and there was a new one from Marc.

> Just made the reservation for dinner with my parents. You ok for tomorrow night at 7:30?

Crap. I had pushed dinner with Marc's parents out of mind. I hadn't even made a hair appointment with Denisha. I pulled myself fully away from Lisa.

"Lisa, I'm sorry about all of this. I know it's a lot. I've . . . I forgot all about dinner with Marc's parents tomorrow night, and I don't even have a hair appointment." I buried my face in my phone, trying to rapidly compose a text to Denisha to secure a same-day slot. "I just hope my stylist can fit me in," I mumbled, more as a prayer to myself than to Lisa.

"Well, why don't you just wear your own hair, then?" Lisa said with a smile. "Let Marc's parents meet the real Tabitha."

"Oh no," I heard myself say. *Oh no?* Lisa looked puzzled.

"Well, why not?" she asked innocently.

"Because . . . because . . ." I stammered. But I had no answer. I had to get my hair done because that was what I had learned to do. That was what I learned would make me presentable, acceptable, accepted. And that was what I wanted. I wanted Marc's parents to accept me, even if I wasn't so sure anymore who the real *me* was or if I'd ever get to be her.

"Trust yourself, Tabby," Lisa called after me as I left her office. Denisha texted back. She said that if I could make it before six p.m., she'd fit me in.

I walked down the hallway in a rush to grab my belongings from my office and race to my car.

21

MY FRANTIC CALL AND LAST-MINUTE SPRINT TO THE SALON DID A great job of replacing my workplace worries with a more immediate panic. In spite of everything, Denisha had done a great job styling my hair. The only thing she couldn't seem to do was transform the itchiness of the wig into complete comfort. But the next evening, the styling held up nicely. No reasonable mother would have any objection to this hairstyle covering the head of the woman carrying her grandchild.

Marc's "I'm outside" text interrupted my last once-over in the mirror, searching for any lingering final flaws that could make his mother dislike me. I knew that I'd be congenial, kind, sweet, and friendly enough to ask more questions than to speak about myself. I wasn't sure what Marc had already told her about me, and I had no idea what she thought about our relationship, or how much she knew about it. I asked him if it would be strange for her to be first meeting me so far along in my pregnancy, but he said both his parents understood. I was happy to know that his father was able to make the trip in from Florida in spite of his poor health. When Marc described his condition, I wondered if he'd even be able to meet our baby. Finally, I'd get to see for myself.

Marc sent his parents to the restaurant in a car separately. I assumed it was so he and I could speak privately on the way. Things had been awkward since the Jewelry Mart. The time that we were spending together had started to stretch apart with decreasing frequency. Sometimes he was busy; sometimes I was. Still, I felt relieved that he hadn't spoken of marriage again. I was happy to keep the details of my doubts and uncertainties to myself.

"Hey, Tab," Marc said with a warm smile as he opened the passenger door for me. "You look great—your hair looks . . . amazing." He beamed, looking at me up and down, and helped me to offset the weight imbalance that my giant belly created, making it difficult to gracefully slide into his car like I used to.

"Thank you," I said teasingly before I kissed him hello on the cheek and wiped away the lingering gloss of my lip print with my thumb. His compliments gave me some assurance and calmed the nerves building in my gut. "Do you think your parents will approve?"

Marc turned to me and took my hand. "Tabby, they're both going to love you. I promise." And with that, he slid the car into gear and set us off into our evening with Yvonne and Horace Brown.

We made small talk along the way, catching up on baby movements, kicking, and my usual sleeping discomforts over the past few days that we hadn't seen each other. In the silences, I kept wondering what Marc's parents would be like, especially his mother, and what kind of grandparents they'd be alongside Jeanie Walker. If you took my mom's version, this baby had only one grandparent and that was *that* on that. Reality would be much more complicated.

Marc had picked a nice restaurant, not too nice, but nice enough. I took it as my first impression of what to really expect from his parents. I anticipated a down-to-earth, conservative, middle-aged Black couple. When I finally saw them, that is what I got. Well, mostly. Marc's mother, Yvonne, was a beautiful deep brown like Marc, dressed conservatively, like an old-school teacher, with coarse salt and pepper hair that had clearly been on rollers the night before. It was Marc's father who surprised me. He was fairer skinned than what I expected and far more frail-looking. He barely filled out the clothes he was wearing, and his face looked gaunt. It was easy to see his illness carried about him almost like an invisible presence. The newness of strangers made me uneasy, but I showed them both my best smile.

"Tabitha! Finally . . . Let me get a look at you." Marc's mother took my hands and spread my arms open so she could examine me. Just before I felt uncomfortable, she pulled me in snugly for a hug. She squeezed us together as tight as a sandwich before finally letting go.

"It's so nice to meet you, Mrs. Brown, Mr. Brown," I said, as cheerfully as I could manage. I appreciated the reassuring warmth of Marc's hand on the small of my back. "Marc has . . . Marc has told me so much about you." I smiled again, trying to remember what Marc had actually told me. He didn't speak much about his family, other than his confession that his father was an alcoholic and his family dynamic could be ugly. Gauging from the people in front of me this evening, I didn't see one hint of that. But working in news all these years, I knew, if nothing else, that looks could be deceiving.

Once we were past the awkwardness of introductions and greetings and through the logistics of seating and ordering, I started to breathe with relief that maybe this night was off to a good start. But then, somewhere between a near-empty platter of fried calamari and the grilled salmon entree that I'd only just ordered, the question came out of nowhere.

"So, Tabitha, do you go to church?" If only I could have performed my most-wished-for miracle and again turned water into wine, I would have. Still, I took a sip of the former from the glass in front of me.

"Ma'am?" I directed my question toward Marc's mother, who was looking at me with curious intensity.

"I just wanted to know if you go to church," Mrs. Brown repeated. Then she turned to Marc. "That's a reasonable enough question, isn't it? People do still go to church these days, don't they?" I watched as Marc visibly double swallowed his water. Unfortunately, there was not a drop of alcohol on our table.

"Mom . . . d-don't you think we could save that one . . . you know, for another time?" If I didn't know better, I would have sworn I heard a small stutter come from Marc as he tried to deflect his mother's inquiry. I put my hand on his arm and squeezed gently.

"I think it's a fine question." I tried to sound soothing in spite of my sense that the truth of it wasn't quite what Mrs. Brown wanted to hear. "I'm not a regular churchgoer. I'm Christian, well, I was raised that way, but my broadcast schedule for work isn't always as predictable as church services are." I searched around the remaining crumbs of calamari to find something to put into my mouth and occupy it before I said more.

"Well, dear, you *make* time for Jesus," Marc's mother challenged back at me with a look of innocence. As my response, I just smiled at her. What more was there to say? Sure, I hadn't been to church in a while, but her conversation wasn't making the proposition any more inviting.

"Mom!" Marc had tensed up completely, and I watched as he seemed to pull back his reaction. He continued more calmly. "Mom, I think what Tabby is saying is that she goes to church when she can, as do I. Let's not make a big deal of it."

"Well, that would be a first." Marc's father interjected with the first full sentence I'd heard him speak the entire night. His voice was quiet, and his eyes met no one else's at the table.

"Just what is that supposed to mean, Horace?" Marc's mother had turned to her husband in a flash. I would have never thought she could move that quickly. I tensed up and looked at Marc for his reaction. He seemed frozen, like a deer in headlights. The entire scene was like watching a car crash in slow motion, one part of my life colliding with the reality of another. I felt my mouth drop open slightly. I closed it quickly and tried to pretend like there was something of interest on my empty plate. Where was that salmon?

"You know damn well what I meant, Yvonne." Marc's father surprised me as he met his wife's stare-down with intensity. "Now, let the girl just have a peaceful evening. No need to go prodding into every corner of her life, like you do with everyone else." I turned back to still-frozen Marc. I wondered if this was a window into his childhood, or if his childhood might have been even worse.

"I'm only trying to ask basic questions, Horace. I can't understand why you don't want to know if your *only grandchild* is going to be baptized!" Her voice had lifted into the octaves of panic. Yvonne's eyes brimmed with the glint of tearfulness. The baby kicked me from the inside, spurring me into action.

"Mrs. Brown," I offered timidly. Something deep within whispered to me to keep my mouth shut, but I pushed ahead anyway. "Our daughter . . . your grandchild, will certainly be baptized. Marc and I haven't discussed it yet, but there's no reason to think that we won't be upholding traditions. Just because I don't go to church regularly doesn't mean that I'm not a Christian."

Mrs. Brown's face softened.

"Hmmm . . . well, that's . . . good to know." It was all she said before she took a sip of her nearly empty water glass and fell silent for a bit. I didn't have to wonder for very long what came next. "Well, I guess that's something . . . especially since . . . as I understand it, you two won't be *married*."

At his mother's words, Marc's face turned ashen. His mouth opened and closed again in a goldfish-like cycle. I leaned forward to speak, but before I could say anything, I felt Marc's hand on my forearm, easing me backward with downward pressure. Then he leaned forward instead.

"Mom, Tabby and I always planned to get married, even if we are doing things a little bit out of order." *We did?* When had Marc and I ever planned to get married? I could feel the heat rising in my face.

"Well, I should hope so, you two!" Marc's mother seemed to be satisfied with his assurance, even as I sat stunned by the bald-faced lie. "Tabitha, I hope you understand, this is a new experience for Horace and me. Marc has never let us meet any of his girlfriends, so to meet you so, so . . . pregnant . . . I just don't understand why you two couldn't have just done this the old-fashioned way."

I debated telling Yvonne the truth, the full truth of it all, but Horace looked like he needed a drink. I could only imagine what kind of nuclear war would result in bringing Jeanie Walker and Yvonne Brown together.

"I've been trying to get a ring on Tabby's finger for a while, Ma! We had to start somewhere!" Marc gave a fake laugh that I'd only heard a few times before—once when I caught him trying to put an empty carton of milk back into the refrigerator. I shook my head, remembering the simplicity of having a sperm donor. Now I had a not-even-mother-in-law who was going to be counting my church visits and the days to my wedding. The thought of the conversation with Marc in the Jewelry Mart gave me a shudder.

By the time my salmon entree finally arrived, I had little appetite and no patience remaining for Marc and his mother. Other than his early commentary to his wife, Marc's father either sat quietly nursing his water or was up again, headed to the restroom. Although the balance of our time together was filled with relatively banal discussion, between Yvonne's judgment and Marc's lies, I had reached a tipping point.

"Will you be joining us for breakfast in the morning, Tabby?" Marc's mother sang at me with surprising cheer. I made up a flimsy excuse about having to work and tugged on the back of Marc's blazer, hoping he'd get the hint. There was ready to leave and then there was my version of ready to leave, which was inching toward urgent if I was going to stay polite. If I could have walked home, I would have. Thankfully, as we wrapped up, Marc's parents accepted his offer to send them back in a car so that he could drive me home, just the two of us. For the first part of the ride, we sat in relative silence. Maybe he was as unsure about what to say to me as I was to him. But eventually, I found my words.

"Marc, what was that?"

Marc turned to look at me quickly and then refocused on the road, his hands noticeably gripping the steering wheel just a bit tighter. His lips pursed, then relaxed. At first, I thought that he wasn't going to answer me. But he did.

"Tabby, try not to let my mom get to you. I mean, I used to be scared as hell of her when I was a kid, but she's really a sweetheart. She means well. I guess you can imagine when my dad was healthy, the two of them going at each other could be . . . a lot."

"I really had no idea, Marc." I patted my head for some relief. My scalp had decided to make me feel as uncomfortable on the outside as I felt on the inside.

"Come on, Tab, it wasn't that bad," Marc said with a sigh. The anger started to rise in my spirit even as I prayed for calm and patience.

"Not that bad? Marc, it was humiliating! I can live with the judgment and stares in the coffee shop and the grocery store, and even at work sometimes, like a ring on my left hand is the *permission* I need to be pregnant. People who have no idea about my circumstances or the choices I had to make. I can even deal with the viewers who seem to feel entitled to opinions about how I wear my hair. But your mother and even you—why did you lie to her? You never wanted to talk about the idea of marriage until the week before your parents arrived. In fact, before our little surprise, I could barely get you to think past your so-called 'options' to even focus on being in a relationship. But now your mom thinks that we 'always planned' to get married?"

Marc pulled up smoothly into my driveway and turned off the ignition. He unbuckled his seat belt and turned to face me.

"Don't you want to talk about this inside?" he asked me, his face softening. I very much did not. All I could think of was being alone to gather myself and figure out how I got so far off my original plan for my original goal. I wanted to have a family. There was a reason why Marc said no the first time and a reason why I said no the second time. Only one of those reasons had anything to do with me. Finally, I understood completely and everything; the inconsistency Marc had been showing and the unease I felt, it all made sense.

"No. I'm sorry, but I don't. There's nothing to talk about, honestly. You need to figure out why you felt the need to lie to your mother about something basic and fundamental. You never wanted to get married, but because of her judgment, now you do? I understand *everything* now." And I did understand. The Jewelry Mart and the timing felt strange to me for a reason. It didn't feel *real*. It felt forced and rushed.

After Marc's statements tonight, I realized that it was all a performance—not for me, but for Yvonne.

"Look, Tabby, it was just something I said in the moment, and I was trying to . . . trying to just defuse the situation. Make it a little lighter, you know?"

He had no clue.

"Marc." I sighed his name as much as I spoke it. I turned to face him completely and took his hand in mine. "There was a time when the worst thing I could think of losing was you." His eyes lit up. "Now I'm sure that the worst thing I could ever lose is me."

Marc made a gesture to protest. I touched his lips gently to keep them closed. I had more to say.

"You and I both know that I'm not your choice, Marc. I never was. If I hadn't gotten pregnant, there'd be no us. And this baby can't be the only reason there is. I've seen enough marriages that didn't work. We can be partners for our child, Marc, but let's leave marriage where it should be. Save it for the woman you love, who's really your choice. And I'll save it for the man who chooses me because he sees me. Not because he feels like he has to."

Marc's mouth dropped open. After a few attempts to speak, he finally closed it and studied me closely. Deep down, he had to know I was right. Even when reflected in imperfect words, the truth holds its own power. I hugged him tightly, as tightly as my belly would allow, and pushed the car door open to step out. Marc sprang up.

"Wait, let me help you." In less than a flash, Marc was out of the car on his side and around to mine, reaching in to help me pull myself out of the seat. We both stood there for a minute, looking at each other. "What now?" he whispered. For once, in months of uncertainty, I felt like I finally knew the answer.

"You be you, Marc, and I'll be me. And we will raise this child as partners and *friends*." I pressed his hand between my palms and then pulled him in the direction of my door.

"Tab, I . . . I . . . don't know what to say," he stammered his words quietly, sounding more uncertain than I've ever heard him. In the man standing in front of me, I could see the little boy that Marc used to be, and probably still was in many ways.

"You don't have to say anything," I told him, unlocking my door. He stood frozen near the steps. I flipped the porch light on for him so that he could see his way back to his car clearly. "Good night, Marc," I said as gently as possible while I pushed myself inside the doorway. "You don't have to say anything, but if you do, to me at least, from now on just make sure it's the truth."

I closed the door behind me and leaned my back against it to keep my body from collapsing. All I wanted to do was get in the bed and forget the night. But, given what I'd said to Marc, there was something that I needed to do first.

I walked through my house, dropping layers of my clothes along the way. My shoes stayed by the door. My sweater landed somewhere between the living room and the kitchen. My dress came off in the hallway. Finally, stripped down to my underwear, I stood in front of my bathroom mirror. I reached down to rummage through the drawer of random knick-knacks scattered about through its contents. I felt the cold metal of bobby pins and the prickly bristles of my hairbrush. Toward the back, my fingers wrapped around exactly what I was looking for and pulled out a glistening pair of scissors, sized just right to clip every bit of that wig off my head. I might have to make it my costume for work, but at least at home, at least in my own time, I could be free of it.

I pulled and snipped, twisted and contorted, until every piece of string sewing down my assumed identity had been severed. The wig dropped to the floor almost silently. I could feel the air swirl through the cornrows on my head, and my fingers found their way into every open nook to scratch and relieve. The braids had loosened so much that I found it easy to unwind them from each other, pulling my kinky tendrils to freedom. They felt glorious, like thick grapevines hanging from my scalp. I let my eyes linger on them lovingly. This moment was *my* truth. Here I was, the real me—unfurled, free, unrestrained, wild in my spirit and natural in my appearance. I could finally see . . . myself.

22

"Wait, so tell me that one more time? You said you broke up with Marc? Again?" Laila looked at me in the way that only she could, showing pure confusion, but making me crack up with laughter.

"Girl, yes!" I said, pulling on her elbow. "Come on so we can get a good spot in the back of this class. You know I'm too big to be doing yoga in front of everybody."

Laila had agreed to meet me at the local yoga studio in Leimert Park for our Saturday morning workout. Working on her startup company, I'd never known her to be busier. I'd gone entire months of my pregnancy without seeing her. I was less concerned about Marc and my latest developments than I was with making sure our yoga trip hadn't been in vain, in time catching up and in exercise. All of the sistas had shown up with their luscious curves in colorful attire, ready to spend their Saturday morning self-care in a cultural mash-up of hip-hop music and yoga poses led by an afro-sporting instructor whose smile seemed lit from within.

"So is this your breakup hairstyle?" Laila smiled teasingly at me.

"Funny, but no!" I shot back, my hand fluffing the rawness of my unstyled pouf. "I had just had enough of that damn wig and anything stuffy after dinner with Marc's mother. I'll have to put it back on for work though. Maybe make do with a wig cap and bobby pins." I rolled my eyes. Laila laughed. "I'll probably go back to Denisha in a few weeks, after the baby shower."

In mid-laughter, Laila's face fell.

"What's wrong?" I asked. Laila, Alexis, Ms. Gretchen, and I were scheduled to leave in less than a week to go to DC for the baby shower my mother was hosting. I already knew my hair would create a conversation with Jeanie Walker, but I hadn't expected Laila to catch on to my concern so quickly. "Girl, you think my mom is going to trip about my hair?"

"Actually, Tab, I've been meaning to talk to you about the shower," Laila said solemnly. Just as I was ready to ask her what she meant, the class started. I made a mental note to ask her after.

Yoga at my size was harder than I thought it would be, but the instructor gave me extra attention with modifications that made it all doable. I finished the class with a slightly winded sense of accomplishment. Laila still looked like her usual former track athlete self, with the post-workout glow accentuating the freckles popping against her deep honey-tanned complexion. Her hair looked great grown out from the halo of short curls I first saw on her just after she'd cut her hair. Without her dreadlocks, her Korean features were more prominent than I'd ever seen before, but there was still no mistaking her Blackness. If nothing else, no matter what anyone else saw, Laila was always clear that she'd lead the definition of who she was and what she was. She looked gorgeous, and happy.

We toweled off and made our way to one of the newly opened coffee shops nearby. Each of us grabbed a green tea to take gingerly to our comfy table set up in the corner. Laila pulled a protein bar out of her bag and offered me a bit with a gesture. I shook my head to refuse, wondering when she would bring up the baby shower again, or if I should. Making memories of the bigger moments seemed more important, since I hadn't seen her much over the past several months, but she was busy growing her news website and it was really beginning to take off as a business. Both Alexis and I would have loved to see so much more of her, but we understood that sometimes in life, you had to seize the moments that were available. I decided to risk the subject.

"So . . . what was it you wanted to tell me about the baby shower?"

Laila looked up at me, showing a bit of surprise in her eyes. She glanced down at her teacup, took a sip, and then met my gaze again. She took a deep breath before she spoke.

"Tabby . . . I . . . I've been meaning to tell you . . . and I hope you understand." I braced myself for her words to follow. Laila's shoulders melting into a slight slouch. She continued, "I can't go. To your shower . . . I can't make it. I'm so sorry."

I could feel disappointment rising in my throat, but I

reached out to hug her. Her news was a letdown, but I could find my way into understanding. I'd been there before, trying to get my own career going. Work had caused me to miss so many life events, just the same.

"It's okay, girl, I understand if you have something for work. You don't have to feel bad." Laila's face went blank for a minute and before she released a deep sigh, breaking our eye contact.

"It's not because of work," she whispered. When she looked up again, she had tears in her eyes.

"What's wrong, Laila?" Concern dripped from my voice and covered the confusion I felt. If not for work, why would she be missing my baby shower? We'd been planning the trip for months. It was the one thing that she, Alexis, and I were going to get to do together to celebrate my pregnancy. But how could she miss it if it wasn't for work?

"Tabby, I'm sorry, I can't go because it's too soon." As soon as she spoke the last word, I took a sharp breath in. *Of course.* How could I have forgotten? Less than two years ago, Laila had been pregnant. Not that I knew it when she was. I knew only after the hospital stay. It was then that she'd cut off her hair.

The silence between us stole all of the words that should have flowed freely—about loss, and disappointment, and fears. Even as the best of friends, we didn't know how to speak those truths to each other. These were truths about pain that had already fused into bone and been grown over by new muscle that connected directly to our smile. These were the pains that didn't have words. Pains we could only hide but never speak of.

"Oh, Laila, don't cry." I wrapped her in my arms as lovingly as I could to try to protect her from her hurt. It triggered me deeply to see her in this kind of distress, a lingering piece of my own trauma that I wished I could forget. Trauma of that night and so many nights that followed when I was so scared of losing her. "I'm sorry . . . I got so wrapped up in all this, I . . . I . . . didn't even think how hard it might be for you . . . after everything," I whispered.

Laila pushed back from me and took my hands. Her eyes still glistened with tears shining in her eyelashes like tragically beautiful mascara.

"Tabby, you're not mad?" Laila asked me in a soft voice.

"No! Laila, why would I be mad?"

"Because . . . because I know I should be there for you, Tabby," Laila pleaded. "I know I should be. But I just can't be that kind of happy right now. That's the honest truth." Her eyes stayed locked with mine, even as she continued. "Of course I'm happy *for* you, but I can't celebrate with you like that. I've come a long way, but . . ."

With this, Laila let my hands go and focused again on her tea, leaving me to ponder what she'd said. The echo of her words in my mind produced a pang. The thought of not sharing the highlights of this journey with one of my best friends stung. But her selfishness gave me surprising relief. The memory of that day, of her sitting in a hospital gown, small and frail, was something that I never wanted to experience again. It made me wonder how it had happened so gradually in plain sight that I hadn't noticed a thing. Since that day, I'd spent extra effort in careful consideration of my words and actions so as not to trigger more of her pain. If the self-care that kept her alive meant prioritizing her needs over mine, then I'd accept and swallow the disappointment as easily as my next sip of tea.

"Laila, I understand." She smiled. "Thank you," I told her. She looked surprised.

"For what?" she asked.

"For being honest," I said earnestly. "Thank you for being honest."

"OKAY, WAIT," ALEXIS SAID AS SHE SQUINTED HER EYES AT ME. I shifted in the uncomfortable seat at the airport gate occupied by my expanded buttocks as we awaited our boarding announcement. "So Laila really isn't coming?" she screeched. "Tell me again what she said?"

I tried to hold back a long sigh. I'd already told Alexis three times. Once when we met up at the check-in desk and she first asked me where Laila was. Laila was habitually late, so I had to let both Lexi and Ms. Gretchen know that we shouldn't wait on her. But that wasn't the end of it. Alexis asked again, the next time walking through security, and then a third time when we sat down. Since that time, Ms. Gretchen had left us to go get a cup of coffee and "somethin' sweet to munch on," as she referred to it, disappearing into the bustling corridor. With all of the asking, at some point, I realized that Alexis knew that Laila wasn't coming; what she didn't understand was why I seemed to be okay with it.

"Lex," I let out with a sigh, "Laila said that she needed to sit this one out. It hasn't even been two full years since everything happened with her. You know that."

"Yeah, Tab, but it's your baby shower. It's your first baby. She's supposed to be Laila's niece! If she were a *real* friend, she'd be here. That's all I'm saying. There's no excuse not to come. That's like . . . It's like . . . not coming to your wedding or something!" Alexis threw her hands in the air with an exasperated look on her face. The glisten off of her left hand caught my attention. I thought I was imagining things, but after a second glance, it was clear. Alexis was wearing her wedding ring.

I'd been defending Laila to Alexis all morning. In truth, I hadn't really known how to feel about what Laila explained to me about not coming, or about not being able to be fully happy in the baby shower kind of way, although she was happy for me. I'd never heard anyone say anything like that before. I wondered if I could ever muster the courage to tell someone what Laila told me. I'd been to weddings when I should have saved the money. I'd gone to birthdays even when I wasn't sure why I'd been invited. I'd bought gifts for people who'd never so much as bought me a card. But for some reason, I couldn't bring myself to blame Laila for the decision that she was making, even if it hurt. How could I demand the truth from Marc and then punish Laila for giving me exactly what I was asking for? The price she'd pay for being honest and true to herself wasn't going to come from me. Although I couldn't say the same about how Alexis felt. She was upset enough for two people and then some. Now was a good a time as any to try to change the subject.

"Lex, when did you start wearing your wedding ring?"

Alexis looked down at her hand and then back up at me with an expression someone would have if they just realized they'd left home without deodorant. "Oh, yeah . . . I didn't tell you?"

"Tell me what?" I leaned in and was completely surprised that Alexis had been seemingly holding back a big decision of her own.

"Girl, it's not a big deal. Just that getting back together with Rob is starting to make sense to me, for real this time." Alexis said the words as if she were still thinking about what she was saying, even as she said it.

"Wow, Lex. Well, I can't say I'm completely surprised. I mean, after the pool party it seemed clear that he was at least trying his best."

"Yeah, Tab. I'm sorry I didn't say something sooner. It just crept up on me. Just one day I saw my ring and decided to put it back on. And one night Rob was over and I realized that I didn't want him to leave . . . and neither did the boys." For a second, Alexis's eyes looked weepy. She turned away quickly and gave a swipe at her face. When she turned back, she seemed to have instantly reanimated.

"Anyway, I'm on vacation, so we can leave that for later. Besides, Tab, of the two of us sitting here, I'm not the only one who's being surprisingly forgiving. I still can't get over that. Girl, I am the wrong one." Alexis let out a loud sigh that punctuated her point of view.

"Lex, of course I would love for her to be here, but it's just one little party; it's just—" Alexis cut me off.

"No, Tabby, it's not just some *party*. It's an event; it's a milestone. It's our only chance to celebrate your milestone together! I can't believe that Laila would be so . . . so . . . selfish!"

For a second I thought that I actually saw smoke coming off Alexis, and then I realized that it was just the steam from the coffee in her hand as she brought it to her lips.

"Lex, what happened to 'I acknowledge *your* struggle'? We both know what Laila has been through. Maybe this is what she needs to do because she's still struggling."

"Tab." Alexis flipped her hand at me. "We're *all* still struggling."

My thoughts and our conversation were paused by the loud commotion of beeping that drew our attention to the walkway in front of our gate. It took only a few seconds to recognize the blond hair of Ms. Gretchen in her bright pink leisure suit and matching sneakers, perched upon the back of the motorized transport cart stopped before us. She waited while the male driver came around to help her down and make an offer to escort her to a seat. I'd seen her move faster on her own to get her nails done. I wondered if something had happened until her eyes met mine with a very obvious wink. And then I realized Ms. Gretchen wasn't walking slowly, she was flirting.

"Thank you, honey," she purred at him, arriving next to Alexis's and my seats. "Here, you take this with your handsome self." She pressed a small wad of cash into his hand and held on to it. "You know if I were these girls' age, I would be passing you my phone number." While a rosy blush mounted the man's face, Ms. Gretchen beamed and blinked her eyes at him. Just before it turned awkward, she finally let go of his hand and shot him a sultry expression as she turned to glide down into the open seat next to me. After a pause, it

seemed like the young man remembered that he was supposed to walk away. With a final wave, the show was over.
Ms. Gretchen turned her attention to Alexis and me. In spite
of the deep conversation we had just been in, I couldn't help
but let out a small chuckle.

Alexis leaned across me to address Ms. Gretchen.
"Ms. Gretchen, you won't believe what's happened since
you've been gone." Ms. Gretchen looked at Alexis and raised
a sculpted eyebrow into some of the fluff of her golden
bangs. Alexis continued, "Tabby is trying to tell me that it's
okay that Laila's not coming! I mean, what kind of friendship
is that?"

Without a word of reply, Ms. Gretchen took a sip of her
coffee and offered each of us some of whatever was in the
white paper bag she was holding. Alexis and I both refused.
"Hmm . . ." she said. "Suit yourselves!" she said as she dove
in with her hand, producing a piece of muffin between her
canary-yellow nail tips.

"But, Ms. Gretchen, what do you think?" Alexis insisted.
Ms. Gretchen looked at her and then back to me and then
back to Alexis.

"I don't spend too much time thinkin' too much about
other folks' business," she said, just before popping the muffin bit into her mouth. She took so much time with the production of eating that I thought for sure she'd said all she
had to say on the matter. But then, finally, she continued.
"Sometimes, you can't tell when a person's hurtin'," she said,
"so you just have to take their word for it." Alexis leaned back
slowly and then sat forward again.

"But Tabby's hurt now too! Aren't you at least a little up-set, Tab?" Alexis frowned at me.

"Of course I wish Laila were here!" I turned to Ms. Gretchen and then to Alexis, trying to show how much I meant those words. "But I also want Laila to take care of her-self because we both know she wasn't before."

"Well, there you have it," Ms. Gretchen said before put-ting another piece of muffin into her red-lipstick-rimmed mouth, this time licking her fingers.

Alexis leaned back again and pretended to flip through a magazine from her bag. I knew her well enough to know she didn't read that fast or turn pages that aggressively if she wasn't upset. I loved her for standing up for me, but I had big-ger things to worry about beyond Laila. In just a few hours, we were going to all have to face Jeanie Walker, and I could only imagine if Alexis's reaction was bad, how my mother would take the news—not just that Laila wasn't coming, but also that I had broken up with Marc.

"On behalf of our airline, we'd like to welcome you to the boarding area for flight 1152 to Dulles airport." I heard the announcement come over the loudspeaker, startling all of us. "We'd like to start our boarding by inviting those passengers who need a little bit more time or extra assistance."

To my surprise, Ms. Gretchen bounded up and was mak-ing her way spryly to the gate. "See you on board!" she turned and said.

"But Ms. Gretchen!" I protested. "This is just for special boarding." She turned back to me.

"Honey!" she said with a laugh. "They said this was for

passengers who need *extra time*. At ninety-three years old, I can use all the extra time I can get!"

With that, she turned back and in a swath of matching pink, sauntered her way to the gate, her blond hair bobbing through the door.

23

JEANIE WALKER WAS VERY EASY TO SPOT WHEN THE THREE OF US arrived at the baggage claim area. She stood with a small army of baggage handlers with multiple carts in tow. My mother herself was armed with flowers, balloons, and a WELCOME HOME!! sign so big that it made my cheeks flush.

"Tabby Cat!" My mother rushed over to wrap up as much of me as she could in her open arms. That amount wasn't much, as my beach ball belly had very much taken over the front of me. In contrast, my mother was no bigger than she'd ever been at any point in my life, likely still a perfect size four.

"Look at you! You're so . . . round!" she said, smiling into it, studying me closely. Her smile faded when her eyes reached the top of my head. "Oh! Your hair!" The sharp inflection of her tone gave away the disappointment she was clearly trying to hide. "Are those . . . little braids?" The evening prior, I'd done a very careful job of twisting my hair—two strands, small sections, and a brand-new leave-in gel styler oil combination that got rave reviews among the bloggers. I wanted my hair to dry overnight into the perfect twist-out for the next day's event. Clearly, my mother wasn't a fan of the intermediate step.

"Mom, these are twists, for a twist-out. They're still drying, but it'll be cute tomorrow, you'll see."

"Not to worry, Tabby Cat, I made an appointment for you anyway, just in case," she muttered while shooing over the baggage handlers from their posts. They descended upon us, grabbing bags and arranging items. My mother continued her hugs and greetings, extending her ebullient welcome to Alexis and Ms. Gretchen while we walked to the car.

"Now, Ms. Gretchen, we can put you right here in the front," my mom said, gesturing to the open front passenger side door of her large black Mercedes SUV. Ms. Gretchen hesitated and then shook her head, heading for the back seats.

"No thank you, honey!" she said. "I much prefer to sit in the front of planes and the back of cars!" My mother looked genuinely confused for a moment, but I knew that the good hostess programming would take over and block any protest.

"Mom, we can give Lexi the front, it's fine." Alexis turned to me with a frown.

"Or I could just sit in the back with Ms. Gretchen," Alexis said, through a clearly forced smile.

"Company up front!" my mom interjected. Alexis trudged to the front and did as she was told. She knew as well as I did that adulthood didn't change the rule that instructions from your best friend's mother were to be followed as if they came from your own. I laughed a bit to myself and slid into the back next to Ms. Gretchen.

Down the road, my mother caught my glance in the rear-

view mirror. "So, Tabby," she said. I braced myself, knowing what was coming next. "I thought that four of you were
coming, rather than three. That's why I brought the truck.
Where's your other friend, Laila?"

I could hear Alexis muttering something under her
breath, and I hoped that she'd otherwise manage to keep her
mouth shut.

"Laila couldn't make it," I said quickly. "Something came
up, and she . . . just couldn't get here." I held my breath, hoping that my flimsy explanation had been enough to close
the subject. My mother would never accept the truth of what
Laila told me, and even more than Alexis, she'd be questioning how I could let that slide. No matter what she said about
Laila, it'd still be better than questions about Marc.

"Well, what about Marc?" *Shit.* I could see my mother's
raised eyebrows in the mirror.

"Mom, it's a baby shower. Marc wasn't invited."

"Well, you know he's always welcome. I mean, I was hoping that the baby's father would make a surprise cameo. I
know all the ladies would love to meet him!" Her cheeriness
about it grated against my reality.

"Mom, I can assure you, Marc is definitely *not* coming."

"Now, Jeanie, when are you going to stop us over for some
Maryland crabs?" I heard Ms. Gretchen's voice float out from
my left. I turned to look at her and caught her wink in my
direction. Her hand reached over and patted mine, lingering
there for just a little bit. I relaxed back into the comfortable
leather and let out a deep breath. The rhythm of the tires
beneath us gave soothing vibrations as I let the conversation
carry on without my input.

I watched the colorful blur of passing trees, cars, signs, and roadway through my window until my reflection caught my attention. I saw me—my face, and my short natural hair, the nearly dry twists flopping slightly with each bump. This was what triggered the disappointment that I saw in my mother's face. This version of me that had to be protected with new laws, that triggered letters from viewers at work, and that I had hidden under wigs and shame for months. This version of me was literally itching to be set free. This was the me that I needed to love and to be loved; it was the me yearning for acceptance and a space to rightfully occupy. This was the me that I desperately needed to be enough.

I let my eyes close and leaned my head back against the headrest. My mother's words, *I made an appointment for you,* rang in my ears. Tomorrow, my baby shower would be filled with family I didn't remember and my mother's friends I didn't know. I wanted to show up as the me I did know, but I'd have to fight for her. As backup, I knew I had Ms. Gretchen and Alexis, and deep down, even though she wasn't with us, I knew that somewhere back home in Los Angeles, Laila was there rooting for me too.

As we pulled up to my mother's expansive Potomac mini mansion, I realized that I'd forgotten how large it was. When we last lived under the same roof, we'd shared no more than eighteen hundred square feet. Compared to the expansive property in front of me, it seemed like the entirety of that house could fit into the master bedroom suite.

"Wow, Ms. Walker! I mean, Mrs. Williams!" I heard the

surprise in Alexis's voice as she turned to my mother wide-eyed from the passenger seat.

"Well, isn't this a spread!" Ms. Gretchen chimed in.

My mother slowed down our rolling descent along the driveway with a pleased look on her face that I managed to catch in the rearview mirror. She'd come a long way and deserved the pride I could see reflecting back. Dusk was settling and the accent lights made the house look regal with all of its windows and landscaping. The large elaborate wood and glass door first demanded your attention and then elicited the strongest desire to be let inside. It was nice knowing that this must be similar to the reaction that my mother enjoyed from all of her guests. After everything, I was happy that she'd at least gotten her own version of my dad's new life. Here I was, arriving at my mother's very own happy ever after.

The heavy door in the front opened as we pulled up, and the general emerged from behind it with a welcoming grin and literal open arms. He rushed out to greet my mother with a kiss and then the rest of us with his usual brand of reserved affection.

"Come in, come in!" My mom gestured all of us toward the glowing entry while the general unloaded our bags. My work schedule hadn't allowed me to make many visits, but I certainly knew how to find my usual room. My mother had taken the liberty to decorate it in the same shade of pale pink as the one I had as a little girl in Los Angeles.

My mother led our caravan up the winding staircase focused around the foyer's glorious chandelier. Set up high above, it twinkled prismatic rays of light that danced all around us like an elegant crystal disco ball. My feet sank deep into the lavishly thick carpeting. The opulence of the surroundings reminded me that I was thousands of miles away from my own starter home in Los Angeles. Perhaps the events of the weekend were because of me, but all of it wasn't *for* me—there was no mistaking that this was my mother's weekend too.

In each room—and all of us had our own—a plush robe and slippers awaited on the bed, wrapped in an oversized bow. While I could hear the separate squeals of delight from Alexis and Ms. Gretchen, my mother followed me into my room and set about straightening an already immaculate setup.

"I've been collecting the cutest baby clothes!" she said to me as she refolded a towel and placed it on the dresser. "I just wish that you had let me come and help you get ready for the baby—I had a whole scrapbook of ideas for the nursery!" My mom smiled at me wistfully.

"I know, but I did have some help," I said quietly. "My little sisters have been staying over a lot more frequently. They definitely pitched in with the setup—I was impressed with how hard they worked on it!" I tried to make the whole thing sound as lighthearted as possible, even though the subject matter was anything but.

"Oh?" My mother's voice raised to a high pitch. "Your *little sisters*? You mean Diane's kids? That's new." I had a million simpler explanations that I could have offered, but in this moment, the truth was all that made itself available.

"Evidently, my dad is not taking Granny Tab's death very well." I watched my mother's face cloud as she processed what I'd said. Her features contorted through a rainbow of emotions until she settled on what looked like resignation.

"Well, unfortunately, Tabby, that's not a surprise," my mother said tersely. "Leopards don't just change their spots when they get a new wife, a new family, or a new house in Calabasas."

"I . . . I don't know," I told her. "I mean, I can't imagine. Honestly, I just want to stay out of it. I do what I can to help the girls. I remember very well what that situation was like." The words felt like sand in my mouth, having to speak them to my mother. I could see what I imagined to be the shadow of memories flicker in her eyes, the remnants of the same pain that another family was trying to navigate.

"And what is Diane doing?"

I listened for the contempt I expected to hear in my mother's voice, but to my surprise, it wasn't there. I heard something else. It was something that sounded like compassion—the kind that can only extend from one woman to another when a shared experience outweighs the differences between them. I recalled Diane's drawn face at Granny Tab's funeral and how much worse it had looked every time I'd seen her since. It was almost as if she were fading right before my eyes.

"It seems like . . . maybe like she's trying to hold things together as best she can." My soft defense of Diane sounded strange, especially in conversation with my mother. Every time before, Diane was the enemy that we could always agree on. But of late, I'd only felt sorry for her. Seeing the reaction on my mother's face, I quickly added, "I've mostly stayed away from my dad and Diane's, but I have tried to help her out by having the girls over more."

"Hmmph." My mother sighed as she refolded the same towel for what seemed to be the third time. I wondered if there was any hint of vindication there, knowing in that moment that the woman who'd been the mistress in her marriage was now likely walking in the same shoes as she had. Now she had something else in common with my mother, something I'm sure that none of us expected.

"Well," my mother said suddenly with the saccharine sound of forced happiness, "let's not worry about them for now." She put the refolded towel down and drew her face into a smile. "This weekend is about you!" She spoke as if the very moment was its own celebration. I smiled back at her. Other than the presence of Alexis and Ms. Gretchen, this weekend didn't feel like it was for me at all. Something about being in my mother's house felt like I was an observer in my own life.

"So, Marc's really not coming?"

"Mom! No, Marc is really *not* coming." I tried to hide the edge creeping into my voice.

"Am I not supposed to ask?"

"I'd prefer you didn't."

"Well, I just hope that the two of you can figure things out. Sometimes it's not how you expected, but everything can turn out so perfectly. Isn't that what you wanted?"

I let out the deep sigh that had been building in my chest. This was the question that sat constantly in the back of my mind. The question that I thought I'd answered the night I had dinner with Marc's parents. And still, this was the question that I reconsidered every day. There was what I wanted, and there was what I was supposed to want, and I still couldn't tell the difference between the two.

"Maybe . . ." I turned to look at my mother. "Maybe my idea of perfect has changed." A shadow of confusion crossed my mother's face and then, startled, we both turned to a noise at the door. Alexis barreled into the room, gushing words in our direction.

"Oh my goodness, Mrs. Williams! The monogrammed robes! And the slippers! And the basket! I just love it!" My mother's face broke into another large smile as she stood up to meet Alexis's open arms with a hug.

"I'm so glad you like them. Just a little something to make you feel at home." My mother kept walking toward the door and turned back to Alexis and me. "I'm going down to make sure that there's something edible coming off of that grill! Otherwise, we're having pizza for dinner." With that, she left the room.

"Tab!" my mom called back, "I made you a salon appointment for the morning! Plenty of time to get your hair done before the shower!"

Alexis and I looked at each other for a moment before my eyelids closed involuntarily and my resigned thoughts translated to a slow shaking of my head.

"You're going to get your hair straightened?" Lexi looked at me with wide eyes. I reached up to touch my hair. It felt smooth and crinkly, the organized texture of my twists would make for a great hairstyle in the morning. I couldn't wait to see how it would turn out, especially now that my hair had grown. I wanted to look at photos from a life milestone and finally see myself in them.

"Girl, I don't want to, but I'm too tired to fight that battle with her tonight. It's just a baby shower, so if that's what I have to do to get through this weekend, then—" Lexi took advantage of my pause to cut me off.

"Tabby, do you know what looks best when you wear your hair natural?" I shook my head. I had no idea what she meant. "It's your face. Your smile is bigger, and you look more relaxed and at ease than I've seen you maybe even since we were kids. Your mom just wants the best for you, and she's pushing what she's been taught that is."

"And I'm about to be a mother."

"And you're about to be a *little girl's* mother."

I sighed. I'd just see what my hair looked like in the morning. If the takedown of my twist-out turned out as cute as I expected, maybe the issue of the hair salon would take care of itself.

Alexis pushed her own hair from her face. As she did, the flash of the ring on her hand caught my eye, reminding me that we had a very big topic to discuss that had nothing to do with hair at all. I gave her a playful push on her shoulder and picked up her left hand.

"Lexi, when are you going to tell me what's going on? Last time we talked about it, you still hadn't decided about Rob. I'd started to think we'd all seen the last of this ring." Alexis looked down at her hand as if she'd never seen it before.

"I was going to say something, Tab, I really was." Alexis continued to look at her left hand, turning it from one angle to the next. "You remember how we were talking about breaking that dish from my wedding china set?" She looked up at me. I nodded. I remembered that conversation and wished I'd had a better answer for her at the time. She continued, "I just realized something about that idea of a broken dish."

"You mean wondering if you could ever put the broken dish back together again or would there always be a piece missing?" I asked her.

"Exactly. I had that broken dish and I tried to fix it, but I couldn't. I was thinking about that, and I got to looking at my wedding china and wondered, if I couldn't fix that dish, would the whole set be ruined? Like, would it bother me that it would always be missing that one piece? And guess what, the broken dish couldn't be fixed. So, you know what I did?"

"Threw it away?"

"Yeah, I threw *that* dish away. But not before I ordered a new one. And that's when I realized." I raised an eyebrow, hoping she'd continue. "I realized that my marriage wasn't just a dish, Tabby. My marriage isn't even the whole china set. And no way I'd throw away my whole set of china because of just one broken dish. It'll never be the same, but that might have made room for something new—something better. Only time will tell."

I thought about Marc and then I thought about Diane. I understood Alexis, but I had so many reasons not to agree.

"Lex, do you *really* think that you can trust Rob? After everything?" I instantly felt the ache of guilt as I saw the hurt welling in my best friend's eyes. She turned her gaze upward and blinked. I hadn't meant to make her cry. She dabbed quickly at the corner of her eye with her shirtsleeve and took a deep breath. Then Alexis brought her eyes to meet mine again.

"Yes," she said softly. "At least, I have to try."

IN SPITE OF A VERY COMFORTABLE BED AND A BIG DINNER, COUR-tesy of the general's skills on the grill, I'd slept very little and ended up watching the sunrise outside the window of my bedroom. As hard as I tried to push the racing thoughts out of my mind, I couldn't help replaying scenes from my life, hoping for some assurance that everything would somehow work out all right.

The mixture of anxiety and excitement tickled their long tendrils around my insides. While this baby shower felt like a milestone, it was only an event. Looming much larger in the distance was the reality of motherhood and the weight of the responsibilities it carried. Maybe it was being in such close proximity to my own mother. Maybe it was being ensconced in this pink room that so closely matched my childhood bed-room. It made me think about what kind of child my daugh-ter would be and everything I learned about life that would and should change the ways I taught her. I thought about what I would spare her and the harshest realities to shield her from as long as possible. I wanted her childhood to teach her that a magical life doesn't have to be a fairy tale. But first, I'd have to make that true for myself.

The creaking of the floor outside of my half-opened door interrupted my thoughts, and I shifted my gaze from the chandelier on the ceiling to the doorway. Soon, the blond fluff of Ms. Gretchen's head popped into my field of vision.

"Good morning, honey!" she effused in my direction in a slight whisper. "I'm so glad that you're awake. I dreamt about your grandmother last night, and I wanted to tell you before it wandered out of my mind this morning." She smiled slightly brighter and sat down on my bed next to me. I was impressed that she'd managed a full face of makeup this early.

"I was just thinking, Ms. Gretchen," I said, arranging my body to face her, "I wish my daughter could know her . . . and I wish she were here. Even for this."

"Especially for this, honey," Ms. Gretchen said, waving her hand. "I just met your mother, but I'm sure this will be quite a day." We both laughed. "Well, I think your grandmother is here somewhere, watching over you, smiling down on you. I don't remember much about what she said in my dream, not specifically, you know. Only that we were sitting there at the table, talking like we usually did, and all she could talk about was Tabby Two, Tabby Two." Ms. Gretchen's face broke into a huge smile. She took my hand in hers and put the other on my shoulder. "So she's here, honey! And she's thinking about you. I think she'd want me to tell you that."

In that moment, it was almost as if I could feel my grand-mother's warmth. "Thanks, Ms. Gretchen, I needed to hear that." I reached up to give her a hug. We separated at the sound of a rap on the bedroom doorframe. My mother breezed in holding a cup of coffee marked at the rim with the stain of her red lipstick.

"Good morning!" she sang brightly. "Today is baby shower day!" She moved deeper into the room and busied herself opening curtains and pulling shades, flooding the room with the full light of the still-rising sun. Ms. Gretchen and I both gave our morning greetings in return.

"Now, Tabby"—my mother turned to face me with a concerned look—"you'll probably have to hurry if you want to make your hair appointment. You can't be late, because you know it can take a while."

"Hair appointment?" Ms. Gretchen said, turning from my mother to face me. "Tabby, I thought you did your hair before you left! Aren't you going to just unravel those twists you have? I bet it's going to look so cute!" Ms. Gretchen gave me a wink.

"But it's your baby shower! Tabby, you were going to get your hair done, right? In a press and curl, like you normally wear it on television!" The smile on my mother's face seemed to tighten.

"Mom, I only started wearing it straight again because viewers were complaining about my natural hair. I was planning on wearing it natural today, honestly. I spent a lot of time on it already. Can't we cancel the appointment?" Having Ms. Gretchen next to me was giving me a flow of extra energy, creating a lifeline and a slight chance to stand up against my mother's wishes. Normally, some battles didn't feel worth fighting and this would be one of them. Still, watching my mother's face fall and the expression of disappointment was hard to bear. If she insisted, I'd go, even as much as I didn't want to.

"You could cancel, Tabby, but why would you want to? Don't you want your hair to look lovely for pictures?" My mother's words were the final cut into my spirit. If she was so insistent, maybe there *was* something wrong with the way that my natural curls looked. And maybe the viewers who hated them were right all along. I started to adjust myself to get up, but Ms. Gretchen's hand on my shoulder resisted and pushed me back into my position on the bed. To my surprise, she didn't let up her pressure. Instead, she turned fully to face my mother.

"Jeanie, I think her hair is beautiful just the way that it is. And I think you'll love it when you see it all teased out and fabulous! Wait until you see those curls come out, honey! Plus, that baby that we're celebrating, she's growing hair just like her mother, even right now as we sit here . . . strong, healthy, and beautiful. And if we can't celebrate that today, and Tabby can't, then what exactly are we are celebrating?" Ms. Gretchen concluded with a demure smile.

The look on my mother's face, I would never forget. It showed every expression from shock, to surprise, to regret, to embarrassment, to anger. I waited for what scathing words she'd have in return.

"Well," she said slowly with a deepened tone. I braced myself for conflict. Her eyes narrowed. Her lips parted. I feared the worst. It was almost in slow motion as she exhaled loudly and let her shoulders drop. "Tabby, it's your hair. You do what you want with it." With that, she turned and walked out of the room, leaving Ms. Gretchen and me in stunned silence.

"Ugh!" I brought my hand up to cover my eyes in exasperation and relief. The release of tension from the room made me suddenly exhausted. Ms. Gretchen patted my shoulder.

"That was from your grandmother," she said.

"Thank you, Ms. Gretchen, you were right on time."

She started to get up from her seat on the bed. "Tabby, I'm going to let you get ready. Honey, you decide about your hair. Never mind all these ol' opinions. Just remember that what you see in the mirror, that little girl you're carrying, that's what she's going to see. Whether you love it or hate it, how you feel, that's how she's going to feel." She gave me another pat and stood up with surprising grace and ease for her age. The yellow on her fingertips flashed like its own sunshine as she moved to make her way out of the room. "I guess I'm gonna see if Jeanie can spare me a cup of coffee, that is if she doesn't send me packing back to the airport!" Ms. Gretchen turned with a wink just as she walked out of the room.

Standing in front of the bathroom mirror in my mother's house, I pulled off my sleep bonnet and watched the twisted-together coils of curls tumble out. I'd painstakingly done my own laborious styling the night before leaving Los Angeles. I'd stood in front of my mirror with my leave-in conditioner, my oils, and gel, picking the best combination of potions, applying them carefully to nourish my textured strands and coax them into shiny, lush coils to air dry. I felt the buzz of excitement as I untwisted each of the sections of my hair, revealing collated pieces of riveting, kinky lengths, each looking unique as a fingerprint. I chose which sections to separate, to fluff, or to twirl around my fingers for more definition. In this embodiment, I was truly myself, in a style that nobody else could replicate. I'd studied each one of those curls, separating some for more volume, each decision made with today's mood in mind. I had preened and primped—to emerge in a perfectly imperfect configuration for today.

In that mirror on the morning of my baby shower, I

thought about all of the time and effort I'd put into my hair up to this point. Even when I wore it under the wig—there were still hours of deep conditioning, trimming, scalp massages, and tender care invested into coaxing out the length I'd attained. This wasn't just my hair. It was a reflection of my work, of trial and error, of education hard discovered on social media channels and in salon side conversations. This, on my head, was my own Garden of Eden. It was my God-given paradise that I needed to protect, nurture, and name. Today, I would name it strong and healthy. I would name it perfect. I would name it love and beauty so that my daughter could come into this world and call hers the same.

24

"TABBY, YOU LOOK BEAUTIFUL!" ALEXIS CAME INTO THE BEDROOM just as I was stepping into my shoes as the last touch on my outfit. I gave her a fake camera pose and smiled. My belly felt like it was sticking out a mile.

"You look great too, Lexi!" Alexis smiled and looked down at her ring. I looked at it too. Seeing it there now meant so much more than any of the times before. Now it represented Alexis's decision and her forgiveness. That ring was how she wore her heart on her sleeve. She noticed my gaze. "You know, I'm still getting used to seeing you with your ring on. I realize it took a lot to make that decision."

"Tab, last night I was thinking, and you're right. It did take a lot to make that decision. The whole time I was separated from Rob, I thought that I might meet someone else who'd be so much better."

"Well, girl, you didn't give out too many chances. You only went on what, like, two dates?"

Alexis laughed. "Yeah, you're right. But I lost thirty pounds, got massages, bought myself flowers, and made space to think and meditate. Plus, I reorganized my house!" She described all of these simple things as if they were the greatest luxuries in the world. After a pause, seeming to savor the memory of it all, she continued. "Tab, I feel like I did meet someone, I met Alexis. I met the grown woman version of myself, and she's the person I get to keep, married or not married. And"—her smile grew wider—"new Alexis won't take no shit either."

We both laughed. "Lexi, I've never been Rob's biggest fan, but I've always been yours. I have to admit, he has been putting in serious effort. I'm happy for both of you and the boys too." I stepped forward to hug her, accidentally awkwardly tapping her with my belly which made us both laugh all over again. We had to adjust into a different configuration but managed to embrace each other all the same.

All of a sudden, Alexis fell silent and her face illuminated as if she had gotten the best news of her life.

"Tab!" she exclaimed. "I just had the best idea! I think Rob and I should have a rewedding. Nothing big, of course, not like my birthday party where he gave me that car. Girl, no. Something fun, small. A party with our friends and family to celebrate!"

"Did someone just say celebrate! That must mean I'm right on time!" Ms. Gretchen popped in, this time in a flash of canary yellow matching the glossy color of her nails. We all stood in the middle of the generous bedroom, admiring each other with silent approval.

"I did, Ms. Gretchen, I said celebrate!" Lexi gushed. "And you're invited too!"

"I might be old, honey, but aren't I already here?" Ms. Gretchen looked from Alexis to me with confusion.

"No, Ms. Gretchen, another celebration! I think I'm going to have a rewedding to my husband, Rob!"

"Oh goodness, honey! You had me thinking I'd finally gone senile! Well, I've had a couple of weddings. I celebrated my marriages at the beginning and the end, but I don't think I'd consider marrying either of those suckers *again*. Couldn't even if I wanted to, since they're both dead." Ms. Gretchen chuckled to herself. "But you know what I learned in all these years? Some people change, and some people don't. Change is for the living. You just have to make sure you got someone that can head in the right direction."

Ms. Gretchen's words made me think about my dad. And for some reason, thinking about my dad made me think about Marc. My dad was on the verge of imploding his family from the inside out, again. I wondered, even if he couldn't, could I change? Or would I always have this part of me, frozen at nine years old, petrified that someone would devastate me with their departure? I wanted to make sure that my own daughter would never have the look I recognized in my sisters' faces as they spent weekend after weekend at my house. I had thought that Marc and I could have a fairy-tale ending. But maybe some fairy-tale endings were just the princess, in her own palace, doing exactly what she wanted to do, for herself.

"Whatcha over there thinking so deeply about?" Ms. Gretchen's voice snapped me back into the moment.

"Yeah, Tab, what's wrong?" Alexis echoed.

"I just thought about Marc for a moment. Maybe I should have invited him?" I looked from Alexis to Ms. Gretchen and back again. Ms. Gretchen shook her head.

"Nah," Alexis said. "Tab, we're good, just as we are."

2 5

FLANKED BY LEXI ON ONE SIDE AND MS. GRETCHEN ON THE OTHER, I made my tentative entrance into the baby shower. My mother had managed to transform the lower levels of the enormous home into a wonderland of soft yellow. I could never figure out how Ms. Gretchen always managed to color match to the occasion. As we descended the stairs, more and more flowers came into view, cascading down the walls from invisible attachments, turning the foyer into its own delicate garden that led to a tent in the expansive backyard. My mother had truly outdone herself. Inside the tent were food stations scattered about, a table covered with a cornucopia of treats as the centerpiece. My stomach grumbled as my eyes danced across the pastel-colored petit fours and cake pops on display, to the glass jars of candies of all varieties, to the various setups of cakes and other desserts. At the round tables neatly arranged in the center, each of the place settings was carefully labeled and the chairs were cloth-covered with bows. Even the centerpieces had the mark of delicate attention and design sensibility. It was all so much more than I would have ever dreamed.

"Well, damn," Ms. Gretchen said quietly under her breath. I turned to her and smiled.

"Wow, Tab!" Alexis exclaimed excitedly, gently pulling on my arm. "Your mother really went all out! This is better than some people's weddings!"

"Classic Jeanie Walker-Williams at her finest," I said. "Now I'm convinced she must think I'm never getting married."

Alexis set off in the direction of my mother, who was chatting with some of the early arrivals in the corner. As she walked away, I noticed a four-piece musical ensemble setting up in another corner. I could hear Alexis call out to my mother on her way over, "Jeanie! This is amazing!"

Ms. Gretchen squeezed my hand. "Now, you be you today, okay?" She smiled at me as she spoke. "No matter what happens, we're on a plane back to LA tomorrow!"

I laughed. "You must think I'm nervous, Ms. Gretchen," I teased back at her.

"Well, hell, I'm nervous, and it's not even my baby or my shower. I haven't been to something this nice since my hair was its natural color!" It was my turn to squeeze her hand.

"Let's just try to have a good time, Ms. Gretchen. We'll make it our own little celebration. At least you get to have champagne." I gave her a wink and watched her set off in the direction of the champagne bar. I felt another person come beside me and take hold of my elbow. I didn't recognize her, but she was dressed immaculately, and if the jewelry she was wearing was real, it could have easily made up my baby's entire college fund. .

"Well, you must be Tabby, the guest of honor," she purred. "It's such a pleasure to meet you! And look at you, aren't you cute! You're all bump, not an ounce of extra weight on you!" She leaned into me further to add in my ear, "That's what those LA men like, am I right?" The woman looked down at my bare hand. I surrendered to the feeling of embarrassment and braced for what was next. "I guess that's the new thing, to get married after the baby, right? Do you have a date in mind?"

"Um . . . not . . . exactly," I stuttered, trying to buy some time for an answer.

"Well dear, just make sure you don't let him take too long. Sometimes they like to drag their feet. Get him down the aisle while he's still excited about the new baby. That's my advice."

"Worth a million bucks." I gave my best fake smile. "So nice to meet you, and thank you for coming, Ms. . . . ."

"I'm Carolyn, Carolyn Carpenter—a good friend of your mom's." She slid away from me, waving in the direction of my mother, and sauntered off. I could only imagine what the rest of the day would bring.

"Tabby! Tabby, come meet some more of our guests!" My mother called to me just as I had decided to try to sneak a cake pop. I walked over to where my mother was holding court with a group of well-dressed women. "Tabby, I want you to meet my friends. This is Ms. Gladys, Ms. Bernice, and you already met Ms. Carolyn." I nodded to each of the ladies politely.

"Well, isn't your hair cute!" Ms. Bernice said to me as she reached out to fluff one side of my curls. I tried not to look annoyed.

"I tried to get her to the hair salon, but she insisted on doing it herself. I guess this so-called 'natural' look is in these days."

"Oh, yes, Jeanie," Ms. Gladys chimed in. "My daughter hasn't straightened her hair in almost three years. I have to say, it's down her back now, longer than ever. I think the kids are onto something." My mother looked surprised.

"Well, my Tabby has always been more daring than I have. I'm so proud of her." I turned to look at my mother like she was speaking a foreign language. She put her arm around me and continued, "And Marc. I'll be spending a few months with them in Los Angeles once the baby is born." I tuned out as my mother recounted all of Marc's credentials and accomplishments and none of my own. The ladies learned that he'd attended Stanford, but not that I'd recently won an Emmy. Eventually, I excused myself.

I found Ms. Gretchen sitting at a table near the champagne bar, happily sipping from the flute in her hand, observing all around her with a bemused expression. "Hey, Ms. Gretchen, how's it going?" I sighed and sat down.

"What's wrong, honey? You tired from standing?"

"I'm tired from existing. All these women want to talk about is Marc. It's almost as if his existence makes me real. Otherwise, I'm invisible. They want to know when I'm getting married more than they care about when the baby is due. Or my hair. It's my hair! Just like the viewers who sent letters, everyone feels entitled to some kind of opinion on my life. Why does what I do matter to them so much?" Ms. Gretchen put her champagne glass down and patted my hand.

"Tabby, this probably won't make much sense to you, but they all think in some way or another that they mean well. Even your mother. But you're doing something new; you're following your heart. Them, they're following the rules."

"Ms. Gretchen, I'm not being a rebel. I tried to follow the rules. But the rules weren't getting me what I wanted. I'm just trying to make a space for me to be myself."

"Stories aren't written about women who follow the rules, Tabby. Stories are written about women who break them and show us all what's on the other side. The world runs on that magic. Don't let anybody limit you with what they can't handle. We're all rooting for you. All of us. Even the ones who don't seem like it. You know what? When you need some extra courage, you need to get yourself a red cardigan."

"What am I going to do with a red cardigan?"

"Oh honey, I just mean that as a figure of speech. I had an old red cardigan that I brought with me to Los Angeles when I first started teaching. I didn't know how to make those kids listen to me, and some days I had a hard time getting through a lesson plan. I just told myself one day that I was going to wear that red sweater, and they were going to have to pay attention to me, just like they did everything else red—the bell, the stoplights, and the fire trucks. Red to me meant authority, and if I couldn't find it on the inside, I sure was going to wear it on the outside." Ms. Gretchen took another sip of her champagne. "So I put on my red cardigan and went into that classroom. I don't know if I was right about the color, or if the kids just decided to behave that day, but it was my best day.

And every day after, since I'd done it that first time, I knew it was possible, so I stuck with it—all the way until I retired."

"Well, I don't have a red cardigan, Ms. Gretchen."

"You don't need one. Just find something that makes you feel special. I eventually figured out who I was when I wore the cardigan was more important than what I was wearing. Now, I'm gonna get myself another glass of champagne. You want anything?"

I told Ms. Gretchen no, I didn't want anything. But that wasn't entirely true. What I wanted at that moment was a red cardigan of my own.

26

MARC AND I SAT FIDGETY ON THE SOFA TOGETHER IN MY LIVING room, awaiting the arrival of my doula, Andouele. By now, I'd felt as if I'd been pregnant forever, but, at least on paper, there were still a couple of weeks to go before we'd meet our daughter. We'd rehashed our delivery plan over and over—natural delivery, as few drugs as possible, avoid medical intervention. When I told this to my mother, she told me she loved me, but she didn't see how I'd be in this world if she hadn't had an epidural. Personally, I wanted things to be different—at least, if they could be.

In the two-weeks that had passed since my shower, I'd already given Marc the download of the baby shower. I made it a point to mention how often he came up as a topic, which I thought would serve as comic relief but only made him more fidgety. I thought about the dinner with his parents and the conversations both before and after and figured that maybe he just hadn't sorted it all out yet. Truthfully, neither had I.

Still, if we were going to be co-parents, one of the two of us had to address whatever heaviness there was between us.

"Marc"—I turned to him openly—"is there something wrong?" He looked surprised. After a beat, he took my hand in his and adjusted his position on the sofa.

"Tabby, I've been thinking a lot, and there's something that I've been wanting to say to you, to give you, but it's never seemed to be the right time." I felt a pang in my gut that, for once lately, wasn't cramping or the baby kicking me. It was panic.

"Marc, you're not—" I was cut off by the doorbell. *Thank God.* The tension in my body drained, and I rocked myself forward off the sofa to answer the door. A backward glance on the way revealed a still-nervous-looking Marc, sitting on the sofa with clasped hands. Even though I'd met with our doula several times before, his nervousness was contagious. Although I had a feeling that it wasn't purely about our shortly arriving baby.

Andouele stood at the door, regal as ever. Her mere presence had its own calming effect on me. I invited her over to sit with Marc and me and introduced them. I didn't want to waste any time. We were getting close to birth, I could feel it. And I still had so many questions.

Andouele felt around my stomach. "Oooh, the delivery isn't far away. Have you made your preparations?"

"My bag is packed, and Marc and I have been going to classes at the birthing center. I'm hoping for an all-natural birth. I've just been so afraid that things will spiral out of control. I'm worried that the pain will get so bad that I won't be able to say no to an epidural if one is offered to me." It felt good to speak these uncomfortable truths out loud. Andouele nodded with understanding. "I just want to do the right thing for our daughter."

"Momma, you're the one who makes the decisions. We're here to support you. On birth day, you are the star of the show. You and that baby are all that matters. And that means what you want is all that matters."

"I guess that means I'm just the decoration," Marc interjected.

"Trust me, most of my clients' male partners say the same thing," Andouele replied with a small chuckle. "Just because you're not centered doesn't mean you're obsolete. Tabby," she continued, "what's most important to remember is you have so much more power than you think you do. And for that baby's sake, you have to claim it."

"I guess I'm also afraid of making the wrong choice."

"The only wrong choice is the one you make for somebody other than you or your baby."

"Hey! So I get no say at all?" Marc spoke up again. It seemed like his feelings were genuinely hurt. Andouele twisted to look at him but said nothing. He followed up his comment with laughter that filled the awkward silence. "I guess I'm really a nonfactor," he said quietly, and sank back into the sofa cushions.

Two hours of Andouele's mix of cheering section and birthing self-help library went too quickly. At the end, Marc and I both walked her to my door. She cushioned her departure with warm, engulfing hugs that seemed to stop the world for the seconds that her arms wrapped around me. For everything that could go wrong in childbirth, I knew that I'd be in good hands.

As we closed the door, my mind went into checklist mode, thinking through the birth and everything that would come after. I turned to Marc with a smile.

"You know, somehow we're going to have to childproof your bachelor pad," I teased, giving Marc a playful push of his shoulder. The look on his face was not amused. "I mean," I added quickly, "of course we'll have a nursery in both places, but you're welcome here whenever you want, Marc. I didn't mean—" Marc cut me off before I could finish.

"Tabby, you've made it clear what you want and don't want. I know you don't want to marry me and . . ."

"Marc!" This time the hurt on his face was unmistakable. "I didn't say I didn't want to marry you ever. I didn't say never, I just said that we don't have to get married now just because other people think we do. If we do, I want it to mean something, to be something that we did for ourselves. Not for anybody else. Not even for our daughter."

Marc studied me, his eyes surveying my face with every word I spoke. It was almost as if he was looking for something. Eventually, he gave a reply.

"Come here for a second," he said quietly, taking my hand. "I have something I've been holding on to, trying to find the right time to give it to you. I guess if I wait too long, I'll run out of time." I looked at him, puzzled, but followed. *He can't possibly be proposing?* The protective gears of my mind started to rumble on the way to the sofa. I felt my body tense up. I didn't want to be surprised, and I didn't want any more complications in our already strained relationship.

We sat down. Even as I looked at Marc for answers, my mind kept on with its rumblings.

"Tabby." Marc's voice cut through my thoughts. He took both of my hands in his, and I turned toward him as much as my body would allow. At this point, my stomach was both an anchor and a barrier to most of my mobility. I managed to face him at an angle. He reached behind him and produced a glossy paper bag tied with a satin ribbon. He held it out to me.

"This is for you," he said softly.

"Marc, what is this?" I asked this of both the gift and the moment before us. Marc looked at me through his long and beautiful eyelashes. I said a silent prayer that our daughter would be so lucky. He smiled at me and nudged the bag closer.

"Look inside," he instructed. I followed his directions.

I took the bag and could see it tremble slightly, betraying my hands. I managed to stabilize it and reached in to produce both a card and a medium-sized rectangular black velvet box.

"Marc, what is . . ."

"Open it," he coaxed again.

I pried open the stiff box and took in a sharp breath. Inside the box was a soft red-satin-cushioned lining that served to set off the spectacular brilliance of a sparkling heart-shaped diamond. Around the solitaire draped the whisper-thin pink-gold of an intricate necklace that looked almost too delicate to hold the jewel it was meant to showcase. It was as gorgeous as any star, one that you would pick to wish on even if it weren't streaking through the nighttime sky. It left me breathless. Marc was grinning, bigger than I'd ever seen.

"Do you like it?" he asked me softly. I struggled to find the words to reply. My anticipation and dread of the prospect of a ring had wound me up so tightly that, coupled with surprise like this, anxiety had closed my throat. "You don't like it," he said quickly. The disappointment in Marc's tone pushed me out of my involuntary silence.

"No! I love it! I'm sorry, really, I love it," I effused. I put the gift on the table and wrapped my arms around him as best I could. When I leaned back, Marc was grinning again, seemingly very pleased with himself.

"Are you sure? I can take it back," he teased.

"Oh no, you will not, Marc Brown!" I shot back at him quickly. "I love it, and I appreciate this so much! It's a push present?"

"If you want to call it that. Read the card." Marc pulled the forgotten white envelope out of the bag and pushed it into my still unsteady hands. I managed to tear into the paper and fold open the card that read *Thank You* in large, swooping cursive on the front. The inside was all handwritten in Marc's scribble, but I managed to make it out. As I read silently to myself, the emotions stirred within, swirling in deep places, threatening to sweep me into overwhelming waters. These were words I could drown in.

"Read it aloud?" Marc asked. I obliged and started over.

"Okay," I said, and cleared my throat. I shifted on the sofa and began speaking his words. "Tabitha Abigail Walker, since the day I met you, you've kept me on my toes. You've challenged me to rethink my actions, my beliefs, and my values, and you've pushed me to figure out what kind of man I want and need to be. I haven't always risen to the occasion. I haven't always shown up when you asked or would have liked, but I want you to know I'm here with you. I'll always be here. Even without a ring, you have me wrapped around your finger. Our daughter will as well. I will always love and support you both. Thank you for being the best mother that I could have ever imagined for my child. Your courage inspires me and gives me the comfort that our little girl will always have a great example. With love always, Marc."

As I finished reading, my hand reflexively came up to cover my mouth, as though I'd lose the magic of the incantation I'd just read. The spell of Marc's words had befallen me. Electricity sparkled in the air between us. We were here, after everything. We'd created a life, and that life had created this moment. I didn't want to lose a second of it. All this time, while I felt her growing inside, she'd been pushing me to create new spaces within that never existed before. Outside of me, Marc was growing as well. But until now, I hadn't seen it.

Finally, after a time of simply looking at each other, Marc spoke. "You want to at least try it on?"

I smiled in a way I could feel everywhere on my face. "Yes, you know I do!"

Marc picked up the black velvet box and gingerly lifted the necklace out of it. The weight of the diamond pendant pulled it down almost into parallel lines. He managed to clasp it and tickle me with its placement around my neck.

"If I was still wearing that wig, it'd be all tangled up," I said, laughing at the thought of it. I pulled out my phone to admire the sparkling addition to my décolletage.

Marc joined me in laughter. "Yeah, you can't wear *this* necklace and *that* wig at the same time." Marc's hands lingered on my shoulders. "You look beautiful," he said quietly.

I felt the warm flush in my cheeks. It wasn't just his words, but my thoughts as well. Tonight, I didn't want him to leave.

"Marc." I spoke to him softly. "Will you stay here tonight?"

"Anything you want," he said, and gave me a gentle kiss on the cheek.

"I know exactly what I want," I said, pushing myself off the sofa and grabbing his hand. I led him back toward the bedroom.

"Oh, you do, do you?" Marc teased back.

"Oh yeah, definitely," I called to him behind me as I waddled down the hallway.

At eight and a half months pregnant, I settled into my bed next to Marc, necklace still on, my swollen breasts and tummy fighting against the maternity sleeping slip that I could just barely still fit. Marc was lying next to me on his back. On my side, I snuggled as close to him as my belly would allow and draped my arm across the ripples of his chest. I pulled my leg over his and let some of the weight rest against his pelvic bone. Finally, I felt comfortable and relaxed into him.

"So you just basically want me as your human pillow, huh?" he said, nuzzling my ear.

"Yup, basically," I said as I drifted off to sleep. "Basically."

27

Walking into my familiar neighborhood hair salon felt unfamiliar on this Saturday. Usually, the salon was a place for transformation. On this day, I really wanted to stay the same. I'd been coming to Denisha since I could remember to transform my curls into straight bouncing styles that looked like the person who I always thought I was supposed to be. I had spent hours and hours shifting from chair to chair to chair, under water, under heat, under hands and effort, all to coax me into the form of someone I no longer wanted to be.

I pulled open the door to the familiar greeting of smells, sounds, and cracked tiles under my feet. Denisha was at her station near the door, putting the finishing touches on a head of iron-turned curls for the customer in her chair.

"Hey, girl!" Denisha called to me.

"Hey, Denisha!" I said. "Hey, everybody," I called out to the rest of the salon. A smattering of replies came back to me from all directions.

"You can have a seat at the bowl. I'm just finishing up this customer and then I can blow you out after your wash and do a braid down," Denisha said as she waved me toward the sinks in the back. I paused. I brought my hands up to touch the necklace around my neck. I hadn't taken it off since Marc put it there. His words teased through my mind. In my purse was my wig. I had only one week left before my maternity leave. *Chris can't fire a pregnant woman, right?*

"Denisha," I said, turning to my hairdresser. "What can you do with my natural hair texture?"

"Oh, you want to wear your hair out?" Denisha asked, barely looking up from her curling, as if I'd said nothing new. "Hmm . . . we could do a deep conditioner and a twist-out!" she said cheerily. After a beat, she added, "And you probably need a trim!"

"Denisha," I warned, "don't go all scissor happy on me." She laughed at my caution.

"Tabby, you and every client got the same thing to say. Girl, you finna wear your hair out again on the news?" Denisha asked me incredulously.

"Girl, when I first saw you on that television with your hair rockin' your texture, I was like, damn!" Denisha's client interjected, suddenly becoming animated out of silence.

"Girl, me too!"

I swiveled around to hear the woman sitting in the chair behind me. Her stylist nodded in agreement.

"Me too!" This voice came from across the salon. An older woman sat with her half-done hair in flat twists.

The chorus around me swirled through my ears like

music. I had no idea these women were watching. They didn't send in viewer letters, but they were watching. And they liked what they saw.

"Denisha, let's go for the deep conditioner, a trim, and a bomb twist-out. I've got a big meeting this week at work."

"Oooh, girl, is it time for a promotion?" Denisha asked.

"Yeah, something like that," I replied, taking a seat in the waiting area. I pulled out my phone. I opened a text and scrolled down to Lisa Sinclair.

Hi Lisa, when's the next women's issues meeting?

After a few minutes, the characteristic ping signaled that Lisa had responded.

Lisa:
It's Monday a.m.

Tabby:
Ok, great, can you put me back on the agenda?

Sure, same topic?

Same topic.

Done. Can't wait!

"Me either, Lisa," I murmured softly to myself as I put away my phone. "Me either."

TRUDGING INTO WORK ON THE LAST MONDAY BEFORE MY MATER-
nity leave made me wonder how some women managed to
work right up to their due dates. If I wasn't on camera, maybe
I would have done the exact same. I couldn't afford to take
any extra time off, not economically or careerwise. Pregnancy was not a penalty box that I could afford to sit in for
longer than absolutely necessary.

In my hands, I carried the donuts I'd bring to the women's
issues meeting. Heading into the conference room, I saw a
small collection of my coworkers, who all perked up at the
spectacle of a built-for-two pregnant woman waddling in with
a box of near-matching width. A couple of them rushed over
to take the box I was holding and place it next to the coffee.
Another woman grabbed my tote and ushered me into an
empty seat.

"Oh, Tabby!" I heard coming from my right side. "I love
your hair!" Glennis Jones, on our writing team, ambled in my
direction with her hands outstretched. I mumbled a quick
thanks, smiled, and braced myself for the attack.

"Oh hey, Glennis!" I heard Lisa's voice coming from the
doorway. "Could you put these agendas on the table for everyone?"

Glennis popped out of her mission and switched directions to grab the small stack of paper from Lisa's hands. A
few people milled in behind her, and she moved swiftly to
get the meeting started. I looked down at the agenda, and to
my surprise, my topic, Appearance Bias, was first on the list.

Lisa stood at the front of the room, calling everyone's

attention to me to kick off the meeting. My palms started to sweat. I took a sip of my tea and then awkwardly stood up to address the room of eyes, each set looking squarely in my direction.

"Good morning, ladies." I spoke the words with lightly caffeinated cheer. A few smiles and good mornings returned to me. I continued, "The topic I'm supposed to talk to you about this morning is evidently appearance bias." I looked down at the agenda, still in my hands. "But the truth is, Appearance Bias is just a title that I made up to sound like it applied to everyone." The truth weighed heavy on my head, and I let my shoulders slump a bit. The paper I was holding fluttered in front of me again. I pushed myself to continue. "I did that because I felt like what I really wanted to discuss only applied to me and that none of you would take an interest for that reason." I took a moment to meet some of the eyes that were fixated on me and then took a deep breath. *Stay calm, Tabby.*

Amid baby kicks and some slight Braxton Hicks cramping that had been picking up over the last few days, I carried on. "Somewhere along the way, I realized that sometimes issues are bigger than they seem; sometimes you have to give a person a chance to help, and sometimes you have to allow people to surprise you. So, here goes. My real issue is that this"—I reached up to touch my crinkly, tight textured curls—"this is the way that my hair grows out of my head, naturally. And yet when I wear it this way, viewers complain. They send letters. But worse, we have no policy here that protects me from this. And I think there should be. And maybe this seems like an issue of one, but to me, it's an issue of women, a women's issue, just the basics of personal say over our bodies, and that's why I'm bringing it here, to this group."

I looked around the room and absorbed the silence. Some of the women were looking at me; some had their heads down, fixated on the masterwork that was the bland conference room table. Lisa looked at me with deepening concern and then turned her head with seeming disbelief that no one had so much as made a peep or moved a muscle. As she shifted, a movement to my right caught my eye. It was Glennis. Her arm was raised. I acknowledged her.

"Tabby," Glennis said thoughtfully, "I know a bit about the CROWN Act becoming the law in California. If you'd like to do a report on that, I'd like to support you on the writing side." She gave a warm smile.

"Thank you, Glennis," I said, and looked around the room for more hands. Lisa now had hers in the air as well, and then I saw several others. And then a few more popped up. My nerves started to melt into appreciation. I hadn't even expected acknowledgment, let alone validation of my issue. The participation was overwhelming.

"Lisa?" I said in her direction.

Lisa cleared her throat, put down her coffee cup, and started to speak. "Tabby, I believe I can speak for all of us in saying thank you for bringing this issue to light. I know it's not easy when you think it's something personal, but that's how all progress starts. The purpose of this group is to make this workplace better for women, and that means *all* women." Lisa paused for a smattering of light applause in the room. "For my part, let's make sure that your segment is on the evening news. I'll talk to my producer and make sure I get to introduce it." She beamed at me. "In fact, it might be a little bit risky, but we might be able to get it on tonight, before your maternity leave." Lisa winked.

Even when she finished, there were still hands in the air. Where I thought I'd be lucky to have even one, there were many. On this day, the reward for my risk came in the form of unexpected offers of support. For my trust, I was able to gain help and alliances. In this moment, within this group, my vulnerability was met with protection. Here, in the same room where I often faced workplace rivals, somehow I'd also found a family.

As the meeting wrapped up, Lisa made her way over to me, flashing a thumbs-up.

"So that was your big idea, eh?" she teased me with a sly smile. "Sharing your CROWN Act story?"

I laughed and shrugged my shoulders. "Hey, I figured what the hell, right? Worst that could happen is people say no, or nothing at all!"

Lisa looked at me quizzically. "Tabby . . . no? Why would anybody say no? Among all of us here, you're an Emmy-winning journalist! Your Daequan Jenkins piece is still referenced. Of course people are clamoring to work with you!" She beamed and gave me a playful tap on my shoulder. "You're a star, girl!"

I beamed back at her and started to make my way out of the room.

"I'll let you know about the broadcast. I'm going to talk to my producer now." I nodded my acknowledgment. "By the way, Tabby, I love that cardigan!" Lisa called back to me. I looked down at what I was wearing.

"Oh, thanks!" I said back from the doorframe. "Someone much wiser than me told me that red's my color."

FOR THE FIRST TIME SINCE THE EARLY MONTHS OF MY PREGNANCY, I stood in the ladies' restroom, overwhelmed by waves of nausea. Thankfully, this time, I didn't feel the need to hide it from anyone. Plus, there was no time to be secretive. With my pulse racing and anxiety flooding my veins, I had just a few minutes to prepare myself for a broadcast that might just get me fired.

Lisa had managed to convince her producer to include the segment she'd proposed in the meeting. It was risky for both of us, but as an anchor, Lisa likely had an employment contract with a termination provision and was in a much better position than me. I wouldn't have that kind of contract until my next promotion. Depending on what happened in the following hour, it might be a promotion I'd never see.

Taking deep breaths, as much as I could manage with the baby against my diaphragm, I tried to calm my nerves enough to give my makeup a final touch-up in the mirror. The crinkly curls in my twist-out were still poppin', and I said a silent thanks to pregnancy hormones that made my hair grow like a weed. I welcomed the still unfamiliar way that, just in accepting my own reflection, I felt a sense of freedom, more than ever before. I exhaled.

"Get it together, Tabby," I told myself sternly in the mirror as I applied my lipstick. "It's not just for you anymore." This was the truth I knew for certain. Almost on cue, my cell phone pinged to signal a message from Lisa.

"Ready?" the text prompted.

Like so many things in my life recently, my own answer to that question wasn't particularly relevant to the events that would soon play out. I typed a quick reply to say that I was on my way down to the news set. With one last smoothing of my outfit around my ripe baby belly, I headed out the door.

During my walk, which was more like a waddle than it had ever been, I ran through my talking points. Lisa and I planned to introduce my story as a human-interest segment. With the coordination of her producer, as a favor, we had managed to slot it in pretty seamlessly. The wild card was Chris. Only very occasionally would he actually sit in for the evening news. Usually, he'd watch from his office or the control room. As long as he wasn't there and wasn't watching, we'd be clear.

Turning the corner into the space of the television studio, Lisa was already seated at the anchor desk, arranging her papers and checking her teeth. I loved how meticulous Lisa was about her teeth. When it came to appearances, broadcast news had a strong history of near-irrational focus on details such as these—whiteness, perfection, the "ideal." Standing on the edge of the news set—natural hair, pregnant, Black, and single—I was a complete contradiction of the entire profession. But still, there I stood, ready and willing to tell my truth.

Toward the middle of the broadcast, the production coordinator came and connected me to the hidden microphone that was clipped just inside my sweater. The earpiece was placed in my ear, with wires tucked underneath the back of my hair. After a quick audio check, the news producer cued me for when I'd be up. The countdown was officially on. There was no time left for regrets or rethinking. Chris had mercifully stayed in his office. The coast was clear.

"Tabby, five minutes, okay?" the voice said into my ear. I felt the pang of nervousness ripple through my gut. I closed my eyes and tried to relax. I'd been seated at the broadcast desk many times, but something was much different about being the subject of the interview. Not just any interview, but an unannounced and unauthorized interview in a segment that our news director knew nothing about. So, something was also different about risking your career on it.

"Tabby, they're ready to get you seated. Your segment is next," the producer's voice warned, prompting me toward the news set. Lisa was doing her standard during-the-break refresh when she saw me and frantically waved me over. My heart was pounding in my ears.

"Come on, you look great!" she said with the ebullient precision of someone still in teleprompter mode. "Same game plan?"

"Yep," I said. "Same game plan."

"We're back on in twenty seconds," the producer's voice said into my ear. Lisa gave me a gentle rub on the arm as she swiveled back to a forward-facing position, and I awaited the red light on the camera in front of us. It was showtime.

"Welcome back to *KVTV Evening News*. I'm Lisa Sinclair. With us this evening, for a very special segment, we have our very own Tabitha Walker, whose reporting has earned her a coveted television award, among many other accolades. We're used to seeing Tabitha on location, but tonight, she's here in the studio with us to discuss a topic that's recently come to the forefront in California, New York, and several other states—it's something that many of us take for granted, the right to choose our hairstyles." Lisa turned to me, and I saw the pan of the camera, letting me know I was squarely in its view. All the usual last-minute thoughts ran through my mind, but I took a quick breath and steadied myself. If Lisa and I could pull this off, this would be our moment to make a difference. Or it could be how I lost my job on live television.

"Welcome, Tabitha," Lisa said to me with a big smile. By instinct, I instantly snapped into my camera persona.

"Thank you, Lisa," I said, beaming back at her, "I'm really happy to be here to discuss this tonight."

"What some of our longtime viewers might have noticed is that you recently made a change to your hairstyle, which I personally loved, by the way." I nodded with a quick thanks, and Lisa continued. "But what surprised me as your friend and colleague was that this wasn't just a simple switch of style to you, this was a big decision, one referred to as 'going natural.' Is that right?"

I smiled on the inside at Lisa's introduction. It was so much better than I expected. I took a beat to gather my thoughts. I decided, *What's there to lose? I might as well give the honest truth.* I broadened my smile, ready to bring it.

"Yes," I said back to Lisa, as brightly as I could, "it was not a decision I made, or even felt like I could take, lightly. I think that there's a perception, a pervasive perception, in the television news industry that so-called natural textures, or even curly hair textures are not as professional, not as polished. So, challenging that bias wasn't an easy decision to make. I had to trust myself; I had to trust our viewers, and I had to make the decision that was ultimately best for me."

Lisa considered my words. I watched the tick of her mind in the split seconds before she returned to me with the next questions. She was making a game-time decision. I braced myself for what she'd say next. The lights of the studio were bright and hot, but it was the tension of the risk we were taking that made me start to sweat. I kept my focus trained on the red light on the camera and remembered my smile.

"To mention our viewers, is it fair to say that you've gotten feedback?" Lisa asked me, teeing up the question. The way she phrased it, I realized she was making it my choice—whether or not I wanted to air the station's dirty laundry. I considered my options and decided to take my shot.

"I *have* gotten feedback, Lisa," I said. "I've gotten feedback from viewers who made it known that they finally felt seen, once they were able to see me embracing my natural hair. I've gotten encouragement and acceptance, overwhelmingly." I paused. *Should you say it?* my mind warned. I decided to continue. "And there have been some viewers who expressed *strongly* that they preferred my hair straight."

"And for us in the studio and viewers at home, can you explain what your choice of going natural means to you?"

"Lisa, it means freedom. It means not having to hide who I am or what I look like from anyone, including myself. It means me having a say over my own body. I think it's important for viewers to understand, this is not some kind of radical change. It's actually just the opposite. It's simply my decision to stop making changes through heat and chemicals and other transformative agents to make my hair texture something it's just not. It means *finally* deciding to be comfortable in my own skin, and I think that's something everyone can relate to."

"That *is* something we can certainly all relate to," Lisa replied. "And with these latest developments, the great thing is that you do get to decide. In California, under the CROWN Act, that decision is protected." Lisa gave me another huge smile. "And," she added, "I think you always look gorgeous." Lisa turned to her co-anchor, Don. "Doesn't she look great?" Don gave her a bobbleheaded, smiling nod. She turned back, facing me and the camera. "We look forward to bringing our viewers a much more detailed report on the CROWN Act once you return from maternity leave. Thank you so much for sharing such a personal perspective on this story."

I gave my thanks and waited while Lisa and Don closed out the broadcast. Soon the little red light on the camera extinguished, signaling that we were no longer transmitting. Shortly after, I felt the cooling relief signaled by the loud click that switched off the brightest of the studio lights. While Lisa and I laughed and high-fived our congratulations to each other, we completely missed the approach of a very red-faced Chris Perkins. As we both looked up, he stood in front of us, obviously fuming.

"You changed the segment," he said through his teeth. All of the color drained from Lisa's face.

"Of course we did! We had the perfect personal perspective right here, in house," Lisa said, more forcefully than usual.

Chris looked from Lisa to me and back again. He leaned

in our direction, placing all of his stubby fingers on the desk in front of us.

"I need to see both of you in my office. Now." With that, Chris turned around and walked away briskly.

Lisa and I turned to look at each other, speechless.

Shit.

WE BARELY SAID A WORD TO EACH OTHER ON THE WALK TO CHRIS'S office. I wondered if this was how Lexington felt being sent on the long walk to the principal's office. Lisa and I both knew that we'd taken a risk in our decision, but instead of mischief, it seemed like the right thing to do. It felt like courage.

Just a few steps from Chris's office door, Lisa whispered to me, "Tabby, whatever he says, let me take the blame for it. It was my segment, my anchor slot, my decision."

I frowned back at her.

"Lisa," I hissed. "You can't take the blame for something that was my issue to begin with."

"I have a good contract. And you have a baby to worry about." She pulled me forward by my hand. Before I could protest further, she added, "Plus, every problem can't be your problem, remember? Let this one be mine."

In years of covering local news, it wasn't often that people surprised me—both in the field and the office. Lisa made for a welcome exception. It had been the worst time of my life when I'd first said to Lisa, "Every problem can't be my problem." It was at my breaking point, and an outburst that I wasn't proud of. But it was honest. In this moment, perhaps one of my most professionally vulnerable, it would take more than a wall full of Hallmark cards to express what it meant to me that she remembered.

I let myself be pulled into Chris's office, fully aware that no matter who took the blame, between the two of us, statistically, I was most likely to bear the brunt of the repercussions. The station couldn't afford to lose a high-profile star like Lisa Sinclair. But they could easily explain away the loss of a Tabitha Walker, even if I *had* won an important award. We were in a world where memories were short and brown faces could go missing for ages before anyone even thought to notice.

Chris shuffled papers from the tall, unruly stacks that covered his desk. He seemed to be looking for something among it all and barely paid attention to the two of us as we sat down. His face was still redder than usual, but the flaming color seemed to have receded from the bonfire state of earlier. I was going to be late for my birthing class but had no choice but to sit there and wait for Chris to eventually acknowledge us. Eventually, the shuffling settled, and he finally looked up. My feet firmly touched the ground, but I felt small enough that it seemed as if they were swinging.

"Explain," Chris said simply, hands still and clasped on his desk in front of him.

I started to speak, but Lisa spoke first, cutting me off as she'd promised to do in the hallway.

"Chris, the segment was my idea. We usually do a human-interest story, and I thought what better than . . ." Chris held his hand up to stop Lisa from talking.

"Lisa, I want to hear from Tabby." My heart skipped two

beats. Lisa opened her mouth and closed it several times. I took as deep a breath as the chair and the baby would allow.

"Chris," I sighed, "on the one hand, you tell me to fight for my perspective. But, when I do, I'm also the one who has to also make the space. Every single time. Because that's what it takes. Either you're going to allow and support my efforts, or you're not. But you can't say one thing and do another. It's not fair. And frankly, it's exhausting."

"Do you think it's wise to cause controversy before your maternity leave?" Chris asked with a raised eyebrow.

Lisa took the opportunity to interject. "Chris!" she said with exasperation. "It was my segment. I used *my* discretion and asked Tabby to be my guest to discuss an important topic." Chris swiveled his head to look at Lisa squarely.

"With all due respect, Lisa, and you're a great anchor, but not a damn person is going to remember you anchoring that segment. All that they'll remember is Tabby and controversy. If complaints come in, they'll be about Tabby, not you. If the ratings go down, you're on every night. It'll average out. But if they go down, which segment will stand out?" Lisa dropped her head.

"Tabby's," she said quietly. Slowly, heat started to build in my core. Chris's words triggered an emotion beyond frustration that made me want to scream. I clenched my fists to hold on to my peace and tapped my foot on the floor to stop my mouth from releasing the words on the tip of my tongue—words that I knew I'd quickly regret. I felt a welling rage, an anger swelling that I hoped I could control but wasn't even sure anymore if I should. I stood up.

"Chris, in case you haven't noticed, I'm nearly nine months pregnant. And I'm late for my birthing class. You don't have to worry about any more surprise segments from me because I'll be on maternity leave. Is there anything you need me to know? Because otherwise, all I have left to say is good night."

Chris said nothing, so I turned to leave. I'd had enough. As I walked out the door, I heard Lisa's voice.

"It isn't all about ratings, Chris," she pleaded.

"It is to me," said Chris, his voice quickly fading as I increased my pace toward the exit.

28

MY HANDS WERE SHAKING, EVEN GRIPPING THE STEERING WHEEL. Residual anger left me clearheaded and laser-focused on the road ahead. The light cramping around my belly served as a reminder that not only was I late for birthing class but there were also more important things than Chris Perkins. I took deep breaths but still needed to blow off more steam.

"Call Laila." I made the brusque command of my phone and soon heard ringing through my car's sound system.

"Hey, Tab," Laila said, sounding a bit distracted.

"Girl, you busy?" I hoped she'd say no, even though she was always busy these days.

"Just working on this site. Tryin' to make a dollar out of fifteen cents," Laila sighed back at me. "What's up?"

"I'm just leaving work, that is, if I still have a job, and heading to this birth . . . to meet Marc, you know for class."

"Tabby"—Laila laughed my name—"you don't have to tip-toe, you can say you're going to *birthing class*." Laila's emphasis

on the last two words rang out through my car. She was probably right to call me out.

"I'm sorry, girl, it's just been a long day. I didn't mean
anything by it."

"I know you didn't. I'm just a little tired of being overpro-
tected. Don't worry, I'm getting pretty good at telling people
exactly what I need."

"Just when I thought you were already all-the-way-live,
girl, somehow you got rawer." I let out a laugh as I spoke to
try to lighten the air. Somehow too much truth too fast could
start to feel like blocks of emotional concrete, stacked one by
one on your chest. I was thankful to hear the clear ripples of
Laila's laughter dance through my car. Our relationship had
adjusted to new boundaries, but the well of friendship had
deepened also.

"Lah, you're so lucky to be doing your own thing. My news
director is the worst. He asks me to take chances and then
punishes me for them. He tells me to stand out but doesn't
protect me when I do. If I wasn't about to be on maternity
leave, I would have quit today before I even walked out the
door." I knew I was yelling, but it felt good to yell. It felt good
to let my emotions take their honest course, not simply the
route of tears down my face, but through the sound of my
voice, unthrottled and loud.

"Tab, I've been trying to tell you, *fuck* that station, come
work with me!" Laila made a staccato delivery of her directive.
She softened her tone as she continued, "Seriously. You're too
good for them. You need a national brand anyway. At least
write a column. You could write about your experiences with
your natural hair on the air. People need to hear it."

Her words rang with truth in them, but I laughed.

"I need the health insurance," I said.

"Yeah, your pregnant ass does," Laila teased back. "But during your maternity leave, you should write a few pieces for the site and see how you feel about it. I'm going to stay on you until you say yes."

"I know," I mused aloud. "Or maybe I should just marry Marc, quit my job, and be a stay-at-home mom."

"Actually, that sounds like the fastest way for you to become a millionaire to me," Laila shot back quickly. "You're the only woman I can name who would say 'no sir' to the wealthy man that she originally wanted to marry after they got pregnant. Girl, make it make sense!"

"Well, I guess, never say never. So many decisions, so little time." At my words, we both shared another welcome laugh. "Will I see you at Alexis's rewedding on Saturday?"

"Girl, yes, because unlike you, Alexis would never forgive me missing one of her 'life events.'" I hoped that Laila would never know just how right she was about that.

PULLING UP TO THE BIRTHING CENTER, I TOOK A FEW DEEP BREATHS in the car to try to relieve the ebb and flow of anxiety that was serving to exacerbate the mini contractions and cramping that I had gotten somewhat used to over the past several weeks. *Relax, Tabby*, my mind repeated to me. Eventually, my breathing slowed, and I was relieved to note that even after everything, I was only fifteen minutes late.

At the door, I gave an embarrassed acknowledgment to the instructor, who was in the middle of explaining pain coaching to the room—an audience of pregnant women and their support partners practicing breathing exercises. I identified Marc, who was by his lonesome, sitting on top of a birthing ball in a collared shirt, breathing along with the rest of his mostly female classmates. When I had let him know that I was running late, he told me he'd "take notes," but this wasn't what I'd expected. I stifled my laughter but made a mental note to tease him about it later.

"I think you're in my seat," I whispered. Marc was so engrossed in the exercise that he'd barely noticed my approach. He seemed startled to be pulled out of his deep breathing rhythm.

"Oh! Hey, sorry. I was just trying to memorize these techniques for later," Marc whispered back with an intense look on his face. Evidently, once an honors student, always an honors student. Marc got up quickly and offered me his place on the birthing ball. He took a seat in an adjacent chair. Sinking into the give of the ball provided such relief in my lower back that I released a too-loud sigh, noticeable to some of my neighboring classmates. Late pregnancy had taught me a new definition for pleasure, which most times was simply relief from any of the many ways I'd learned one could be uncomfortable. I turned my attention to the instructor.

"Now, if you've chosen this birthing center, hopefully you've already made your decision *not* to have an epidural." The instructor paused and turned to look around to the dozen of us in the room. "Hopefully so, because we don't offer epidurals here. That, ladies, is for the hospital only." I remembered my decision and conversation with Andouele. She'd warned me that the pain could become intense. The discomfort I'd been experiencing from my body's so-called "practice contractions" seemed like something I could manage. The potential pain level of labor wasn't enough to outweigh the risks as I understood them to be. I noticed others around me nodding. I wondered if they too had made similar considerations. Either way, here we were, all together.

"In this birthing center, you'll have several options. We offer water birth, squatting, and almost any of the birth positions that are most comfortable to the mother, including use of birthing balls throughout labor, similar to those that most of you are seated on this evening . . ."

The instructor continued for the length of the class until it was time for one of the "potty breaks" that would precede a tour of the birthing facilities. After the tour, Marc and I decided that we'd make our final selection for birth preferences. Although we'd planned to do it together, we both had a tacit understanding that for the labor portion, "we" would actually mean me.

"Hey, baby daddy." I gave Marc a playful nudge in the arm as we waited for the tour to start. He seemed to be distracted.

"You know, Tab, I was just thinking . . . Are you sure you don't want an epidural? I mean, those breathing exercises were hella intense. That pain must be no joke."

I gave a pretend frown. "What, you don't think I can handle it?"

Marc shook his head and gave me a sly smile. "I think that you can handle anything—except maybe getting here on time. I saw your text about going rogue on the segment tonight. What happened?"

I felt my eyes roll a full circle and let out a dramatic sigh.

"Don't get me started. Of course, Chris again. He holds it against me for expressing my perspective, and he holds it against me for conforming. I can't win."

Marc chuckled. "Did anyone else besides him figure out that you and Lisa hijacked the broadcast?" He barely got the words out before he cracked himself up. I gave him another nudge in the arm.

"It's not funny, Marc!" I protested. "If we hadn't done that, chances are I would have never gotten a chance to address the viewer comments, and I'd have been stuck doing some dry-ass report on the CROWN Act without giving viewers any perspective on why it's even important or needed."

Marc put his arm around me and pulled me in close to him. "I get it. I'm sorry for teasing you. I'm glad you added your own experience. Most people wouldn't understand the significance because it doesn't affect them. That's true." Marc gave another sly smile. "But you do have to admit, that shit you did was kind of gangsta."

"You trying to say I'm a studio gangsta?"

Marc shifted to look at me squarely, his long eyelashes slung low over his deep brown eyes. "I'm trying to say I'm proud of you, Tabby."

"So, does that mean I make a pretty solid baby mama after all?" I teased.

"More than that, Tabby, much more."

Marc and I both turned to the sound of the instructor announcing the beginning of the tour. It felt natural to take his hand as we exited the room toward the hallway. After all, we were in this together.

29

ON THE MORNING OF ALEXIS'S "REWEDDING," SHE WAS A BUNDLE of nerves. I, on the other hand, was a bundle of waddling discomfort. If I hadn't thought that she'd disintegrate into a pool of sobbing emotion, I'd have taken the pregnancy option to cancel. My back hurt, my feet were swollen, and my nose looked like I'd had a reverse nose job to make it bigger, wider, and the focal point of my face. Still, she was my best friend. As my phone rang, I figured that this would make Alexis's seventh time calling that day. I was more than relieved to see Ms. Gretchen's name instead.

After I answered, her voice rang out loudly from the other end of the receiver.

"Good morning, honey!" she chirped. "Now, I wanted to let you know that I'm just going to get us a car from my place, and I'll come and pick you up like I did last time on the way to the airport. Is that okay?"

"I'm so glad you're coming to get me, Ms. Gretchen.

Honestly, I feel so big and tired this morning, you might have to drag me out of here!"

"Well, what do you expect in the final stretch! If it were me, I'd sure be at home. I'd imagine your friend would understand. Well, actually, now that I think about it, that girl Alexis probably would not." She laughed.

"I think you're right about that, Ms. Gretchen." I recalled Alexis's response to Laila missing my baby shower. I hoped that Laila would make an appearance today. If she knew what was good for her, she would.

"Okay, honey! I'm gettin' my nails done, but I'll see you this afternoon. They want me to pick a color—do you remember what her first wedding color was?"

"Sure, Ms. Gretchen, her colors were pink and gray."

"Well, I guess I'll do pink, then, no sense in gray. Nobody has time for that, and honey, I need all the time I can get!"

By the time Ms. Gretchen arrived, I'd managed to take a nap and then finally stretch a cloth tent around my body that I hoped people would believe was a dress. I congratulated myself for putting on makeup when I would have loved the extra minutes for another quick sleep. Pregnancy was exhausting, and being at the start of my maternity leave seemed to make me want to fight it less. Even though Marc would be arriving late, I felt relieved that I could leave with him at any time when my feet just couldn't take it anymore. The things we do for our friends.

I walked out to greet Ms. Gretchen in the waiting car at the front of my house. I could see through the window that she'd not only picked pink nail polish but a near-fluorescent color that seemed to light up the entire back seat. She was wearing the same magenta dress that she'd worn at Crestmire for the Senior Prom. I smiled at the memory from the earliest days of my pregnancy, a stark contrast from my frontloaded, fumbling entry into the car.

"Cute dress, honey!" Ms. Gretchen patted my leg as I joined her in the back seat.

"Come on, Ms. Gretchen." I gave her a side-eye glance. "You and I both know I look like an orphaned sea animal."

Ms. Gretchen smiled. "Honey, you look like a pregnant woman who's ready to pop! And only a fool wouldn't think that was beautiful. Next time you feel some doubt, you just put on some red."

"Oh, Ms. Gretchen, I did that. It worked just like you said it would, only that it might have made me a little *too* bold!"

Ms. Gretchen kept her smile, even while her face took on a stern look. "Now, honey," she said, looking at me intently, "you're a full-grown woman, so you ought to know, there's no such thing as too red—or too bold."

LEXI'S REWEDDING VENUE WAS A FAR CRY FROM THE ELABORATE location of her first wedding almost a decade prior. In fact, this event venue wasn't even as posh as the hip restaurant where we celebrated her last big birthday fête. Perhaps in the interest of time, as an ode to the backyard barbeque that just might have cemented their reunion, Rob and Alexis had found a quaint Italian villa-esque location on the edge of Westlake. It had a transportive indoor-outdoor rustic ambiance that I might have picked out for my own wedding, if I were ever to have one.

Ms. Gretchen and I made our respective ways out of the car. Even at her age, she moved more quickly than me toward the door. Trying to navigate the cumbersome weight of my front and not trip on my way in led to an incident of another type. I ran directly into a thin-framed man who was trying to hold the door open for us.

"Oh, I'm so sorry, ma'am, excuse me." He blinked at me through his glasses. I blinked back and then took a sharp breath.

"Todd?" I couldn't believe my eyes. And even though it would have been fair to expect to see a man I'd previously dated, given that I'd met him at Alexis's birthday party, he might as well have been a stranger from a distant planet. That was about as much contact as I'd had with exes, other than Marc, once I got pregnant. Before my pregnancy, Todd and I had a promising brunch date followed by canceled plans that neither one of us had taken the initiative to reschedule. I was too stuck on Marc. Maybe he had someone else too. We hadn't seen each other since.

Todd squinted at me. "Tabby?"

I nodded vigorously and then looked down at my belly. "Yep, plus one." I looked back up at him and gave the best smile I could push through the awkwardness.

"Plus two, actually." Ms. Gretchen stood in the space between us to make her way in the door while Todd and I stood frozen. "Tabby, I'll be inside. Nice to meet you, *Dr.* Todd." Todd looked a little confused but moved a bit to make room for Ms. Gretchen to breeze past us. He ushered me inside the doorway behind her.

"I—I can't believe . . ." Todd stammered.

"That I'm pregnant?" I raised an eyebrow at him. "Don't worry, it's not yours," I joked, trying to lighten the air.

Todd laughed. "I . . . I definitely wasn't thinking that."

"How have you been?" I asked as a hurried follow-up.

"Good, good." Todd answered me distractedly. I followed his eyes to my left hand. At this point, I was used to the glances. "How about you? Still single?"

I hesitated. The answer was complicated, so choosing the simplest version seemed to make the most sense at the time. "Yep, still single. How about you?"

"Um, single. Busy with work mostly." He made a motion to usher us further in. "Wanna make a move to the inside? Maybe we can catch up some more later on?"

"Sure, that sounds good, and plus, I'm starving!" I was glad that Todd had made the discomfort of an unexpected reunion relatively easy and efficient to get through. Although we'd gone out the one time after we met, sparks never flew as much as I'd wanted them to, especially during the era of recurring breakups with Marc. Todd didn't seem to have a date, but Marc would show up eventually. Then Todd would understand that my simple answer wasn't so simple after all. But there was no way he was still interested—who'd be thinking about dating an about-to-pop pregnant woman anyway, right?

"You look beautiful," Todd added as we separated toward our respective table assignments.

"Thank you," I said, sounding a bit more flirtatious than I'd intended to. As he walked away, I breathed a sigh of relief and hoped that the evening didn't get any more awkward. It was already too late by the time I'd remembered that God had a very strange way of answering my prayers.

30

I WAVED FRANTICALLY AT LAILA WHEN I SAW HER APPEAR IN THE wooden frame of the French doors. Ms. Gretchen and I were seated in the cozy charm of the brick-walled event space. Vintage chandeliers provided flattering and romantic rosy light. We'd been chatting among ourselves and with the other guests nearby. For the sake of my sanity, I was glad that Dr. Todd was seated in the adjoining outside courtyard. Laila found her name tag at the place setting next to Ms. Gretchen.

"Wow, Tab, look at you! You must be due any day now! Ooh, don't get up, I'll just . . ." Laila made her way over, arms outstretched to awkwardly embrace me in my seated position.

I gave Laila a teasing smile. "I'm still a couple weeks from my due date, but we're close."

Laila gently touched my belly. "Don't let me forget to give you your gift—I left it in my car."

"You didn't have to get me a gift, Laila!"

"Tab, yes I did. Just because I didn't come to your shower doesn't mean I wouldn't get you a gift! You've been amazingly supportive through everything, and it meant the world to me that you understood." Laila shifted tone quickly. "So, are you ready?" I reached over to hug her.

"Girl, I think so," I mused. "My maternity leave just started, and you know how I left things at work. I'm just looking forward to having some downtime to really get ready and get that place out of my hair—literally and figuratively."

"Well, don't you look splendid!" Ms. Gretchen interrupted our conversation with her comment to an approaching Alexis, who had been making her rounds to greet the guests. Unlike her first wedding, this event had no ceremony planned. Alexis wanted it to be a great party with dinner and dancing. It was meant to be "a celebration of love and family," as she described it to me. Considering how quickly the event came together, it was surprisingly well done.

Alexis squealed her excitement as she approached Ms. Gretchen and then me, but when she reached Laila, her demeanor noticeably chilled.

"Hey, Laila, *really* glad you made it." She sounded genuine, but after almost thirty years of friendship, I could hear the unmistakable undertone. I wondered if Laila noticed too.

"Well, I knew you'd *never* forgive me if I didn't." Laila gave a singsong reply back to Alexis. I realized that I was holding my breath. Alexis, Laila, and I hadn't been in the same place since before my baby shower. I'd forgiven Laila's absence, but I had no idea if Alexis had.

"Yeah, Tab is a lot more forgiving than me. But you probably know that already." At Alexis's words, Laila frowned slightly but said nothing.

"Well!" I interjected, attempting to clear the chill that set-

tled between us. "We're all here now! Another chance to celebrate love, life, and happiness." My forced cheer was obvious,
but I hoped that my friends would take the hint.

For a few moments, no one spoke.

Finally, likely because she suddenly remembered it was
her day, after all, and we were in fact all there, regardless of
the events of my baby shower, the bright and glowing smile
returned to Alexis's face. I let out a small sigh of relief. Out
of the corner of my eye, I saw Laila's shoulders drop. The previously escalating tension seemed to drain, replaced with the
energy of happiness and celebration.

"You girls can stay here if you want to, but my champagne
glass is empty." Ms. Gretchen pushed past us in a flash of
pink, with a half-full flute in her hand. We all laughed.

"Ms. Gretchen sure got the hell out of Dodge," Laila said
to Alexis and me, her eyes twinkling with a hint of amusement.

"But as far as the champagne, she's got the right idea!
Drink up, ladies, it's an open bar!" The merriment had fully
returned to Lexi's voice. "Oh! But I guess not you, Tabby . . .
or, actually, you either, right, Laila? Oh well, there's plenty
of nonalcoholic drinks. We're going to start dinner in a little
while and then we have the *best* DJ, and I told him we need a
bunch of old-school jams. If I'm going to remarry Rob, I need
to hear some Jodeci, okay?"

"Girl, I'm starving. If I didn't know better, I'd think I was
eating for three." My stomach growled right on time to emphasize the point.

"I'll send the hors d'oeuvres tray your way," Alexis said
with a wave. "And I'll see you both after dinner on the dance

floor. We're not doing any big speeches or toasts or anything. Just one acknowledgment and a thank-you, and then it's time to get down!" Alexis made a shimmy in her tight-fitting dress that showed off her compact curves. "Tabby, you gonna be okay dancing?" She looked at me intently.

I laughed. "I'm sure I'll be fine, Lexi. Maybe it'll be good to get some exercise." I looked at my phone. "Hopefully Marc will be here by then . . ."

Something about the moment, or the occasion, made me feel more vulnerable than usual. I didn't just want Marc there as a dance partner; I wanted him there for support.

AT JUST ABOUT THE END OF DESSERT, THE DJ SIGNALED A CHANGE in the flow of festivities. Alexis and Rob appeared on the small dance floor holding microphones.

"Hey, everybody," Rob bellowed into the mic. The attention in the room quickly shifted. "Alexis and I aren't going to take too much time away from the party, but I did just want to take a moment to say a few words about what we're here to celebrate." By now the room was stark silent. We all knew more or less about Rob's indiscretions that made this night a necessity and a miracle of its own sort, but I was sure that none of us were quite sure what he was going to say about it. He continued, "When Alexis and I got married, almost ten years ago, that union didn't come with an instruction manual. And neither did our boys. We had quite a few ups and some real setbacks." Rob looked at Alexis. "Some *real* setbacks." He turned again to face the audience. "In fact, it's fair to say that some shit got real, and we almost didn't make it. But we're here today, thanks to the love and prayers of friends and family. This celebration is about you as much as it is about Alexis and me. So I'd like to propose a simple toast. To the unbreakable bonds of family and the miracle of love." Rob raised his champagne glass to all of us in the audience, and then to a beaming Alexis, who clinked hers against his. I lifted my water glass in solidarity.

Alexis raised the microphone to her mouth. "I know that you all know how much this night means to Rob and me and how much we appreciate you sharing it with us. We also appreciate the support in all the ways you've shown up for us, especially in recent months, from childcare to advice, and everything in between. It takes a village to raise a child, and evidently, it also takes a village to keep a marriage together. So, from the bottom of our hearts to the bottom of your drinking glasses, we thank you all." Alexis signaled for the cheers, clinked her own glass with Rob's, and then took a few steps closer to the DJ, pulling Rob with her. "But now we want to really get the party started. So we're going to ask the DJ to play some carefully selected songs from back in the day, and I'd ask our friends to please join us." I felt my face flush. *Crap, Marc's not here yet.* I cursed the timing. For a minute, I didn't move. I could only imagine ambling over to the dance floor, trying to wiggle the mass that had taken over my body.

"Tabby, would you like to dance?" The voice surprised me, but I knew who it was right away. Standing above me was Dr. Todd, hand outstretched. In the moment, it was an offer I couldn't refuse. I nodded and placed my hand in his, first to be helped to my feet, and then to be led to join the others on the floor.

"I think I can make it through one song," I whispered to Todd.

"Don't worry, you'll be fine—just think of it as taking a nice walk." He smiled at me. I remembered the charm and kindness I'd seen in his eyes when we first met. I couldn't help but wonder what would have happened if I hadn't been so caught up with Marc and if he hadn't been caught up with work.

On the dance floor, the thump of the beat called for a slow two-step. Todd's arm could only wrap around me so far across the back, but he held me as close as he could, joined by our hands, and mastering the rhythm, we swayed into unexpected enjoyment. I started to compliment him on his dancing, but my eye caught a familiar face at the door. Marc was standing there, and for a second, our eyes locked.

"Shit," I murmured under my breath.

"Everything okay?" Todd turned me a bit, removing Marc from my view, but not in any way from my mind. The panicked feeling began to spread outward from the center of my body. Even in spite of the uncertainty in mine and Marc's relationship, and the innocence of the moment, I felt like I was doing something wrong.

"Yeah, everything is fine, just that . . . just that . . ." The feeling of panic and dread in my body turned into a spreading warmth in my underwear. I was literally peeing my pants. The world stopped briefly as I felt the liquid starting to make its way down my leg. I struggled to find words to reply to Todd and swiveled my head frantically for the nearest exit to find the restroom.

"Tabby, are you okay?" Todd repeated, the look of concern deepening on his face.

"I . . . I . . . need to get out of here," I pleaded. "I really need to get to the ladies' room." I gave Todd a wild-eyed look. "Like, right now."

Todd looked down. I was mortified at what he might see beneath me. I pushed my legs together, deathly embarrassed by the idea of forming a pee puddle on the dance floor. "Tabby, how far along are you?"

"Thirty-eight weeks, why?"

"Have you been feeling any cramping?" By now, Todd had his arm around my shoulder.

"Of course! All night, but that's been the same Braxton Hicks I've been feeling for weeks now, right?"

Todd started directing me off the dance floor. "Tabby, I think your water just broke. You don't need to go to the ladies' room, you need to go to the hospital."

31

IF TODD HADN'T BEEN A DOCTOR, I WOULD HAVE NEVER BELIEVED that the flow of liquid from my body was my water breaking. It was nothing like the dramatic gush of my nightmares that I'd seen in so many movies and television shows. But what I saw down there on my trip to the ladies' room wasn't anything close to what I'd expected for pee panties. I'd learned enough in birthing class to be sure. I was definitely in labor.

When I emerged, Todd escorted me from the ladies' room back to the table. I didn't want to make a scene, even in a circumstance where there was no good way not to. *Where in the hell is Marc!* What if he was mad at me? Oh my God, what if he left?

The marked seats for Ms. Gretchen and Laila were empty as Todd led me back to my seat.

"Tabby, sit right here, as comfortably as you can. I'll go get your friends. Is there anyone you need to call? A doula, your family? You can tell them to meet us at the hospital."

Us? Oh no. I realized our conversation earlier. I hadn't told Todd about Marc. "Um . . . Todd, about that, there's a . . ."

"There you are." A familiar voice floated from behind me, interrupting my words. Familiar hands fell on my shoulders. The look on Todd's face was as effective as a mirror in confirming to whom the voice and hand belonged.

"There's Marc," I said quickly. "Todd, meet Marc. Marc, this is my friend Todd." Marc and Todd gave each other an awkward nod. I turned to see Marc glowering. I felt like a small animal stuck in the middle of a predator's cage fight. The twinge in my back quickly brought me back to the true emergency. "Marc, I was just on the dance floor with Todd—"

"Yeah, I saw that . . ." Marc said through slightly clenched teeth. I could see him bristling.

"And my water broke." Suddenly, Marc looked like he'd seen a ghost. He jumped to attention.

"What? You're in labor? What are you doing sitting there? Don't we need to be on the way to the hospital?"

Todd jumped in. "She's all right, man, you have some time."

"What the fuck do you know?" Marc growled at him. I'd never seen him this intense.

"Marc!" I failed in my effort to stand up between them and managed to simply raise my arm instead. "Todd's a doctor. He's a friend of Rob's." My heart started to race again. Marc still looked like he was going to swing.

"Hey, why don't I just let Alexis and Rob know what's happening, and . . . Was that your aunt that you came with?" Todd was making his offer and walking away at the same time. I relaxed only slightly and only briefly as the regular cramps I'd been feeling from time to time surprised me with increasing intensity. I winced. Marc instantly dropped down into a squat to meet my eyes.

"Shouldn't we be getting to a hospital?" He took my hand in his with urgency and sincerity in his eyes.

Laila rushed over to us, followed closely behind by Ms. Gretchen.

"Tabby!" Laila was breathless, as if she'd been running. "I heard you're in labor?" I could barely answer when Todd returned with Alexis and Rob in tow.

"Tab, are you okay? Do you need us to drive you? What are you still doing here?" Alexis was turning around frenetically as if the world no longer made sense to her. All of a sudden, everyone was looking at me.

"Guys, I think . . . I'm having another contraction." Those were the only words I could manage. At that, Todd perked up.

"Is anyone timing them?" Todd walked over to me, looking at his watch. "Tabby, I think we need to get you to the hospital now. It seems like your labor is progressing pretty quickly."

Marc was frantically tapping on his phone. "The directions to the birthing center say that it'll take us over an hour to get there at this time." I'd never seen him look so worried.

"Los Angeles traffic, of course," Alexis said, sounding both frazzled and exasperated. Over her shoulder, I watched the other guests dancing to the beat of the DJ, oblivious to both the fact that they were dancing on the site of my water breaking and that there was a pregnant woman in the room going into what was evidently accelerated labor.

"Let's just get her over to Cedars," Todd commanded.

Marc gave him a look that might have been a felony in several states.

I started what breathing exercises I could remember, not so much to manage the pain, but to try to calm myself down from the mounting tension, especially between Marc and Todd. I thought that at least if I went into labor on-site, it would stop them from going to blows. Todd was the doctor present, and that should have been a relief. I'd never expected Marc to be the jealous type, but something about that made me feel things that I was sure I'd have to evaluate later. More pressing matters were at hand, literally. We were about to have a baby.

Laila came over to my side and touched my arm. "Tabby, are you okay? Can I get you some water or something? Maybe some ice in a cup to go?" She looked concerned. I hoped that the situation wasn't too much for her.

"Thanks, girl, that would be great. Are you sure?"

"Of course I am. I'll be right back." Laila shot off in the direction of the venue's kitchen. Of everyone, aside from Todd, Ms. Gretchen was the only person in our huddle who seemed entirely calm but was clearly eager to get our little show on the road.

"Well, what are we all standing here waiting for? Should I call an Uber?"

"Ms. Gretchen, no need to call a car, you can ride with Tabby and me in mine." Marc stepped forward and put his arm around her.

Ms. Gretchen grinned. "Glam-maw is riding in style!"

Another wave of pain hit my lower back. "Ooh!" I grabbed Marc's arm with an overwhelming urge to get up and walk.

"Are you okay, Tab? Start your breathing. It looks like all the dancing you were doing set your labor in motion." I couldn't tell if Marc was being sarcastic or genuine. I decided to take the generous interpretation.

"Marc, on your way to get the car, can you please call Andouele? Let her know we're going to the hospital instead of the birthing center?" Marc nodded.

"I'm going with you!" Ms. Gretchen called out, following Marc toward the exit. "I'm too excited to just stand still!" I could still hear her talking to him as they walked. Seeing her made me think of Granny Tab. Somewhere, somehow, I knew she was there too, and maybe she'd make sure we'd be okay.

AFTER A RIDE FILLED WITH BOTH SWERVING TURNS AND CONTRACTIONS, I was as happy as one could be in my situation to pull up at the doors of the hospital. Never mind that I thought Marc was going to wind up driving through them.

"Marc, did you call Andouele?" I hoped that he had and that I'd see her in the lobby waiting for us. So much was already so different from what we'd planned. And now that we were at a hospital rather than the birthing center, there was so much more that could change . . . At least Andouele could help me hold on to what mattered most.

"She didn't answer, so I left a message," Marc said curtly.

"Well, you have enough people here already for a damn basketball team," Ms. Gretchen called from the back seat. "What's she gonna do that the doctors can't, honey?"

"That's just it, Ms. Gretchen, I'm hoping Andouele will save me from the doctors doing too much."

"Don't worry, Tab," Marc said, opening his car door. "You'll be fine. I promise. Stay here while I go inside and get some help." Just then his cell phone rang. "Andouele," he mouthed at me as he pointed to the phone in his hand. He popped in his earbuds and turned for a light jog toward the hospital doors.

True to her word, Andouele was there, right as she said she would be. The conversation we'd had months prior in the café ran through my mind. She'd told me that not just during birth, but after was when things would get the most overwhelming. When I'd need to ask for help. I felt another contraction rip through my body, reminding me that I had a lot to focus on right now—later would have to wait. And with all the flurry around me, I hadn't been paying attention to the baby movements. I had lost track of how much time had passed since my water broke so unceremoniously on the dance floor with Todd. Where was Todd, anyway?

Alexis ran up and tapped on my window. As it descended, I watched Rob walk through the hospital doors.

"Tabby, are you okay? Is Marc going to get a wheelchair?"

"Lexi, isn't your party still happening? What are you doing here? You could have come later."

"No, I couldn't. Tabby, there's no way I'd miss the birth of your first baby. We paid for a DJ and an open bar. Nobody will even notice we're missing." I reached out to take Alexis's hand. "How far apart are your contractions?"

"I don't know, about four minutes, three maybe?"

Lexi raised her eyebrows. "Oh shit, Tab, you're close." She

swiveled toward the hospital door. "Where is Marc with that wheelchair?"

"I don't know, Lex. Maybe I should just walk in?"

"Yes!" Ms. Gretchen called from the back seat. "You two go in, and I'll stay here with the car and wait for that Marc to come on back out. By the time he gets here, I'll be the one who needs a wheelchair."

"Not for a long, long time, Ms. Gretchen," I panted back at her.

"See you on the other side, girls!" She waved us on, and Lexi and I waddled arm in arm through the sliding glass doors that had been all that separated me from the next chapter of my life. Whatever happened in there, nothing would ever be the same again.

EPILOGUE

To: "The Village"
From: Marc Brown
Subject: Baby Brown Is Here!

We'll be sending a more formal announcement shortly, but I just wanted to let our friends and family know that **Tabitha Evelyn Walker Brown** was born at eleven p.m. last night. Our little beauty came into this world measuring twenty-one inches and weighing eight pounds, two ounces.

The stork arrived just two and a half hours after we walked into the hospital. As some of you know, we got there just in time! Tabby championed through an all-natural birth (although I think she threatened to kill me twice). Both she and the baby are healthy and doing fine.

We can't wait to see you, and for you to meet the newest addition to our family. We are already so in love.

—Marc

ACKNOWLEDGMENTS

I WROTE ACKNOWLEDGMENTS IN MY FIRST NOVEL AS IF I'D NEVER get the chance to write them again. It reads like the longest yearbook caption ever. I'm sorry—I was a newbie. Still am. And yet, I have the great fortune of having another go at it, which means most importantly that I've had the opportunity to write and publish another book. For this, I have boundless thanks and gratitude—and a much better grasp on brevity.

To my incredible team at Harper Perennial: Amy Baker, Sarah Ried, Megan Looney, Kristin Cipolla, Heather Drucker, and Lisa Erickson, along with Jackie Kim and Stephanie Moon and everyone who has been a part of this journey from sales to production to copyediting to design, I have so much appreciation for everything that you do.

Thank you to my agent, Lucinda Halpern, for the invaluable support, cheerleading, and wisdom. Also to Ashley Bernardi, Samantha McIntyre, and team Nardi, along with continual thanks to Dawn Hardy for helping me establish my author platform.

Thank you to the many readers, reviewers, book clubs, bookstagrammers, and podcasters who have made this journey so much more than the isolation of writing and have turned it into a community affair. You bring a joyous finish to every manuscript because it means we'll have something new to talk about.

And there would be no *BGMBM* without the incredible bookstores and librarians who first supported *BGMDE*, even when it had a green cover. Thank you for connecting me with readers and making dreams come true.

Finally, thank you to my family and friends for your unending support and encouragement. You keep my cup full so that the words can flow.

ABOUT THE AUTHOR

JAYNE ALLEN is the pen name of Jaunique Sealey, a graduate of Duke University and Harvard Law School. Drawing from her unique experiences as an attorney and entrepreneur, she crafts transcultural stories that touch upon contemporary women's issues. She is the author of *Black Girls Must Die Exhausted*, her first novel, which she calls "the epitaph of my thirties." A proud native of Detroit, she lives in Los Angeles.